DEMIURGE
a novel

Sheldon J. Pacotti

Other Works by Sheldon J. Pacotti

γ

A near-future novel in which a failed genetics experiment leaves dozens of Los Angeles teenagers ailing, vengeful, and determined to reinvent humanity their own way.

EXPERIMENTS IN BELIEF

An eclectic collection of stories, spanning three continents, the past, the present, and the future.

CELL: EMERGENCE

An action/arcade video game featuring a "massively reactive" biochemical simulation of the human body and custom "dynamic voxel" technology.

Contents

Preface to the 2014 Edition

Times have changed since I wrote the introduction to the 2000 edition, which in places reads like a wild-eyed manifesto. The most relevant development is the emergence of digital stores—for music, movies, and of course books. "In ten years we will know whether legislation will be strong enough to preserve the capitalist business model," I wrote in 2000. Well. The digital store appears to be society's answer to many of the questions raised in this book, and it came as a surprise to many of us who lived through the first years of the World Wide Web, when it seemed like society was about to be stood on its head by an invention greater than the printing press.

The social changes have been vast, and they're continuing, but of the artists in 2000 marveling at the prospect of connecting directly with fans over the Internet, I don't think many envisioned massive online stores tended by major corporations. Yet artists have gotten their 70% (pretty good, historically speaking) plus discoverability and customer service, and consumers are even going along with the deal. This suggests to me that between the radical viewpoints of this novel compromise might be possible. Society has an answer, as I said, and if you bought this book legally maybe you agree with it.

Yet—the tension remains. We are imposing our own idea of commerce on products with a negligible marginal cost. The materialist in me does wonder whether the non-Euclidean reality of the digital world will ultimately have the final word.

Sheldon Pacotti
Austin, Texas: January 2, 2014

Preface to the 2000 Edition

The court battles being fought this year over .MP3 files are just the beginning. The pace of change in the entertainment industry will only accelerate, and within ten years the entrenched powers may well throw up their hands and go sliding down their mountains of mud into an angry ocean. The capitalist system faces its first genuine threat since communism—a shift in the means of production so unexpected that even Marx may be sitting up in his grave and raising his bushy eyebrows. In ten years we will know whether legislation will be strong enough to preserve the capitalist business model, or whether the means of production itself will ultimately impose its own phenotype on our institutions.

A complete transformation of civilization is surely decades away and probably more. In *Demiurge*, global democracy and capitalism are thriving in 2996, exactly 1000 years after I finished writing the book. Our economic system may very well last that long—and may, in truth, be the most efficient and universally beneficial way to organize ourselves—but its apparatus, evolved during the Industrial Revolution to accommodate the manufacture and distribution of physical products, will increasingly rely upon legislation to preserve structures that would otherwise not survive in the "New Economy." The copyright battles over .MP3's are the examples of the day. A second copy of a song file is "free" in an economic sense because it takes no work to create it. Financial compensation for the artist is possible only if the community accepts an external set of rules that allow the definition of a "price" as a secondhand representation of the work that went into recording the song.

The preceding characterization may seem overwrought. After all, the author's copyright has been with us at least since the Statute of Anne in 1710, and law enforcement has been effective—at least in Western countries—at preventing illegal copies from circulating and therefore at preserving fair prices for entertainment products. The difference in the

New Economy is that the risk of making and distributing illegal copies is approaching zero, as is the cost. A hundred and fifty years ago, if you wanted to pirate a Dickens novel, you had to set up a printing press, hire workers, do a print run, and physically transport a copy to each buyer. You needed capital. Making illegal copies involved financial risk and the centralized mass production of literature made it quite probable that the authorities would discover a pirating operation and shut it down. A would-be criminal faced the double risk of losing money and going to jail.

Today, with decentralized systems like Napster and Gnutella, the individual crook does not need to make a capital investment, nor does he need to make the large number of copies that would attract lawsuits or police. He can operate with relatively low risk, downloading a few '80's punk tunes every few days and nothing more. If millions of people behave the same way, we suddenly have a law enforcement nightmare. Copyright—as wise and beneficial as it may be, and as much as this author, in publishing an eBook, would like to see his own work protected—may in fact be an institution too expensive to maintain in the digital age. And where does that leave the producers of entertainment, who need food and lodging just like the rest of us?

In *Demiurge*, I complicate the question by making a somewhat "soft" SF extrapolation to a time when everything can be copied like an .MP3 file, including physical objects and people. I look at the stresses that would be placed on a capitalist system—founded upon copyright—that had survived into a wholly digital age. In 1994, I set out to write a straightforward adventure story, but I found that I had to do quite a bit of prediction and social engineering before I could even begin. Perhaps other writers and fans of science fiction will recognize that as just part of the process, but it came as an unexpected challenge to me. Even the most basic aspects of a character's life—such as the character's job or aspirations—had to be justified in the framework of a radically different economic order. That I was able to sketch out a detective story at all depended heavily on the laws and software of the fictional world government, which made sure every person had at least one foot in real life and real time. As the New Economy moves forward, I think we, too, will rely increasingly on legislation and software to keep us at least partly in familiar surroundings. The open question is whether any government or software company has a chance of succeeding.

I don't know if the book has an answer. As I said, my intention was just to put down an entertaining adventure story, which was a difficult enough challenge as it turned out—and only time will tell if I succeeded in doing even that much. Perhaps the fate of *Demiurge*, the eBook, will have more to say about the future of copyright than *Demiurge*, the novel. If the book is still an eProperty in a few years, with a price and readers who actually pay money to read it, then maybe some of the old conventions will have found a way to survive.

I do think that a technology that allows individual artists to securely distribute their work without the interference of media conglomerates will be a great benefit to society. The real enemies here—if we must pick sides—are the lackluster middle-aged bureaucrats who serve as the gatekeepers of taste for everyone on the planet. Or, rather, the stockpiles of capital that allow mediocre businesspeople to cram lousy movies like *Armageddon* down our throats. The key word is "capital." Capital won't go away, nor will the promotional advantage it affords artists, but it will no longer be *necessary* for commerce. Artists will have options other than assimilation by AOL-Time-Warner. They won't have to suck down that ten percent commission; they will be able to keep one hundred percent of gross, if they choose. Why would a writer give away ninety percent of the revenue of a book to pay loggers, paper mills, printing presses, truckers, managers, and the pimple-faced kid behind the counter at the local bookstore when he no longer *has* to? To be sure, there will always be advantages to signing up with the Big Boys, but the very idea of bigness will face direct competition from microscale enterprises, some, like Pacotti Publishing, consisting entirely of a single shmo who claims to be an entertainer of some kind.

So, dear readers, dear potential customers, help make micro-capitalism a genuine alternative for artists and consumers alike. Help eliminate meddling businesspeople from the transaction between creator and consumer. Pay for this book! Refrain from copying it or—heaven forbid!—looking for editions that may have already been copied. Think of the meager price of this novel as a few bucks in the tip jar of your favorite local musician, or the tip jar at the sandwich shop, or the one at the bar on the corner. Accept the small transaction as a convention from a bygone era, for in the end we may need to rely more on our heritage and common understanding of fairness than on any technical or economic apparatus.

Readers of the world, UNITE! Buy electronic!

Sheldon Pacotti
Austin, Texas: June 15, 2000

DEMIURGE

demiurge: 1. **a.** *in Platonism*: the subordinate god who fashions the sensible world in the light of eternal ideas. **b.** *in some Gnostic systems*: an inferior not absolutely intelligent deity who is the creator of the material world and is frequently identified with the creator God of the Old Testament. 2. something (as an institution, idea, or individual) conceived as an autonomous creative force or decisive power.

— *Webster's*, 1997.

demiurge: 1. a device for assembling or "printing" a molecular structure.

— *Webster's*, 2497.

demiurge: 3. *In "culturalist" psychology*: the personality type associated with creativity, solipsism, and daydreaming.

— *Webster's*, 2997.

Chapter 1

Matter is simply frozen information . . .
> — Timothy Leary, *Pataphysics Magazine*, 1990.

The villagers had taken the bait. Paul came out of the desert covered in dust, beads around his neck, braids in his hair . . . He climbed to the top of the mesa alone, under the high scorching sun, and begged to see their little settlement, licking his parched lips and managing to tremble—genuinely—from exhaustion. They had no idea what to do with him. The American Indian body—though recognizably the work of a fashion designer—gave him the look of the land, their desolate home for almost a decade, and also gave him a very hip, reformist look—a distinct advantage.

"I come from the north," he told the men who met him at the top of the mesa. "I'm from a settlement behind the Snakeback. They've sent me to make contact."

The men exchanged looks, shading their eyes to better see him, as though doubting that this was happening at all, then one left to find the village leader. The other man directed Paul to a stone on the edge of the mesa.

Paul sat down, relieved for a chance to rest, while the man withdrew to a high crag, where he could keep watch. From the stone Paul could see as far as he had traveled, farther even, perhaps a hundred miles. Shabby little houses stood here and there, isolated by the absence of roads but looking crowded together, though this was perhaps the most underpopulated place on earth. Among them he spotted places he had stopped for directions, only pretending to be lost in order to stir up gossip. He could also see the long bending scar of the riverbed he had followed two miles in the wrong direction, stalling for time, waiting for word of his coming to reach the village.

They had been warned, he was sure. The question was what they were going to do about it. Most likely, they thought he was telling the truth, that he was from a new settlement of "logoffs" just digging into the sand and learning to live without credit. He was banking on it.

A girl came up the side of the mesa, panting and carrying a gray metal cylinder on her back. A small boy followed, blonde like she was, too young to be one of her friends.

He watched them navigate the steep rocks, surprised to see that the device the girl carried was a demiurge. The machines were getting smaller, more portable. She walked up the slope with such agility that he guessed she must have grown up carrying such devices, probably too young to have ever known the days before solar fusion, too young to find the device even unusual. She carried it like a part of her body, like some high-tech mutation, amazing to parents but invisible to children. A strange way to grow up, he thought. Had these kids ever been to school? The girl maybe, not the boy. Either way, they were creatures of the desert now, half-savages, gods in some ways, animals in others. He could hardly blame them. They were just living the lives their parents had given them.

The girl—maybe twelve years old—recognized him as a stranger right away. She dropped the demiurge onto the gravel at his feet and with alarming directness asked who he was.

He pointed to a low ridge of hills. "I'm from over there, behind the Snakeback. There's a settlement like this one. We're trying to live like you do."

The girl examined the place where he had pointed, very intent, believing everything he said.

Though fooling people was Paul's job, lying to children always seemed a little unfair, even unkind. Yet he could not put on one show for the adults and another for the children.

She asked, "Are there many people?"

The boy interrupted, holding up a small brown lizard, beaming at Paul. The lizard squirmed and kicked its legs like extra fingers. The boy grinned, expecting Paul to say something.

"That's quite a little critter you have there."

The boy laughed shyly and looked away. "You want me to make you a sandwich?" He knelt beside the machine and told it to open up. He tried to put the lizard inside, but it slipped out before the door could close. He caught it again with a brutal swipe of his hand. "It needs carbon," he explained, talking about the machine.

"I'm not very hungry. But thank you."

The girl was still examining the Snakeback, intent as a hawk, maybe looking for signs of life she had missed before. "What's it called?"

"We don't have a name yet. We don't even know if it'll work out."

"Are you here to see my dad?" She looked at him, serious.

"Is your father the leader of the village?"

"I guess. He brought all of us here, a long time ago."

"Then—yes, I came to meet your father."

The boy had gotten the lizard into the demiurge. The machine vibrated greedily, sorting the animal's atoms into separate compartments. "Tell it what you want," he said.

"I'm not hungry. Maybe later."

The kid squinted against the sunlight to see Paul's face.

Paul added, "That's very nice of you, though."

The kid kicked around in the dirt, then he retreated to the girl's side, hugging her leg to say he was ready to go. Paul had not meant to be rude. "Maybe something to drink," he amended. "That thing have enough silicon to make a glass of ice water?"

The boy did not smile as he came back, but he seemed proud to command the machine to make water. He delivered the glass to Paul with solemnity, holding it with both hands, as though he were performing a ceremony, a timeless rite of friendship. Paul accepted the glass with both hands, hoping he had passed the test.

The girl allowed the boy to make the offering, watching how Paul behaved. "Sure you're not hungry?" she said.

"This will be fine. Thank you anyway." He took a long drink of water, grateful.

"I'll get our father," she said. "You wait here."

"I'll be here."

She lifted the demiurge onto her back.

He could not resist asking the question that had been on his mind since he had first seen them. "Is he your . . . brother?"

3

The little boy did not seem to be listening, but the girl gave him a sudden look, old enough—he realized too late—to know the implications of the question. "I'll get my father," she repeated, and headed for town.

They left him at the mesa's edge, sitting on the rock, hands wet from the cold glass. He looked over his shoulder. Fortunately the man was too far away to have heard his little slip. "Talking to kids," he muttered to himself. Christ. He might have just thrown the investigation with an inappropriate remark he had made to a couple of kids. Got to keep your guard up, he told himself.

Two men from the village appeared, armed with laser tubes. He figured they had talked to the girl and would take him to a cave to flash a hole through his head. Instead, they led him to a two-story rock compound molded from a single expanse of stone, molded into a jagged façade like rimrock in order to fool the spy satellites—which it might have done, if the rooms inside had not been so conspicuously rectangular. In addition to portable demiurges, the village obviously had some nanotech construction agents.

Marcel Pizarro, the founder and leader of the settlement, was indeed the children's father. Paul had been sitting in the man's high-ceilinged antechamber only a minute or two when his gaze, drawn upward by the murky inverted palace of the chandelier, fell from wrought-iron hexagons hung with long banner-like rubies, opals, and bloodstones to the boy and girl, who were conspiring together upstairs in the shadows behind the ivory balustrade. They should have been tucked away in some far corner of the house, where Paul was sure the father had tried to put them, but he said nothing. The ugliness of this meeting would be nothing compared to the ugliness that would follow.

Marcel, coming through the room only once, tended to mysterious matters of state while Paul waited, seated in one of a pair of straight-backed chairs pushed against a wall, the half-empty glass of ice water on his knee. The men who had met Paul outside of town, having additionally armed themselves with what looked like goo guns, stood against the opposite wall, stone-faced, positioned like a pair of statues, so still that candles could have been balanced on their heads. A third man, morphed into a long-haired baboon creature, paced in a far corner, nervously pulling his fingers through the tangles of his poorly groomed hide. By the time

4

Marcel and his wife, Anita Stone, finally arrived, thin modern laser tubes strapped to their hips, Paul had a working theory that the villagers did not entirely trust their new Indian friend.

"We've heard of Snakeback," said Marcel, sauntering to the center of the room like a gunfighter. "How've you heard of us?"

The children had moved forward, showing their faces between the scrimshawed balusters.

Paul said, "You've been making a go of this thing for a few years now . . . or so we heard from your neighbors."

"We have an understanding with the people in this area."

What assurance, thought Paul, amazing . . . Marcel really believed he could trust the locals, who had been tight-lipped, certainly, suspicious . . . Maybe he *could* trust them with a secret; after all, in ten years no one had filed a report with the police. Widespread sympathy for logoffs was a new wrinkle no one at the World Police had predicted. "We asked around," Paul said anyway, sticking to the story, "looking for others."

The baboon-morph, crouched in its safe dark corner, spoke to Marcel. "Right. The first thing you do when you log off is put up a flag, blow a bugle, call out to the whole area . . ."

The slang usage of "log off" still bothered Paul. These people wanted to believe that leaving society was like leaving some big evil computer, but in the "online" world you could be sitting at your table eating a sandwich and never be inside a computer or even say a word to a computer. "Logoffs" tried to make their crimes into some grand statement about technology, when really they broke the law out of plain selfishness. They wanted free food, free clothes, free entertainment—

"Take it easy, Gary." Anita Stone was calm and her voice even, though her fingers were doing a dance up and down the laser tube. "We're pleased to make your acquaintance, Mr. Kruger. This county could use a few more faces. Tell us about Snakeback."

"We don't call ourselves Snakeback. We don't call ourselves anything, actually. We're very new and small, so new that we don't even know where to begin building a village like you have here. I was sent to ask for advice."

"You came to the right place," said the baboon-morph named Gary. "Bald Mesa's the best. Ask anyone."

One of the men who had greeted Paul said, "Something tells me you're looking for more than advice."

Paul grinned and drew his long black braid onto his breast—yes, the costume was there; he was in disguise. Nevertheless, the gameplan they had made in Phoenix was turning out to be a stinker. The idea had looked great on a holodisplay in the conference room, but he could see now that no stranger, no matter how well-scripted, was going to tempt the villagers to traffic illegal technology, let alone reveal where they had originally acquired it. "Okay. So here we are, not quite able to trust each other," he said. Everyone stared at him. "You're right to be careful. And you're right that we want more than advice; we want much more. We're a new settlement, with only one offline demiurge, no nanoplast, no way to build houses or anything larger than a loaf of bread, and—" He shifted his eyes around the room, as though afraid to admit the truth. "And we're sterile as mules, as sterile as the day we were born. No one in our group has ever had a child." He waited, hoping his speech would at least buy some sympathy. "When we heard about Bald Mesa, we knew it was our only hope. We need help." Anita's fingers halted their dance, resting on the laser tube.

He stood up. "Maybe I should go."

The villagers drew their weapons. Reflexively, he glanced up at the children, who had not moved. Their eyes were drinking in the spectacle as though it were a holomovie thriller, making him want to say something, step out of the scene, stop them from seeing the inevitable violence, the laser-slicing of a human body, the lightning freeze of gray goo—but he could wait. He could hold the role together a moment more.

"If we offered you fertility pills," said Marcel, probing, "or if we help you out with offline technology, we've committed a felony—or is it treason these days?"

"Just kill him," said Gary, thankfully the one unarmed person in the room. "He's seen too much, even if he is who he says he is."

"It was a long shot," said Paul, trying to sound defeated, praying that Banks, who was tuned in via a bead-sized transmitter on the Indian neck-lace, had not waited for the baboon-morph's comment to launch the raiding party. He calculated that about ninety seconds remained to his life. "But we were desperate. I won't come again, or tell anyone I was here."

6

"Tell us who you really are, Mr. Kruger," said Anita. "For all we know, you're a cop."

"Just get it over with," said Gary. "If he's a cop, then he's bugged, and if he's bugged . . ."

"If I'm a cop," said Paul, "it's already too late for all of you." He gave the shaggy baboon-man a serious look. Go ahead, buddy, he thought to himself, growl at me all you want. Live it up. Enjoy your last day as a monkey; I'm paid to pick up junk like you every day, and I know to the microgram how much shibboleth we're going to find in your monkey hair follicles. More than enough to get you changed back into a human and beamed to prison, you demented freak. "If I'm a cop," he added, "A raiding party is on the way and will be here in a few minutes."

He let his strong, authoritative voice fill the chamber. He wanted the feeling of announcing just what had happened to all of them, before he died. They had the guns, but this was the end for them, the absolute final end. For years they had scrabbled in the wilderness, kept their lives small and unseen, like shadows under the rocks, hoping to hold on just long enough to grow old and pass away like primitives, or wishing, like capricious teenagers, that the world order would come crashing down, as it did in music meld-movies, freeing underprivileged people everywhere. He gave them all a very obvious, fearless, searching stare. The villagers were understanding now. Yes, the police are here. None of you will ever have jobs or families again, and your illegitimate children will be taken away, put into datafiles. They will be half-alive for a day or two, during your short miserable time in court, then they will be deleted. You have already killed them, by lying them into existence.

Marcel's naturally aged face was a page of creases and lines, a chronicle, drawn by deformations of gravity, the sun, the sadness of having children who for all their years had hidden in the dust, no chance of ever growing up: Paul could see the years of anxious fear at the corners of the eyes, worn there like seams in old leather, the way feeling must once have shaped the faces of all primitive human beings. Marcel raised the laser tube, the crow's feet deepening, his eyes dark as bullet holes in glass, a tick below the eye, twitching, twitching again, a break happening somewhere inside him: the final break, it seemed to Paul, the bright shattering end that happens when a person has lost everything but life itself.

Paul closed his eyes, sensing defeat but calm, thinking how much worse this moment must be for the villagers. He had simply blundered, not done his research, whereas the villagers had thrown up a phony life all around themselves and their children, a life that would soon fade away, like a dream. At least Paul would forget this place and everything that was happening. The precinct would reinstantiate the most recent backup of his body, the person he had been when he beamed off to the assignment.

The little girl shouted, piercing the chamber, drawing everyone's attention. Startled, he opened his eyes, thinking the laser gun had fired. "No! Don't!" she cried, not moving, not even standing. Her silent face looked down on everyone, pale, painted with light like a moon, small and clear and beautiful. She had been there the whole time, watching; she had been high above their heads, aware, judging them all.

"Judith! Get out of here! Get—" Marcel held the weapon on Paul. His sentence hung unfinished, hung in a silent baffled moment over a room of toylike figures, suddenly still, the game called to an end by his daughter.

He would never finish the sentence. A sound like pounding rain filled the chamber, overwhelming them all. Hundreds of autonomic tranquilizer darts, zooming in formation out of neighboring hallways, pounded the bodies of the villagers. The raiding party had landed. Marcel got off one silent swipe of the laser, cutting from shoulder to hip a rookie squad member, who had jumped the gun and now fell to the ground in two pieces. Ouch. The kid would get a kick out of watching the replay at HQ, after his reinstantiation—his first death, Paul guessed.

Marcel redirected the laser tube at Paul, but the darts in his chest and neck took him down before he could fire, clean as clockwork. Paul watched him slump to the floor, the last words he would ever want to say to his daughter buried in his heart.

David Banks, Paul's partner, was next to enter the chamber, running sideways up the curving staircase, his back against the wall, dart pistol clasped in both hands and pointed at the ceiling. He looked like a giant bug in the black diamond-fiber bodysuit. The children ran off, but he did not attempt a pursuit. He navigated the building's full perimeter, securing the premises like a preprogrammed military robot—Banks, the most exacting and dependable cop Paul had ever known.

Meanwhile, a squad of police occupied the antechamber. Since Paul was the lead investigator, one of them handed him a molecular scanner so that he could do the honors of recording the villagers' DNA sequences. He moved through the chamber like a physician, using the scanner to tell the computers in Phoenix who had been found. Biographical files, projected by the scanner's holodisplay, followed him like planets around a star, lives now subordinate to his own, returned to lawful orbits.

He had finished with the drugged bodies and was paging through the files with touches of his fingers when Banks finally came down the stairs, escorting the children by the hands. The boy fought like a lamb being pulled by its front hooves, his head jerking around with bewildered terrified side-glances, his eyes flashing wetly, dark, wild. Poor wretch, thought Paul. No one was going to make the effort to explain what was happening. He would die thinking his parents had been killed. The girl was a still frame of who she had been, numb-looking, guided to a stop by Banks' leather-gloved hand, not a muscle alive in her face: she understood what had happened and how truly helpless she was.

"We didn't have a chance with these people," said Banks, releasing the girl's hand to lift his visor.

"One thing to be glad about: this place was a fortress of paranoia. We're doing something right. When people don't give a damn whether we find them or not—that's when we have to worry."

The boy began howling like a dumb grieving animal, reaching out his free hand to his mother, who was sleeping on the floor nearby.

"Scan the kid," said Banks.

Paul complied readily; the boy was making everyone uncomfortable. It took only a few seconds to verify that both he and the girl were illegitimate, organic pregnancies induced by parents who had never been granted even the lone child sanctioned by the state.

Paul volunteered to take the kids to the hovercraft's telepod, wanting to supervise the round-up of the rest of the villagers. The boy had to be pulled, but the girl followed, obedient, knowing there was nowhere to run. That left a hand free for the ice water the boy had made him. As they walked, he finished the ice cubes one at a time, chewing swiftly, too hard at times, hungry for the cold after all he had been through.

By the time he had led them into the huge hovercraft, the boy had calmed down enough to talk to his sister. He asked if their mother and father were dead, and she said no, they were just sleeping. They would be okay. When Paul had the computer open the telepod booth's door, however, the boy stepped back, his face growing fearful again, illuminated with light from the machine's pastel-green interior. He asked his sister where they were going, familiar with telepods, probably from holomovies.

The girl took no step either forward or backward. She looked into the empty chamber as though she had expected it all her life. "Nowhere," she said.

Paul had never deleted a child her age. She must have been one of the first born after portable demiurges had opened the possibility of unregistered living. What a life—out here—growing up and learning that you're illegal, believing the opposite as long as you can, the way children try to believe in the Tooth Fairy even after they know it's a lie. For the first time, he was deleting a child who was done trying to believe.

The boy must have heard something in her tone of voice. He became nearly unmanageable, screaming for his father, biting, scratching with his fingernails. When Paul shoved him through the opening, he managed to squirm out before the door could shut, like the lizard the boy himself had converted into a glass of water an hour before. He kicked and squirmed in Paul's arms, full of his sister's anger. Eventually Paul had no other choice than to take a pistol from the gun cabinet and put him to sleep. He held the child until the muscles had fallen completely limp, then he curled the body onto the floor of the telepod. Beside it, he put the empty glass of ice water, thinking he might as well recycle the silicon while he was at it. He told the computer to store a copy of the boy and to delete the glass.

The girl observed the episode very calmly, almost analytically. When the telepod doors opened again, she stepped right into the empty chamber and turned to face Paul. She looked up calmly and said that she was ready.

This is what his job had become: looking into the eyes of an illegal child, always the same child, growing older as the years passed, until he no longer faced an unthinking toddler but a girl with age and understanding, nearly a woman, knowing just who he was and what he was doing. With her motionless gray eyes, she seemed to dare him to think about what he was doing; he was taking her life from her, punishing her for what her parents had done years ago. No one was more innocent than she was, but *she was the crime*, and the crime had to be removed from the world. Twenty years before, she would have been a drug shipment, a stolen datafile, or, at worst, an illegal copy of herself, in need of deletion but only a copy. Now she was a real human being. He was actually killing someone. "I'm sorry," he said. "I have to do this."

She just stared at him, and he knew what she was thinking: *Come on, do it. Kill me. Kill me and everyone else. Kill yourself.*

"The choice isn't mine," he told her, amazed how sick he felt inside, knowing that her calm face, already a face in a photograph, would be only one of many more hundreds to come, faces that would grow older with the years, until he would be looking into the eyes of grown men and women, telling them they had no right to be alive. If the police could not stop the spread of villages like this one, the whole sick world, already black with cancer in his mind, would truly begin to kill itself, creating lives that had to be destroyed, setting two armies of people against each other: the legal and the illegal, two armies thrown onto the planet like pieces in a game by a changing world no one understood. He touched the girl on the cheek, wanting to tell her how wrong everything was, how lost they all were, but it was hopeless. She turned away, disgusted, and he withdrew the hand.

He told the computer to store her data. The door slid shut and she was gone.

To get her off his mind, he took the scanner outside, where the raiding party would be lining up the rest of the villagers. The sun was past its zenith, which meant he would get home late again, for the third week in a row. Hopefully Claire would not be waiting up.

Chapter 2

Method 7: "Get in Trouble"

That is to say, be there. Get in the line of fire. Jump in front of the camera. Have an affair with someone famous. Commit a crime. Even better, be the victim of a crime. Just make something happen. The one resource you have and will always have is the story of your life, which you own, the way you might own a movie script. If an industrial laser burns off your arm, for instance, you own the pain, the arm, the burning, the laser beam, and all the surrounding circumstances. Your life is information. Make it into something marketable. You have value only if you entertain: *entertain or be entertained.* Remember: everyone is a holovision personality. Do something interesting and someone will buy your show.

— Claudia Vanderbilt, *101 Ways to Make the Big Bucks*, 2822.

Claire had the holomovie so large that she hardly appeared to be lying in bed at all. Paul opened the bedroom door and thought he saw a dead body on the deck of a cruise ship, a woman sprawled at the feet of vivacious well-to-do passengers who had perhaps killed her with cocktail-party chatter. She had indeed waited up, though he had warned her that the mission might take longer than expected.

The computer had announced his arrival, but when the telepod doors popped open he had made his own customary announcement: "woo-hoo!" He said it again, in a conversational tone, when he saw his wife: "woo-hoo."

His wife yawned. "Hey," she said, propping herself up on one elbow. With bent fingers she freed strands of hair that had stuck to her lips.

He let the weight of his body fall onto the warm gel mattress. No sand, no dust, no snakes. He would sleep well tonight.

"I take it you lived through the mission. You look beat."

"We lost a cadet—that's it. No big deal. He'll probably think it's great—a silver cross to pin to his desk. The rest of us got sent home with sunburns. I thought the whole point of this job was to get us the hell out of the desert."

The sunburned forehead drew her into a sitting position. She put her palm to it. "Ouch. You should've had the computer delete it."

"I forgot." Paul pulled off his shoes, tossing them against the wall. He didn't have the energy to put them in the demiurge. He would delete them tomorrow. The sunburn, too. He could sleep through anything.

After ordering the computer to turn off the movie, Claire propped herself up against the headboard. "Clay went online, so we have the weekend to ourselves."

"School?"

"He went with a girl named Katherine, a friend from school."

"Good for him." Paul was glad to hear it, and a little surprised. Clay had a slow, secret way with girls, never wanting to admit that they entered his mind at all, at least not to Paul and Claire; maybe this one would crack his shell a little bit. "Do we know Katherine?"

"Dr. Brown mentioned her."

"They talk about girls?"

"Of course. Dr. Brown's his therapist. What do you think we're paying him for?"

Paul lifted his aching legs onto the mattress and pulled the covers over himself. Yes, he should have had the computer give him a fresh body. "Isn't he supposed to make some kind of diagnosis? How's long's that going to take?"

"He made the diagnosis. You were there—you went to that session. We talked about it."

Paul shrugged. He had been to a few of the parental sessions, but he didn't remember Dr. Brown ever saying anything definitive, except that more counseling was needed. "Oh."

"I don't want to go over it all again," said Claire.

"Sorry," he mumbled, rolling over to face her, feeling heavy, like gravity was double tonight. "In the morning . . ."

"Clay won't be back until Sunday," continued Claire. "This is our chance to take that trip you were talking about. I was thinking of *Habitable Mars VII*."

He kept his head deep in the pillow. "They have another Mars?" he said.

"I hear it's spectacular," said Claire. "It's supposed to be even more beautiful than the first ones. Remember when we went to *HMIII*?"

Paul remembered. It had been shortly after their first anniversary. They had climbed a mountain almost four miles high just to camp out under the Martian sky.

He put an arm around his wife, who was stretching out beside him. She smelled like almond oil. She was wearing the same 25-year-old body she had worn when they were dating—straight blonde hair, startling blue eyes, evenly tanned round breasts—a nice body, not the novelty it had been 35 years ago, but nice. It was good to be home. "Honey, I know what you're thinking. We had a lovely time on Mars, but that was a long time ago. I was thinking more of a trip to the Alps, or maybe to an island somewhere near the Equator. Somewhere quiet, offline."

"You can have quiet. Just sit at the bar the whole time—I don't care. And we'd be on scan-time. We could stay a week before Monday rolls around."

"I don't want all the stuff to buy, the things to do."

"God, you sound like you're three or four hundred years old." She punched his shoulder. "Live a little."

"All right, fine, but not Mars. I've seen enough desert to last me a year."

Claire propped herself up on one elbow. "Cynthia and Mark are already there. They've been there a week."

"Mmmm . . . Those chatterboxes? They'll probably be there until they turn green and grow antennas. Let's beam in tomorrow morning."

His wife's warm body moved away. He opened his eyes and saw her throw off the covers and stand up. She walked over to the demiurge, wearing a white nightgown he thought he remembered. In a sharp voice, she told the computer to give her a martini.

While the demiurge hummed away, constructing the drink one atom at a time, he thought about opulent loud furniture, high ceilings, subtle advertisements woven into the texture of carpet, into wall designs, into shadows and reflections, onto his own skin. Not an online hotel room, he thought, not tonight.

15

The gray panel of the demiurge slid open and his wife, as was her custom, removed first the olive, which she ate, and then the drink. When she continued speaking, her voice retained the sharpness with which she had addressed the computer. "I told them to expect us at ten."

He lay very still, letting the mattress form a seal around his body, a suspension-cocoon like the embalming fluid of a mummy, but he could not relax. "I wish you'd warn me . . ."

"I don't see what difference it makes what bed you sleep in." She sat down on a corner of the bed, crossed her legs, and set the martini on her knee.

He would have explained about the mission, the hike through the desert, his brush with death, the murders, but no matter what he said Claire always had the impression that when he beamed to work he was being scanned into some cops and robbers game, a synthetic drama, easily forgotten when the adventure was over. To Claire, even the Eye Award and his continuing planetwide fame for solving the Walls case was like winning a game.

He pulled the covers up to his chin and looked at the ceiling. "Maybe it's just me, maybe it was this investigation—we had to delete some children this time—but, no, I don't feel like going to some idiot's mock-up of another planet. The real Mars is a dead rock millions of miles away where maybe a half dozen people have ever set foot—" He looked at her. "A freezing-cold wasteland where you could survive maybe thirty seconds before suffocating or being torn to bits by a sandstorm."

"They melted the—"

"No one's going to melt the fucking ice caps. It's too big of a pain in the ass." He was yelling. He tried to breath more slowly. He wasn't mad. Not really . . .

Claire was only trying to plan something nice. He understood that much. If she had a nesting instinct, it operated on organizing their time, and he knew this; he was used to it, yet something made him want to scream at the top of his lungs. She made their nest from scraps of billboard, magazine ads, travel guides . . . How did they get buried under such rubbish? It was all they ever talked about; it was their whole world. "I don't want to beam to Mars," he concluded. "Not tonight."

She stared at him. "Fine. I just thought it would be fun, that's all."

When she got back in bed, she faced away from him, pulling the covers tight around her shoulders. She told the computer to shut off the light. He hadn't even kissed her hello. What am I doing? he asked himself. Bickering over trifles . . . letting even the smallest aggravations blow up in my face.

He couldn't put his finger on what made him so mad. He had no reason—no good reason at all—to act this way . . .

He sat up, picked up the clothes he had piled beside the bed, and tried to think of things to bring to Mars.

*

Paul did not see his wife again until over two months later. They had a lovely time in *Habitable Mars VII*, taking rides into the canyons and up the mountains on spry camel-like animals called spider elephants (an enhancement since the days *HM III*), but the following Monday Police Chief Sorenson had an undercover assignment for him, a case of illegal instantiation in which a woman had apparently broadcast several copies of herself across the Net. It was up to Paul to find all the copies and to discover who had provided the copying software.

He stepped into a telepod outside his office at 10:35 am, bound for the Tokyo Hilton, where he was supposed to apprehend one of the copies. Having been killed or maimed thirteen times, and having no memories of ever having been chewed up by the "gray goo" of a goo gun, he was not surprised when the doors of the telepod opened to reveal, not the Tokyo Hilton, but a low, pastel-blue hallway at department headquarters. Time had passed. A copy of himself had been lost.

He faced a very sober-looking committee of high-ranking officials: Michael Sorenson, who was the police chief of the Arizona County Precinct, David Banks, who was Paul's partner, and two people whom Paul did not recognize, dressed as civilians but wearing the official mark of the Beijing World Government: a gold lapel-pin computer shaped like the Kanji ideogram for rebirth. The man looked like a reporter, having lank shoulder-length blond hair and non-prescription glasses—definitely not like a government employee—while the woman could have been only someone of great rank and importance; she was tall and dark with strong Indian features, and every detail of her appearance, from the stiff-looking blue blazer to the considered, sober way she was eyeing him, gave off an easy, practiced air of long-held authority. Paul tried to act nonchalant. "Dead again, huh?" He stepped out of the machine, trying to smile. "Have I won an award? I must have broken the precinct record."

No one smiled in return. Detective Banks came forward, moving his square frame stiffly. Amid the block-like features of his face were two large, startled eyes. "Paul, we have a difficult situation here. You—or, rather, your original—did not die, as far as we know. We don't know where he is, but we think he may be alive. That means—"

Chief of Police Sorenson, a boyish looking man, came forward. "That means a lot of things," he said, his voice surprisingly orotund for the slender early-twenties body he inhabited. "Why don't we discuss this in the conference room."

"That means I'm not legal. Am I—"

"Let's go to the conference room," said Sorenson.

He was an illegal copy. What did that mean? Since only the highest-ranking government officials could duplicate a person, something very serious must have just happened. But where had his original gone?

He would have to wait for an answer. The officials turned their backs to him, mutely obeying the chief's suggestion.

In the conference room, Paul found himself at the narrow end of the egg-shaped table, facing the other four, the focus of a grave tribunal. Sorenson had the computer dim the lights.

"Detective Cramer," began the chief, pacing in the shadows near the wall, "a difficult nine weeks have passed since you first beamed to your assignment. During that time . . ."

Paul interrupted. "My original's been offline for nine weeks?"

"Let me finish. He went online. This has been observed and verified. However, the Bureau of Life Insurance has not received time-stamped copies of his data. The woman's got some sort of cloaking ability. Her data gets moved around by an elaborate system of computer worms and viruses. When we finally decided on reincarnation—" Sorenson turned on his heels—"the most recent time-stamped copy of you at the Office of Life Insurance was, well, you. Your more recent scannings have been hidden by a process we do not yet understand. You see, the case has grown much more complex."

"You mean she's still copying herself?"

The chief nodded, turning on his heels again and looking at the floor. The woman in the blue blazer took this opportunity to introduce herself. She was Chief Batacharia of the World Police, Beijing, and her presence indicated that the case had indeed acquired global implications. "Since my team first began to coordinate this case, about three weeks ago, we've had over fifteen thousand verified instantiations of this woman worldwide, plus several thousand illegal instantiations of other humanoids, some male, some female, some morphed. Interrogation has proved inconclusive, but we think all of these appearances are being managed by the same network of worms."

Paul took some comfort in the boardroom levelness of her voice, but he could not stop his heart from racing. They were dealing with another Walls case, the case of an individual being broadcast to the whole planet—the case that had made him famous, two decades earlier, when he had guessed—only he could know how much of a guess it was—that an employee of Makotomi Telepods had helped Walls write the worm into which Walls had packaged himself, armed with a repeating laser cannon. Millions had died. The government officials called it a "case" only because they were afraid to use the word "war." How could they be so calm now, weeks into a scan-crime with no progress against the underlying technology? Too alarmed to keep quiet, Paul started thinking aloud, "Does the public know? Do we have any code fragments? How many illegals in custody?"

The lower officials looked somewhat embarrassed, but Batacharia continued in an even tone. "The public does not yet know. We do not want to alert the responsible parties, because they could pull the plug at any minute, erase the viral code, and give us no trail to follow, which would leave the Network operating with unknown security holes."

We should shut it down, he thought automatically, instinctively afraid. But it was impossible. Shutting down the Net would alert the criminal, scare the public, upset the economy: the greatest failure possible for the World Police would be the shutdown of the Net. Without demiurges and telepods no one would be able to eat, drink, instantiate clean clothes, or go anywhere. To the public it would seem like the end of the world, like an utter breakdown of society. "This is terrible," he said. "Don't we have any leads?"

"We have no code fragments, no incriminating log files, nothing. The only agent to get anywhere in this investigation was your original, who, as we have said, disappeared."

"How've you kept this hidden from the public? This is the worst security breach—"

"The number of copies appearing is relatively small, only a few hundred per day. Whoever built this system is trying to keep it a secret, meaning that the immediate danger to the public is probably minimal. What we have to worry about are the long-range dangers."

"How do you know only a handful of copies are being made?"

"You can be sure that if this system were being used to full capacity—"

"—the world would already be overrun." Paul was catching up to his own stupid questions. It was hard to accept the fact that everyone in this room, besides himself, had had over two months to digest the situation. The world had gone forward two months; in a way, he had traveled in time. What about Claire? he wondered suddenly. What had she been doing all this time? Did she know what had happened to the original? He wished the officials would just get to the point. His life had just been thrown entirely out of whack. "What can I do? I never even got to Tokyo. Everyone in this room knows more about the case than I do."

Agent Batacharia straightened the gold-plated computer pinned to her blazer. "I'm not sure I can answer that question." She looked to the long-haired man.

The man introduced himself as Spalding Morris, Special Adviser to the Director of the World Bureau of Investigation. "I don't usually become directly involved with criminal investigations. Most of the time, I'm across the street in the peanut gallery." He and Batacharia exchanged smiles, sharing some in-joke about the bureaucracy. "I gave final permission for the reincarnation," he said, grinning uncomfortably. He lacked the poise of his companion, though he clearly outranked her. "To be honest, my motive was to support the precinct here in Phoenix. Though I'm impressed with your detective work, particularly on the Walls case, the Arizona Precinct drew up the plan." He lifted his shoulders like a student wondering if he has said enough yet.

Sorenson spoke to Paul. "You know that you're one of the finest detectives in North America. The decision to bring you back was made by our staff; we were given the responsibility of tracking down your original copy. As Chief Batacharia mentioned, you were the only investigator to get close to one of the illegal copies. We suspect you got her to take you to her point of origin."

"Where's that?"

"We don't know. We weren't able to trace the transmission, and your original never reported back. At first we thought you—he, I mean—was staying undercover, but when a month passed with no word from him, we decided he had either jumped ship or been killed."

"Why would I—you mean I just ran away? What about my family?"

"We think you left them. You see—I wish there were a better way to say this—we know of at least two occasions when you spent the night with the woman, and we have eyewitnesses who claim that you two were—or at least appeared to be—having an affair. Bellboys, a sentry robot, a video of you carrying her through a hotel lobby, that sort of thing."

"What was I—pretending or something? To get her to open up?"

"That's what we thought at first, but now we're not so sure. We think you were lured by a professional con artist into a trap of some kind." Sorenson went on. Paul was not the only person who had vanished with a copy of this woman. Hundreds of average citizens, most of them male and many of them married—were reported to have beamed away with this same "red-haired lady in a videoplastic skinsuit." Also, a smaller but significant number of women had run away with a male counterpart, whose data was being managed by the same worm network. "Now," said the chief, "we can understand why an average, unsuspecting citizen might be taken in, but for you, an officer of the law, to give up your whole career, leave your family, and beam away with a scan-criminal—*that* has us puzzled. We were hoping you would have an explanation. We're looking for marital problems, a family crisis, anything that would predispose you to run off like this."

The four officials looked at him, interested.

"You don't have to answer now," continued Sorenson. "We want you to think about what happened, visit your family, examine the records of the case, and see what you can figure out."

He was overwhelmed. Just forty-five minutes ago, on his personal discontinuous timeline, he had kissed his wife goodbye and beamed to work, relatively secure in his marriage, rejuvenated both physically and emotionally after the trip to Mars—and now he was being told that a copy of himself had not only cheated on Claire but had run off with the other woman! "Does Claire know? Did I—did he—leave a note or anything? How could this happen?"

Sorenson replied. "We told her that you were missing. Though we could have said more, we waited, probably too long, and then the idea of bringing you back came up. We decided to let you explain the situation to her yourself."

"What am I supposed to say? I get to go home, right? Is that what you said?"

"You can go home," said Sorenson. "We want you back on the case full-time, and we think that talking to Claire would be the proper way to begin. She might know more about the disappearance than she has re-vealed to us. Afterward, you can meet a copy of the other woman."

"You want me to interrogate my wife."

Sorenson smoothed his regulation tie against his chest. "We know this will be hard on you, Paul, but we're shooting blanks. We need your input, and in this case you know—or, rather, you *are*—the one who is missing. That should give you some intuition."

"Let me get this straight." He took a deep breath. "You want me to find my original, perhaps get him indicted, and then—what? Step back into a telepod and let myself be erased? I'm an illegal copy. Why should I help you?"

Agent Batacharia answered him easily, an arm on the table, her shoulders canted as though for a press photo. "Certainly. Two copies of a person cannot be allowed to live the same life. Frankly, I was against it. I'm still concerned, but Detective Banks came up with a solution that makes some sense—and is in any case what we have to work with."

David Banks acknowledged the others, a ceremonial gravity on his face, then he looked at Paul, lifting one corner of his mouth—an apology? "Well, it's not much really, just a thought I had." He cleared his throat. "I've known you and Claire a long time. I watched our kids grow up, from babies to having sleepovers to right now being out there somewhere raising hell." Banks allowed himself a moment of reflection. "Seriously," he said. "But I think, from watching our families grow up that way, that I really know the two of you, better than I've known anyone, and, hell, I know you and Claire had some troubles—we all do—but they weren't that serious. You two . . . Whatever happened out there with that scan-criminal, it can't be all that serious. Your original must have lost his mind. I can't believe you'd just up and run out on Claire."

This solemn tone of voice—in David Banks—where was it coming from? Paul's mind raced to catch up. Yes, it must be true: his family had really broken up. He, or his original, had run out on Claire and Clay. "You said you had a plan?" he said weakly.

"That's right," Banks continued with a sheepish smile, "That's what I was going to explain. Well, I got to thinking about you and Claire and the boy, and I started wishing you had a second chance. You know, some time to work things out, time to think a bit. And then it hit me: why not bring you back to work on the case—God knows we need the help—and then, afterward, let Claire pick things up with you, if that's what she wants. Maybe you can work everything out."

Paul could not believe his ears. Banks was sincere, but at the same time Paul could not imagine that they would let Claire, an average citizen, grant life or death to another person. "Is this legal?"

Batacharia replied. "Technically. You disappeared during an investigation. The police can always rule that your original was abducted. If we decide that he was harmed by the encounter . . ."

"I think this is where Mr. Banks is on to something," said Spalding Morris, visibly excited by the creative interpretation of department policy. "We can decide, for his own good, to reset his timeline, in lieu of a criminal hearing."

"The original will accept," said Batacharia. "He'll be guilty of so many crimes that he'll be forced to plea-bargain. Next to fifty years in prison, resetting his timeline will be very attractive."

Paul understood. They were going to do to the original what the courts did to every criminal. He was surprised how sinister it seemed, now that it was happening in his own life. They were going to offer the original a reduced sentence to get him to replace himself with an earlier copy, with Paul himself, a copy from before the crime. They wanted an innocent copy of Paul Cramer, a copy punished for something he had not done, afraid of criminal *impulses*, not just deeds. They wanted a Paul Cramer who could control these impulses, not the dramatic disappointment the original must have been in their eyes.

They had already made him into who they wanted. They knew he would want to live, that he would want to preserve his marriage, and that he would want to find the original. He could hardly wait to get started, in fact. He had the urge to throw a wrench into their scheme, just to show that he was alive, but even if he did something crazy like commit suicide, they would just instantiate a new Paul Cramer, maybe change the parameters of his existence a little. He was their man, he realized. He would do what they wanted.

"Your wife—maybe she would tell you something," added Banks.

"I can't believe this is happening. You're telling me to make up to my wife or be erased."

"Don't look at it that way," said Banks, his large blue eyes startled again. "Think of it as a second chance. You shouldn't even be alive right now, but here you are. You're back. You can put your life back together. This investigation . . . it will be the most important thing you ever do. You won't just be working on this crime; you might actually be able to start over, put things back together for yourself and your family."

Chapter 3

United Earth Bill of Rights

We, the human race, do hereby establish by compact the natural rights of the human organism:

> •**Life**: Every human being fully owns his state of being alive. He may end his life at any time or extend his life indefinitely.
> •**Body**: Every human being fully owns his body. He may augment, modify, or diminish his body without limitation.
> •**Mind**: Every human being fully owns his mind. He may augment, modify, or diminish his mind without limitation.

— The Tsao Tsi Insurgent Army, "Constitution for Homo Sapiens," 2618.

Amendment 80: The freedoms of Life, Body, and Mind extend to all individuals, with the exception of those having a physiological mental illness, either temporarily or permanently, naturally or unnaturally.

—110th Legislature, "The Recreational Drug/Virtual Mind-state Amendment," 2730.

A window on the north side of the house had been open for several hours, maybe a day. Rainwater had made puddles on the parquet floor, soaking in, leaving white rings at the edges as it dried. Paul was too late. The damage was done.

He asked the computer when his wife would be back, but all it knew was that she was at Loretta's and that her visits there averaged about 3.1 hours. It had even less to say about Clay, who had gone with Katherine to some sort of fantasy-adventure simulation.

He asked for a few towels and a salmon dinner, which the computer instantiated together in the dining room's demiurge, the demiurge closest to the spilled water. He dried the floor and the window sill, put the towels, now soaked and heavy, back in the demiurge, and had the computer dissolve them. Cleanliness is next to classiness, he said to himself, admiring the spare, uncluttered house, where from the beginning he had made sure that everyone instantiated only what they needed when they needed it.

How could Claire have been so careless? He was enough of a detective to know it had been her, because Clay never went into the dining room; after school he walked straight to his bedroom and shut the door, coming out only if he was baited with a dinner or a family trip online. It was not like her. She must have left in a hurry.

He had dinner in the cold on the veranda, unable to break his autumn ritual, though now it was decidedly, abruptly winter. The Mediterranean lay like a gray blanket to the horizon, with the sheets turned up along the shore; he sat where a head should have been resting, growing tired. A white storm of seagulls rose and fell, dreamlike, far away. He loved these evenings above the sea, almost could not live without them: the still, soothing hours, which in all his life he had found only here, along the southwest coast of France County, away from all the resorts; it was cheaper land but better in his mind, the ideal place to have spent his family years.

The salmon tasted plain, though he had used the usual meal-file. He ate only half, then fell into thought, sipping warm tea that was soon cold, no idea how to break the news about the original to his wife and son, who had been told that the original was merely missing.

His wife found him there, at last, but not before his joints ached with cold; he had avoided going inside, not wanting to sit around a deserted house, watching holovision and feeling like the only one who lived there anymore.

She woke him with caution, with tender movements of her fingertips on the back of his neck, and with a strange, very meaningful kiss—which bewildered him, since on his personal timeline he had seen her just that morning, not even four hours before. Out of habit, he started to pull away, but she lengthened the embrace, and it was only with difficulty that he accepted what she must have been feeling, an absence of two months real-time, which with regular trips online would have seemed like half a year.

"Well, look at you. Stranger," she said.

The red-orange setting sun, newly free of the clouds, imposed its colors on the sky, the ocean, and his wife's new Asian body, making it even harder to separate this moment from the time on Mars, where the rose-petal atmosphere had cast everything in sensual shades of pink and lavender. She was as beautiful as ever, with the long silver earrings flashing, the earrings Clay had made for her in art class, and for several seconds he just stared into her eyes, wondering how she had been feeling all these weeks, with the original gone, and wondering how all of this could have happened in the first place.

"I've been calling the station every day," she continued, "and all they give me is the same line about 'the wires are down' but that you're still 'in the field.' What does that mean—'in the field'? What's the big secret?"

He looked out to sea. "A new case," he said, needing to start somewhere. "Illegal copies, a security flaw. They're getting desperate. I don't know how to explain . . ."

"You mean you're at work for two months, just working on a case, and in all that time you talk to me twice? What's going on?"

"I talked to you? When? What did I say?"

With narrow Asian eyes, Claire caught sight of him for the first time: caught sight of who he really was. She stared at him with her arms crossed, then she pulled up a chair and sat down. "You were killed, weren't you?"

"Not exactly . . . Not that."

Her face was like brass: the hardness of a woman accustomed to frequent deaths of her husband; she had become just what the *World Police Lifestyle Guide* had predicted she would become: "a librarian of your husband's other selves," the selves of his many lives; she was the knowing part of his world, in any case, and he was just another intruder, stepping back into a life that was not entirely his. Seated, she once again crossed her arms. "Who are you, then?"

"I'm a copy, not even an official copy. Like they said, I've disappeared. They brought me back to help find the original."

He wanted to hear about the original's visit—and how it had been kept secret from the police—but he could not interrogate his wife, not just yet.

Over her shoulder, Claire told the computer to instantiate a martini and some chips and salsa. "Want anything?"

"Sure. Another tea."

She rose to get the drinks and food, which would be appearing in the living room's demiurge by the time she got there.

While she was gone he decided what to say. He began as soon as she reappeared on the veranda, meanwhile helping her unfold a small eating table between them. "Claire, I don't know exactly what happened, but they think my original had some relations—with the copied woman. I don't know—I don't know why—"

Claire tossed the basket of chips onto the small table. A corn chip flew into the air and landed in his lap. She sat down and took a long swallow of the martini, leaving the olive in the glass.

"You didn't start with the olive," he said.

"Hm?"

"Um, nothing."

"Nothing. Great."

This new feeling inside Claire had an astringent effect on her face. Her mouth contracted to a small stitched shape. He was going to have to meet this head-on, whatever it was, whatever the original had done. "Okay . . . Let's back up. What about the original? What did he say?"

"I wonder how long I would have waited. Months? Month after month right here in this house? Strange, I don't think I had one single thought of leaving."

"What happened? Did we fight? Help me." He was beginning to feel guilty for something he had not even done. He took a sip of the tea.

"I don't know if I want to help anymore. Too many times, I've helped you sift through the evidence of your life so you can imagine the parts you haven't lived, pretend that you're alive. . . . I'm sick of it."

"I—I can figure this out. Just take it easy. You're yelling at *him*."

"That's how it always is. You're always changing into someone else, forgetting everything. It isn't going to work this time."

"Well—and what am I supposed to do, then?"

His wife placed her trembling lips to the glass, sipping. "Let me tell you a story," she said, calming down. "I saw one of your dolls today, a Paul Cramer doll."

"I'm sorry, Claire. I can imagine—all these weeks . . ."

"The big doll. The one with the gun that flashes."

He grimaced. The most embarrassing part about solving the Walls case, which had made him world-famous, had been the action figures. Designed and marketed by a small Australian firm, they still sold by the millions. Though the royalties had given him the money for a house on the Gulf of Lyon—and gotten him and Claire out of that wretched middle-class 5-acre plot of nothing in southern New Mexico County—he hated being remind-ed that children all over the world were playing with effigies of himself, talking to them, playing make-believe, turning them into imaginary friends; it was spooky, especially when he thought about the younger kids, each learning his name and imagining him as someone else, often not even understanding what had made him a hero.

"Loretta and I were having coffee when her two-year-old came up to the table, holding you in her arms. You were covered with slobber and she was chewing on your head."

"Poor me," he said tartly.

"Do you know what Loretta said, when she saw her daughter?"

"Considering that I was reinstantiated just a few moments—"

"'There's your husband.' She said it without thinking, of course, and she apologized right away, remembering you'd disappeared, but, you know, I had thought the same thing: 'Look, there's my husband.' I see one of those dolls and you pop right into my head. The strange thing is, when I see the real you I don't feel all that different. You come out of the telepod in your shirt and tie, and you look like a doll dressed up as a detective. They wind you up, you go out to solve crimes, then you come home and go to bed."

Paul did not know quite where this attack was coming from—was she yelling at the original? Certainly the Paul Cramer legend was a huge exaggeration, but *he* had not been changed. He was the same person he had always been. "I can't jump right into the middle of this, mid-stream. Just tell me what the original did—when he came back. I can't argue about something I know nothing about."

"You need to leave. I'm sorry, Paul, but I need you to leave." One hurt, honest look, then Claire had to look away.

"Leave—you mean . . ." There was no question to ask. The weight of truth was on her side.

Claire was no longer trembling. She screwed up her courage and regarded him with finality. "I want you out of here, right now. We'll deal with this—but not on the spur of the moment just because you decided to pop in for a visit."

"Believe me, dear, I—the person I am right now—I want to help. It was David's idea, actually. He wanted to bring me back so that maybe I can figure out what happened—and work it out."

"What does David have to with anything?"

Paul told her about the arrangement, in which she would choose one copy of her husband.

She was amazed. "That's crazy," she said. "Can they do that?"

"I think so."

She shook her head. "Tell them I want a copy from about fifteen years ago." She rose, set down the martini, and pointed into the house. "Go."

She was serious. Paul had known her long enough to realize when he should back down. "At least let me talk to Clay before I go,"

"I don't want you to see Clay."

"Okay," he said quickly, guessing that she was going to need a day or two to cool down, "I'll go."

He went into the living room, set the two teacups—one of which was still full—in the demiurge, and told the computer to dispose of them. While the device hummed, he gathered up his gun, badge, and jacket. Before he could leave, however, the telepod started groaning, building a body. He waited patiently, his jacket folded neatly over his arm. Meanwhile, Claire stood nearby, distracted and looking worried. Maybe it's Clay, he thought. Sure enough, the computer said, "Mr. and Mrs. Cramer, your son is home." The doors came open and a horrible creature came out, a hairy ape-like morph. Paul's hand moved to his gun. The creature would have been stunned cold if the computer had not already spoken.

"Hey, Mom, Dad."

The morph crossed the room, hauteur etched into his cartilaginous face, his fingers brushing some lint off of one arm, as though the ape-hide were a fine dinner jacket. This thing, his son, headed for its bedroom.

"Clay!" Paul leapt in front of the boy, blocking his path. "My God, what have you done?"

"We've been through this before. Remember? Or did you die again?" Clay glared at his father with round white baboon eyes, then quickly pushed past.

30

"Clay! I didn't die, but—wait!"

The boy shut his bedroom door. Paul tried to open it, with no luck. "Computer, unlock Clay's door." There was a clicking sound. Paul pushed open the door to his son's room.

His son was reclining on the bed, preparing to read. "I'm sixteen," he said. "I deserve a little privacy."

For several seconds Paul just stood in the doorway. This fashion, this statement, the building "reformist" attitude . . . what part of all that could Clay know about or understand, at sixteen?

"Yes, Dad, I'm a retroevolutionist. Your very own son."

He felt a hand on his shoulder. "Leave him alone, Paul."

"When did you—"

"Let's go into the other room," said his wife. "I'll explain."

Numbly, stupidly, he groped through his memory. All that came into his head was Dr. Brown giving his pat answers, saying that Clay was a *neurotic demiurge*, lost in a corner of his mind, daydreaming—"hypostatizing," they called it. "There are two types of underdeveloped children," Dr. Brown had said. "Those who hide their feelings, wanting to be invisible, and those who show them to the rest of the world. In cases such as this, we always hope for the second condition, because it opens the patient to change. We have to help Clay learn to express what he is feeling." Paul swallowed, standing like a fool in his son's bedroom, finding nothing to say. He guessed he should have been thankful that Clay had chosen to be visible; the morphing would throw him into a dialogue with everyone around him. Yet Paul did not understand how a child could *try* to break away like this, onto some private tangent, where he might find himself entirely alone, universally resented, even hated. "Oh, Clay . . ." His voice faltered. He had no idea how to say what he meant, not in a way Clay would understand. "What does Dr. Brown say?"

"I don't go to Dr. Brown anymore."

"He doesn't need a doctor," said Claire, her voice more caustic than seemed appropriate.

"When did . . . I thought the treatment lasted six months."

Clay sat up in bed. He hugged his legs and laid his head on his knees. He said to his mother, "Haven't we been through this simulation before?"

"Yes, we have." Claire tugged harder on Paul's shoulder. "Don't make me call the police."

"The police aren't going to throw me out of my own house."

"You're a second copy."

The statement stopped him. It was true: he would have no legal rights until the original was dead. When Claire took his hand, he had to allow himself to be led back to the telepod. Then he had to let her guide him through the opening. "Tell the computer to beam you to Phoenix," she said, stepping back.

"Claire . . . Jesus, I don't understand what's happening."

"Tell the computer to beam you away."

"All right, but listen. I love you, Claire, and I love Clay. I don't know what went wrong, or what we can do, but I'm going to find out."

"You sound like the last Paul Cramer."

"I'll get to the bottom of that mystery, too."

Claire crossed her arms and turned to examine Clay's room, her face glowing yellow for a moment then darkening as the door shut.

He told the computer to beam him to Phoenix. His wife and his strangely silent home vanished behind the telepod's sliding metal door.

Chapter 4

In the realm of fashion, too, the body is gone; all that remains is Image (that is, Moving Image). Videoplastic clothing,
now indisputably in vogue, marks the final replacement of human form with cultural form. We are now precisely as beautiful
as the skies, the blooming flowers, the love scenes—precisely as
beautiful as the *programs* we zap into our clothing, the little
movies we believe communicate something about ourselves, but
which, in fact, rub us out, paint us over with fads, with the
welter of collective, puerile dreaming. When a star on holovision shows her grace and austere taste with a single yellow
butterfly flashing across her black dress, we download the
program, so that we, too, can have her poise, her simple yet
grand elegance. We've all seen the butterfly. All the women of
the world, this year, want to wear that butterfly. Next month it
will be a will-o-the-wisp, then it will be a sea anemone, but the
meaning will remain the same.

— Alice Shin, *House of Mirrors*, 2231.

David Banks met Paul at the Hot Tail, an online bar suspended above a
simmering volcano, their usual place.

By the time Banks had gotten out of bed and beamed in, Paul was four
drinks ahead. He had been staring through the glass floor at the striated
churning lava, the splashing bubbles, the gases, meanwhile mentally narrating the scene at home in different ways, imagining how his friend would
respond. While Banks ordered from a software-rendered waitress in a
diaphanous sequined bodysuit, Paul simply continued narrating, aloud now
instead of to himself. When the waitress left, Paul repeated what he had
been trying to say, "I wouldn't just *run off*. That's absurd and Claire knows
it." Banks nodded back, wrinkling his forehead. Paul added, "I know what
I was thinking when I stepped in that pod for Tokyo."

The girl reappeared with Banks' drink. The Hot-Tail simulation allowed
you to paw the waitresses or teleport with one to a hidden nook on the

crater's rim, or to a bedroom—but Paul and Banks had done it all, in harmless fun, years ago, and they knew how the software responded. No surprises left. Banks took the drink without glancing at her. "Wow . . . so it looks pretty bad? I can't say I had any clear idea what would happen if we brought you back. A hell of a lot of unknowns, I guess."

"It's my *home*." For an instant refill, Paul triple-tapped his glass, no interest in playing along with the "bar" fiction. "My home. I couldn't just walk away. . . . My original didn't either. He must have given some indication . . ."

"The logs are strange. You're very reserved."

"The logs. Exactly. I should look right in his face and see what he was thinking."

"You left us nothing. Honestly—no hint at all."

"I'll fire them up first thing in the morning. I'll have access, right?"

"Of course. We want you on the case, but—"

"I'll start with *him*."

"Paul—"

Paul took a long swallow of whiskey sour.

"Paul, this isn't what I had in mind. I figured you and Claire—I don't know. I gave up on your original weeks ago. I think we should forget about him."

"What are you trying to solve here, Officer Banks? I'm here to catch a traitor."

"And our job is to catch a scan-criminal. Your original—whatever he did—isn't the main suspect." Banks let this sink in. "I should have known Claire would mix you up with him."

"Stella must be a knockout."

"Nothing your wife couldn't wear, if you suddenly got a thing for redheads."

"Yeah . . ." Paul double-tapped the rim of his glass, toying with the idea of another drink. "I just don't understand. It would have to be something else. My original—I must have really got a thing for her."

"Eighty-year-old men don't get *things*."

Paul pushed the glass away. His reflection in the glass was angry—an angry, young man. Whatever he might want to believe, Banks' little quip was the only statement so far that had the ring of truth. "Then we can conclude only one thing. Paul Cramer is on the case. He has found a lead and finds it prudent not to report back to base. He's Paul Cramer. He's doing what the world expects him to do."

"Maybe he is," said Banks, declining his face toward the clear plane of the bar. "Maybe so."

Paul stood up. It was late. He had to let his friend go home. "We'll see tomorrow. When I come in, I want to see everything on Stella, including interrogations. You said I'm cleared, right?"

"Of course. You can also talk to her yourself. The precinct picks up several copies a day."

"Even better."

Paul thanked his friend and said goodbye.

He stayed at an offline hotel so that time would move faster, though he knew nothing could make it move fast enough. He got up early, skipped breakfast, and beamed to Phoenix in time for the pale yellow glow of morning, vast and foreboding, just beginning to reveal the rock formations of Popago Park. He liked the mornings here, before the building got crowded and loud, before the sun made him close the blinds. From the little office he could see the ruins of a once great metropolis, now almost thoroughly reclaimed by saguaro, and somehow it helped him think. Telling the computer to arrange what was known about the case, he prepared to draw some conclusions about the original.

Unfortunately, as Banks had warned, the other Paul Cramer revealed almost nothing about himself or the copied woman. "We had sushi this afternoon," began a typical log entry. "I'm beginning to agree with the people in Beijing. She seems to be someone's pawn, completely ignorant of the copying. A naive but oddly sophisticated woman. How she got mixed up in all this, I have no idea. I don't see what good it would do anyone to beam an innocent woman all over the world. Probably someone is trying to get her back for something, an ex-lover maybe, though I don't see anything cruel about multiplying her lives, especially since whoever did this mapped her old credit card to some bottomless government account. She lives quite well, actually. She seems happy." And so on. Though the original displayed a certain curiosity, he did not seem absorbed, either in the woman or the case. Two hours of viewing logs and other police records convinced Paul that the original's motives were inscrutable. What he would have paid for a recording of the original's visit with Claire. . . .

Nor was there anything illuminating or strange about researching a copy of himself. Over the years he had grown accustomed to reviewing the logs of recently murdered copies. The only difference was that this time the copy might still be alive.

He would have to get answers from Stella, the copied woman. Not directly, of course. If the case logs showed anything, it was that she knew nothing herself (or that she had some magical ability to resist Exegesis, the truth serum). She seemed to be a pawn, inadvertently leading men into some sort of online trap. She could only be used as a starting point. He would have to reenact the original assignment, somehow get her to take him away, to wherever she had taken the original, and there were only two obvious ways of doing that: either find a "fresh" copy, roaming the streets, and try to win her confidence (as his original apparently had done and as dozens of other investigators had been trying to do ever since, unsuccessfully), or make his own copy, a copy tagged with a transmitter, so that even if no one undercover could get close, she might yet lead them where they wanted to go.

The police had failed in this second approach, too, but the lab was continuing work on microtransmitters that might fool Stella's worm network. He decided to give the techs a chance to try something new. The last thing he wanted was to clumsily reenact the original's affair. Banks was right: work on the case, solve the crime, then deal with personal problems, after the facts are on the table.

"It's good that you meet her," Banks told Paul, before the two of them entered the interrogation chamber. "It will give you a sense of who we're dealing with, how she thinks, and maybe how she might be approached in the field. But don't expect to get anywhere with this woman. People all over the world have had her on X, and she always gives the same story." X was short for Exegesis. "She doesn't know anything."

"That was my impression. Is there any chance she's lying?"

"The people in Beijing say no. It's possible, but even intelligence agents don't get that level of training."

The two investigators entered the interrogation chamber. Paul, who had a reputation for keeping cool with even the most uncooperative and hideous morphs, halted in the doorway upon seeing the woman, caught by a very odd, unexpected intuition: *she knows me*, he said to himself, seeing the calm, interested look on her face. But that wasn't it: she was a random copy, picked up that morning. He felt a connection, though—or maybe just a foreboding that he might respond exactly like the original and find himself drawn to her in some unforeseeable way.

He thoroughly scrutinized the copied woman before taking a seat. She was indeed beautiful—tall, well-built, uniquely designed with expressive, idiosyncratic features, with wide-set crystal blue eyes, a sharp, thin mouth, a broad nose—but there was nothing to separate her from any other woman with an artistic taste in physical beauty—nothing, that is, until she spoke. She smiled with an inimitable expressiveness and warmth, and said in a slow, rich, perfectly crafted voice, "An inauspicious beginning, Inspector. I hope it will not color our friendship."

Paul smiled and sat down across from her. Banks sat to the left. "You must say that to all of your interrogators."

She watched him with great tenderness, as though she saw something very sad inside of him. Pulling her long, wavy red hair behind her shoulders, she replied in the same mellifluous voice. "I can tell already, from the way you clench your teeth, that I'm going to like this conversation. You're hiding something."

Her manner was terribly relaxed for someone just picked up by the police, for someone who had been told she was an illegal copy, locked in a cell with two other copies of herself, and told that they were all about to be erased, that their lives were over. Maybe the nature of the situation had not had time to sink in. "Let's get something straight. You're not going to like me." Paul clasped his hands above the table, determined not to show one speck of sympathy. "When I've learned what I need to know, you—and the other two copies of yourself—will be dissolved. Your matter will return to the ducts beneath Phoenix, and within hours your lovely, illicit forms will be restructured into hamburgers, clothing, beverages, and other items required by this province's rightful citizens. It's a terrible thing to do to a person, but it's the law, and it will keep happening to you—to copies of you—until we figure out the secret of the copying software. Do you understand?"

"Not a pretty picture, Inspector."

"Please address me as Detective Cramer."

"Yes, Detective."

"Now I don't want this to take long. I already know your story: You were traveling from Kansas to Vancouver; you're not sure what happened, but now you're appearing all over the planet, continuously, at the rate of several hundred people per day. Your story doesn't check out. No woman of your approximate molecular structure has ever beamed from Kansas to Vancouver, nor does the Bureau of Life Insurance have your structure on file. Whoever you are, you've morphed—or been morphed—and now you're an untraceable component of a very dangerous computer worm."

"I haven't morphed, Mr. Cramer. I look the way I've always looked." She gave him a frank, amused smile.

He glanced at the vital-sign holodisplay, an opaque layered bar-chart projected, like a bowl of flowers, onto the middle of the table. Everything looked normal.

"Maybe you believe it—and maybe whoever programmed these worms was also clever enough to erase the government's files on your original— but that's not what I came to talk about. Whether or not you are a willing accomplice to this scan-crime, you're an integral part of it, performing certain functions every time you're instantiated. I want to know how you fit in and why you behave in such predictable ways."

"Predictable?"

"When you appear, you do three things. First, you find a man who is alone, then you befriend him, then you coerce him to beam away with you. You both step into a telepod, and then—as far as official Net traffic goes—you vanish, never to be seen again. Your male and morphed counterparts—those also managed by this network of computer worms— perform analogous tasks when they appear. This leads me to believe that you are part of a coordinated plan to lure people into some kind of trap."

"I would never be a part of something like that."

Paul gave Banks an inquisitive look.

The detective said, "That response checks out under X. Her responses always do."

The holodisplay still looked normal. Redirecting his gaze to Stella, Paul continued the questioning. "Then how do you explain your behavior? Are you lonely? Manic?"

Stella replied with a small, girlish frown, as much for his benefit as her own, it seemed. "I don't know. I suppose if I met someone I liked, I might travel with him awhile—but not right away, not just like that." She snapped her fingers.

She seemed to be telling the truth, or at least the computer thought so, yet everything about her fit together too well, the flirting, the light-heartedness, the bemusement, even the small things, like the way her videoplastic skinsuit's marine imagery played across the contours of her body, sliding and flowing in strangely sensual swirls, caressing her all over, continuously, making her whole body suggestively liquid with the movements of eels, fish, and seaweed. She seemed dressed up to play a part. "I have before me a psychological profile, Stella, an analysis of your attitudes, tendencies, and emotions. According to this document, drafted by a team of experts in Beijing—" He let the import of the last word sink in—"You have a very common modern illness, a touch of exhibitionism. You not only crave constant attention, you need it to survive. You are—in your 'actress' psyche, as they call it—what others see you to be, almost entirely grown out of their imaginations, written into scenes they want you to act out; depending on how you perform, you're loved or unloved, and at all cost you must be loved. You're like a hologram that fades away if no one is there to admire it."

"That's not true," she said, now serious. "I don't have many friends. I don't date much and I like to spend time alone. A psychologist friend of mine always says I have the 'demiurge' psyche; I'm always throwing together fantasies in my head and then projecting them outward, not the other way around."

"A psychologist friend? Who?"

"The name . . . I don't know. It slips my mind."

The bar-graph of her vitals held steady, as always. She could never remember the names of anyone she mentioned, not even those of her parents. Either she had a remarkable case of amnesia or she had a remarkable talent for lying. "Your copies are not demiurgic," he said. "They appear to want nothing but a man who will love them." Or maybe they just want to break up families, he added to himself. Maybe they *are* demiurgic, trying to impose some fantasy of domestic disorder on the world.

A smile lifting the corners of her mouth, she crossed her arms on the table, engaged by the accusation rather than intimidated. "Maybe they all found special people."

"What makes one person more special than another?"

With a lovely, musical laugh she leaned forward. A large blowfish on her forearm watched Paul with big, curious eyes. "You want to know what I look for in a man? That's my personal business."

"I'd like to hear it. Go on." Paul glanced at Banks, who made no comment.

"Well—" She seemed to be enjoying the line of questioning—"He has to be strong. He has to have a heart." With a mischievous, introspective smile, she was walking the fingers of one hand along her arm, deforming, with each step, the sluggish body of the blowfish. "He has to be gentle. Sincere." She looked up, startling Paul with the clear intensity of her blue eyes. "I like men in authority, Paul. I like dark-haired men, men with dark eyes."

He flushed. Banks was smiling, smug, as though he already knew the secret of this game of Stella's. "Listen," said Paul, ignoring his partner. "Stella, you're a little ahead of me, and I know you're teasing, but that's what I brought you here to talk about. A copy of you and a copy of me have had some relations; they've beamed off together, actually, and—"

"How romantic." Her eyes sparkled. "No wonder you're so interested in what I like."

"I need to figure out what happened. I'm married, and—it doesn't make sense—what would I see in one of your copies? I'm trying to get a handle on you, Stella, because this afternoon I'm going to reinstantiate one of your identical twins. I'm going to watch her, figure out how she picks her victims and where she takes them."

"You make it sound so nasty. Victims? Am I some kind of spider?"

"People are disappearing, and you're the cause."

"Why not watch *me*? Why go to all the trouble to make another copy?"

"You would be suspicious."

"I wouldn't. I promise." She cocked her head to one side and pouted.

"Look, I'm being serious. During this interview I was hoping to learn—oh, I don't know." He stood up. This wasn't police work. He was berating a scan-criminal to find out why he had left his wife.

"Where are you going?"

"The people downstairs will now erase you." Paul left the room, irritated, wondering if Stella had found a way to beat X and knew what she was doing. She seemed terribly confident and conniving. This was something the original had not mentioned in the logs.

*

What bothered him most about Stella's responses was their irreverence. Her two copies laughed off his interrogations, too, though with them he was careful not to stray as far into personal matters. Surely other investigators would have noticed it, the complete lack of seriousness, the ability to joke in the face of deletion; the only clear conclusion he could draw was that she had known about the copying beforehand, that she had had time to prepare, mentally, for everything that was happening.

While the morning's batch of Stellas was being erased, he went through some interrogations that had been conducted in Beijing, looking for verification of his theory. Unfortunately, the irreverence was less apparent in the Beijing archives, and in fact a few of her copies were downright stone-faced, confused about what was going on and cold to the interrogators. Particularly under X, she seemed full of anxieties. His conviction began to wane. He was getting a more complete picture of who she was, and, not surprisingly, it was more complex than what could have been learned from a few interviews. Perhaps he had caught her in an unusual mood, or perhaps—he hated to think about it—something about him had caught her eye, the same something, maybe, that had drawn her to the original. If so, the department had been smart to bring him back. He would be their bait.

He had pretty much finished researching Stella when the computer announced that his wife was calling. "Put her on," he said.

Stella, puffy-eyed on Exegesis and rambling on about her friend in Vancouver, was replaced by an audiovisual hologram of his wife. Her image stood in the center of his desk, cut off at the waist by the polished wood. She had been crying. "Oh, Paul, it's horrible. He's gone."

"Who's gone? What happened?"

"Clay. He beamed to Los Angeles."

The information did not register at first, but Claire's mascara (always perfect, continually retouched by the computer whenever she stepped into a telepod) glistened in long tear-trails, like the lachrymose makeup of a clown. He had to believe her. Their son had run away.

"He left a message. Here." She had the computer run the message. The weeping-willow face of an ape appeared, speaking matter-of-factly. "Don't freak out, Mom. There'll be lots of fruit trees in California. I won't starve. It'll be like the Stone Age, before writing or even agriculture, a more natural way of living. And before long I'll be on unemployment, anyway." The face vanished.

The stiff talking mask was like a cartoon animation: the teeth, the ugly shape of the face, the hair, but somewhere inside that monster was trapped a very scared, confused young man. "You traced the transmission?"

"Of course. I have the serial number of the pod. Paul, how's he going to survive? He's too young to get anything from the government."

"I don't know. I wish—" Paul thought better of what he was about to say, but then he said it anyway. "You didn't have to throw me out of my own house. I can't hardly reconcile things if I'm not there."

Claire pulled her hair into a tight pigtail, looking away, and he had the sense that what was coming was what she had called to say. "Your son's sixteen, Paul. With all the scanning, he's nineteen. Did you know that? The computer just told me. Biologically, he's nineteen. He shouldn't get crap from his parents for every little thing he does that we don't agree with."

Claire's torso, rising and approaching across the wood of the desk, made him twist in his chair. Once again, he felt like he was talking about something he didn't understand. Reading a speech off of notecards. "Okay, okay. Just give me the pod number, and I'll have him picked up within the hour. I'll find out what got into him."

"You will *not* send a couple of goons after our son. I was going to give you the number so that you could find him yourself."

"I'll beam out there, but L.A.'s a big place. If he's offline . . ."

"I'm not going to give you the pod number so that strangers can hunt down our son."

"First thing is we've got to get him out of there, and L.A.'s a different jurisdiction."

"That's great, dear. What *is* your jurisdiction? Am I in your juris- diction? The woman—is *she* in your jurisdiction?"

"I'm not him, Claire. Calm—Claire, calm down. I'm not him."

"You *are* him! You are Paul Cramer! God dammit!"

"One thing at a time. Clay—I will have him found. It's something—in my position—something I am able to do. When he's back home . . ."

His wife had stopped listening. She shook her head and cursed silently, squeezing her eyes shut.

Their son had just vanished into the largest ghetto on the planet, a jungle of abandoned buildings, offline demiurges, logoff campsites; a hardscrabble desperate place, where to survive runaways would do almost anything, steal, instantiate contraband, inform on one another. His wife was not as familiar with the dangers; she had no idea how the situation should be handled. "He'll be okay, dammit. I'll make sure of it."

Claire muttered something and her image vanished.

These last two months—they were a black hole, and they were swal- lowing everything. The more he examined them the less he could see.

The puffy-eyed face of Stella reappeared above his desk. She looked sad and lost, and he wondered if she would ever have any answers for him.

Chapter 5

The so-called "demiurgic personality," this century's pop-psychology tennis ball, comes from the Pandora's toybox of "culturalism," a school of psychological thinking popular in the 29th century. It's our particular misfortune, living in a world that every day looks more like a database, to classify ourselves with totems drawn from computers and their peripherals: the camera, the actor, the construct, the demiurge; etc. Such an enumeration of personality types is as valid as any other, but we should not allow its symbolism to cloud our thinking. Favoring any one of the types is perfectly normal. Likewise, all of the types—not just that of the demiurge—can degenerate into pathology. The purpose of this guidebook, therefore, is not to prescribe the ideal personality for your child (even most demiurgic children are perfectly normal), but to describe the symptoms each of the types produces when it becomes pathological.

. . .

The demiurgic child: The demiurgic child experiences an unwillingness or a discomfort regarding "costumes," that is, in regard to being socialized into a particular role. He wants to believe that his identity is separate from the socializing process, above it somehow, fully *self-created*. Particularly during adolescence, he fails to properly augment himself with surrounding social or cultural materials, though he may try. Ironically, this retardation of the ability to script the self is typically accompanied (technically speaking, "compensated") by a heightened sensitivity to others' "costumes" and cultural artifacts in general. The demiurgic person finishes a movie or a novel—or listens to music—with the absolute conviction that an aspect of his life is illuminated therein. His feelings are projected outward, onto the entire world, where they become intelligible, interpretable. Whether or not expres-sion is private and artistic, the material manipulated by the demiurgic personality to express and understand himself—the psychoplasm—is the entire universe. We all color reality in some ways, but in the demiurgic personality this mental function is overdeveloped, often pathologically. He often loses himself in a fantasy world—either one hypostatized from cultural material or one invented on his own. In such a case (that of the *neurotic demiurge*) he would rather spend weeks alone painting a single painting (which, usually, will be difficult for his peers to "understand") than learn to express himself in conversation. The *psychotic demiurge*, instead of manipulating artistic representations of the world, tries to manipulate the external world itself, as though it were part of his fantasy life, usually failing, becoming frustrated, and often—this is the case of psychotics like Jerome Walls—lashing out with force, trying to kill what can't be controlled or assimilated mentally.

— Maria Lopez, *Understanding Your Child*, 2992.

From the office in Phoenix, Paul watched the operation begin.

David Banks, drifting around an apartment in London, shook out his arms like a boxer before a fight, blowing air through his lips. Alternately, he stood still and played with the buttons on his videoplastic Luv-Shirt, a plain collared shirt displaying sentimentally blurred soft porn.

He was taking his time getting into character. Paul was about to ask for a comlink when with abrupt resignation Banks addressed the computer. "Computer," he said, "instantiate Stella."

He was playing the part of a bachelor. They needed to convince Stella that she had been "poached:" scanned illegally and distributed on the Net. Scanned young women were often coerced into prostitution and delivered—illegally—by "chaperone" programs. This particular copy of Stella would remember being hit with a tranquilizer dart in Tucson, then sleep. Meanwhile, the laboratory had scanned her and inserted a custom-built transmitter into a bone cell in her hyoid bone—the department's fifth attempt at a transmitter that could slip past the software that moved her copies around. They had also inserted a "goo capsule" in case she proved dangerous. Now Banks was going to complete the poaching ruse by pretending to have just pulled her data off the Net.

Arranged over the walls of the apartment were wool tapestries depicting playing cards, firearms, and costumed women. Two dead ferns hung from the waxed beams of the ceiling, and a carefully prepared gloom hung over everything. The only light—other than that from the Luv-Shirt—was the depressing gray pallor of the outside world, which came through a single window beside the telepod.

Banks turned his back to Paul and approached the telepod. Stella stepped out of the telepod very cautiously and said exactly what they had expected she would say. "Where—where am I?"

"Where do you think?" With his fingers, Banks traced a moray eel that was swimming up her thigh. "I like the program," he commented.

With the dread and incomprehension they were counting on, Stella took a few hesitant steps into the room, eyeing the tapestries. "Who are you?"

"Oh boy," said Banks, letting her brush his hand off one shoulder. "I hope this isn't a mistake."

"How the hell did you get my data?"

The detective backed away, crossing his arms over the entwined couple on his shirt. "I thought you were—"

Fully composed, she said, "I'm going to ask you again: where did you get my data?"

"You—you better step back into the pod. I don't want any trouble. You're an illegal copy. I thought that because—well, you were mixed in with all these others, so I figured—"

She came toward him as though she were going to throw a punch. "Kill the chaperone program. I want to leave."

A chaperone program seized control of a telepod between creation and destruction of a prostitute. Would-be prostitutes could not sell their data unless copies of themselves, during extensive quality-control tests, showed absolute fealty to these programs, allowing themselves to be deleted after every job.

Banks said, "You don't understand—if I get caught again . . ."

Stella walked to the window and looked outside. "What city is this?"

Banks made sure she saw him staring then swallowed hard. "Don't. It would be suicide. How far you think you'll get with a dead ID?"

She began walking to the door. "I'll take my chances." When she got there, she turned around and said, "No one touches my data—not you, not anyone." She left, shutting the door gently.

David Banks released a long, joyful sigh. "That wasn't so hard," he said. He went to the couch, told his shirt to turn off, and then addressed the computer. "Bring up the transmitter and get a comlink with Cramer."

Paul brought up his own display of Stella and her surroundings, a dim staircase she was descending, then he accepted the comlink.

When Banks' face appeared, Paul told him he had done a good job. "Thanks. Now it's your turn."

*

Paul watched. And waited.

Considering she had no idea when or where she had been instantiated, Stella was surprisingly brave. She put her credit card right into the nearest streetside demiurge and instantiated a large videoplastic umbrella. The purchase was charged to an obscure government expense account, one of dozens her copies had been known to use.

Even before she got the umbrella open, both it and the skinsuit, in wireless communication, were coordinating a dance of blue and white striped fish over a coral reef. She disappeared behind the dance, naturally not wanting to be seen by some stray surveillance camera, and made her way through an arboretum once known as Oxford Street; without looking, she moved past trees and grass, past iron benches, past the silent facades of buildings, old and new, stone, glass, and silicaplast, gravestones in a well-manicured museum, which to Paul, who had tracked many criminals through ancient cities, always conveyed watchfulness, a faint reminder of how living in cities must have felt, a sense of being examined from all sides. This would make her paranoid. Predictably, she kept to one side, away from the brick walkway, where, risen on pedestals like statues of dead soldiers, glass cases displayed relics from the Age of Machinery, insects covered with sad, accusing chrome eyes, more sad than the eyes of dead soldiers because no machine had ever been a hero: the bodies of drawn carriages, automobiles, locomotives, hovercraft, all the metal once thrown around the human body to make it a functioning, movable re-source. Paul shuddered. The London World Park always upset his nerves. Maybe on a sunny day, when here and there he would have seen another human being, these cages might have aroused some curiosity, but with the park deserted they bothered him, as they would bother her. For this reason, perhaps, she hurried into the first streetside telepod and—without even bothering to invoke the cloaking software—beamed to a resort in Persia County.

It was there that Paul caught up to her, morphed into a handsome black man, his usual disguise. He rented a room on the same floor, where he watched a hologram of Stella soaking in a mineral bath. As a gesture of disinterest, he forsook the hotel room's holographic projector for the far inferior projector on his watch's nanocomputer, projecting the scene on the velvet divan while he ate a complementary falafel sandwich.

When Stella finally left her room, to take a stroll along the resort's crenellated promenade, he followed. A crowd had gathered to watch the sunset, so he had no difficulty approaching; she, too, stopped to watch the sunset.

Getting her talking was easy. She had brought the videoplastic umbrella. "Expecting rain?" he said, pointing his foot at the device, which was leaning against the dusty stone battlements.

"Oh, no." She did not look up. "That was for the sun. I didn't know what time it was." She went back to watching the sunset.

The coldness of her response surprised him. What had he said? At the police station she had been warm, warm and cunning; now she very definitely wanted to be alone. He stepped into the crenel where she was standing. "Ahhhhh," he said, "nothing on Earth more beautiful than the desert at sunset."

She gave him another look, nettled. Then her expression changed. As though finding him a very handsome man (or perhaps a potential victim), she smiled, accepting his sentiment for the desert as easily as she might have accepted a flower for her dress or her hair. She stretched out her arms, letting a hot breeze inflate the oversized sleeves of her white satin dress. She faced the gold dome of the horizon as though she had wings and wanted to fly. "I love the dry heat on my body. It makes me feel like a desert bird."

Paul was pleased. His original had used a similar opening in a rock garden in Tokyo—and had met with a similar response. "You know, it's so rare anymore that I see a real sunset."

"You have to make time."

Stella continued to gaze at the sky. Paul asked her if she was from the desert.

She turned, leaning against one wall of the crenel. With the uncanny expressiveness he had noticed before, she said, "I wish I was. My favorite thing to do as a child in Kansas was to sit on the back porch and watch things—fireflies, or heat lightning. . . . I would've loved the sunsets in the desert, but I guess I would've missed the fireflies."

Paul spun a tale of his own childhood encounters with nature, fictionalizing, something he found easy to do. "I used to watch the sunset at my father's condominium in the Himalayas, where we lived after the divorce. The sunlight would come up the mountain from below my feet, clear as a laser. I wanted to go outside, but of course the air was too thin. It was beautiful." They were quiet a moment. "Did you beam here from Kansas?"

She shook her head, slowly. "I don't know how I got here."

"What do you mean?"

She moved to his side of the crenel, lowering her voice to a whisper. "I shouldn't say anything." She looked at the desert a moment, tapping the tip of her umbrella against the battlements. "But—am I going nuts? I tried to beam to Vancouver. . . . I don't know what went wrong, but I popped out in Tucson, got hit with some sort of tranquilizer dart, then instead of waking up I got instantiated in the apartment of some creep in London who thought I was a hooker." She scanned the promenade rapidly then dropped her voice further. "I'm suddenly—not real. Off on some other timeline."

"Slow down. What happened again?"

She took another glance over her shoulder. When she turned back there were tears. "I—I don't know."

"When did you leave Kansas?"

"Just this morning. I've been getting zapped here and there ever since."

"No, I mean the date."

"Oh." She told him.

Paul had already learned the information from her file. "Miss," he said, putting a reassuring hand on her arm, "that was over thirty-five years ago."

"No." She pulled away, looking for someplace to run, it seemed. "That's impossible."

"Your data must have been stolen, a long time ago."

She stared at the desert, now in shadow. The light was going out. He watched her wet eyes close. This world was not for her.

He was beginning to understand the hook that had caught his original. Like himself—and so few others—she had lived through a temporal discontinuity. She knew the feeling of waking up and not knowing what day it was or who she was supposed to be.

Back at the station, he had tried to learn more about her, what her life had been like, but whoever had intercepted her data had either damaged her memory or taught her to lie under Exegesis; the police had learned only generalities: her childhood had been spent in Kansas County, her parents had been divorced early, she loved animals. "Hey, the cops haven't caught up to you yet. Why don't we go inside and have a drink. That won't trip any alarms if I pay."

She would know—or should know—that there was no way for her to hide for long, but she smiled anyway, and they walked to an outdoor bar located beneath a hanging garden. The night air, heavy with the perfume of overhead blossoms, lent itself to introspection and the telling of long stories. They wandered together through the list of mixed drinks (common ones renamed after local geographic formations, towns, and ancient episodes in Persian history, no longer known or relevant beyond the cadence and ambiance of the words), and though Stella said nothing different from the testimony delivered by her copies, Paul was moved by her loving descriptions of the wide open plains, the North American land once fenced and harrowed by primitive man but now rejuvenated into a vast playground, where she had gone horseback riding as a child. He thought he saw some of that boundless freedom in her eyes. Maybe it was the warm night, maybe it was her deep, unusual voice, or maybe it was the elegant despair with which she accepted her mortality, but within an hour he felt as though he had known Stella for a long time. She had the delight for living of the young, which he envied—even coveted. When she asked about his life, he let the same spirit infuse his lies: he said he was an unemployed drifter who liked to skydive. The night was still young when Stella invited him to her room. "I've never been mortal before," she said. "I feel so reckless."

She led him by the hand through the hotel, just as her copy had led the original through the Tokyo Hilton two months before. By degrees, as they walked, the original's affair lost some of its mystery; Paul arrived at a clear idea of how it had begun, at least. The man without a clear moral code is always susceptible to impulse, he decided. He has nothing to hold him back. Though Paul's mind was galloping, sorting, hypothesizing, running counterfactuals—it was only background noise, and he was numb to analysis thanks to a half-dozen fruity drinks in his system. Knowing that their mischief could lead to the termination of both of their lives—and his disgrace—made his heart pound with a fervor he could not believe. The umbrella trailed lazily over the flagstones, dancing below her dangling wrist. They reached her room, and he followed its tap-dance inside.

He stretched out on the sofa. Even with the transmitter recording everything, he was tempted, tempted to . . . ?

When he looked up again Stella was leveling the sharp end of the umbrella at his chest, holding it like a rifle. "Don't move, Detective. I have a few questions." With her free hand Stella lifted his stun gun—which she must have taken during the walk to the room—and threw it against one wall. "How much do the police know? Tell me everything."

"I don't know what you're talking about." The umbrella . . . ! They had been sloppy.

"Don't insult my intelligence. I let you follow me here so you could tell me what the authorities know." She waited. Paul began to sit up. "Don't sit up." He lay back down.

Banks, tuned in to the transmitter, would be notifying building security right now. If Paul could just stall long enough . . . "What do you want to know?"

"Have you ever been shot with a goo gun? Changing into molecular static is a very slow process."

Paul decided it would not hurt to acknowledge a few basic outlines of the case. "We know that copies of you are appearing all over the planet."

"And?"

"And we've assumed that your data was hijacked, since under Exegesis the story about being from Kansas checks out. But now I'm not so sure. You know what you're doing, don't you?"

"Faster, Detective. More information."

Paul could feel the blood pulsing through the veins of his neck. He didn't want to mention the other copied individuals, the man and the morphs. "You're a fully informed accomplice."

"I don't have time to beat the information out of you."

Paul knew that he was dead, that Banks would never make it. "You want information, you're gonna have to do more than poke me with an umbrella" were his last words.

"Fool."

The next half-minute was the most surreal and horrible moment of his life. If he could have kept the memory—that of his flesh burning, freezing, and then becoming numb gray clay, the pain spreading until that terrible moment when he was half clay, solidly split in the middle, just a head and feet waiting to disappear—he would never have gone undercover again. Fortunately, for him and for the department, this memory, like those of his other thirteen deaths, would be forgotten.

*

Banks watched the scene from the flat in London. He had indeed called building security at the resort, but by the time the lone security guard had arrived, Stella was gone and Paul was a broken gray mess on the couch.

He opened a comlink to Sorenson. "We need to contact the Bureau of Life Insurance. . . . Paul."

Sorenson was standing, on his way out. "How'd it happen?"

"Goo gun."

"Why didn't you use the capsule?"

"Paul had taken a hit. It was too late."

"So this transmitter isn't as useful as we thought. Terminate Stella. We'll use another approach."

"Another twenty-four hours."

"She's on to you and she's dangerous. She killed a police officer."

"We have something. When she beamed away, this time she used the cloaking software and morphed into a bird creature. I think she's feeling safe now. All we have to do is get an agent . . ."

"I don't want another casualty."

"Wait. Listen to this. When she went to the morph boutique, online, the transmitter kept working. The cloaking software doesn't interfere. I saw everything. We could find out where she's taking her victims."

"That's good news. Hmmm. Yes. We're getting data, then?"

"Everything."

"Okay, put someone in the field. Give it another day."

"That's all I ask."
"Where is she now?"
"Los Angeles."

Chapter 6

Even the earliest, lowest humans understood gods and godlike powers. They had a psychophysiological need, like an ant's need to build an anthill, to inflict order and meaning—even sentience—onto the material world. Their brains already held a blueprint for the modern world, an imprinted vision of what, as a species, they were programmed to build. However meager their contribution, they bent themselves toward inventing our modern matter-shaping technology; the sharpened stone was the first blind and hopeful step toward the demiurge. Something about our brains, something about how we perceive and make sense of the world, has *necessitated* our conquest of nature, the fluidification of matter, the empowerment of our voices. We want Mind to rule all we see. We were wired not just to imagine gods, but—perhaps primarily—to build them.

> — Ragiv Ghataria, *God in a Box: The Primeval and How It Shapes Our World*, 2803.

The Los Angeles Forest was barren and knotted with rubble: twisted iron ties, rusted signs, litter—a far cry from "the wild mother" and "unrepentant pandemonium," as it was described in songs. He began to wonder if Joey Gamble and Sound Evasion had ever even been to L.A. He felt closer to Nature in the biome simulations at school, the deserts, the rain forests, Arctic landscapes, though all were meticulously narrated by somnolent museum voices. So far in California County, Nature had been cold, dull, and indifferent to his decision to come here. With even billboards bare of advertisements, the wind uninterrupted by music or narration, trees malformed and suffering from drought—with no order or sense to anything, it was like a simulation that had been left running for decades on a server someone had forgotten to unplug.

He guessed this would be the fate of the places he had rented online, places he would not be able to access for months and probably years, most recently a log cabin for himself and Katherine in *Wizards and Warriors VII*—still out there, being rendered on scan-time, standing silent five hours

for every hour he spent poking around the Los Angeles ruins, every hour
he spent eating with the kids he had hooked up with—a "gang" that had
formed around a guy called Joaquín who had an "offline demiurge."
Hours, days . . . multiplied online and lost forever . . .

Two days ago he had been touching the wick of a candle, pulling off
threads of a cobweb, while he sat at the gashed wooden table in the cabin,
alone, noticing for the first time how dust collected on the candles. An
amazing detail. While they had been gone, the candles, standing in the
mouths of bottles and in wooden holders carved in the village, in a line on
the shelf by the window, in the center of the table, beside the bed . . .
Silently, secretly, they had gathered age—and would continue to do so
until his parents stopped paying the bill. His parents never asked what he
and Katherine had done in *Wizards and Warriors*, perhaps assuming the
obvious. After all—at his age—could he seriously have been excited about
monsters, treasure, magic . . . ?

He had picked a fantasy simulation because he knew Katherine would
like meeting the strange characters in the village. That's all they did:
wander around and try to guess who was real and who was simulated. He
killed a harpy that was eating a poor old woman's cats, but that was as
close to adventure as he came. At night, once, he and Katherine shared the
bed, exhausted from talking and waiting for something to happen, the
candles on the table worn down to stubs. In baggy medieval underclothes,
he lay beside her, waiting. The impossible happened. He could not lift his
hand to place it on her shoulder, though he knew she wanted him to—he
knew it.

He knew it, but he lay there, wide awake, until the moment was worn
out and he could hear the soft whistle of her snoring.

The blue tint of early dawn was enough to wake them. Katherine sat up
and faced the open window, where animations of birds could be heard
chirping. "I gotta get home," she said.

"Yeah—me too." He tried to sound casual, like she did, but could not
prevent the words from jumping out of him in an unnatural rhythm.

"Scratchy mattress." Yawning, she stretched toward the floor to pick up
her tennis shoes, a modern item she could not part with.

"It's feathers. They use bird feathers." He was half-sitting on his
elbows, still waiting.

She stuffed her feet into the shoes and lifted two long laces up past her knee. "That's really cool you got a cabin and everything—I had fun."

"Yeah?"

"Much better than the last time I went to one of these things."

"Yeah—*W & W*'s always a bit ahead—their construct classes are all proprietary."

Katherine finished one shoe. She laughed easily, turning her head to face him. "I still think the butcher was real."

Only now, with the return of conversation, was the moment truly gone. Their voices were precisely the same as they had been the previous evening, only now every sentence felt like a lie. They chatted about the simulation for a few minutes, then Katherine beamed out, taking the shoes with her.

She play-acted better than he did, keeping up their friendly routine. Though at night he would scheme about ways to change the subject and say what was on his mind, the next day, walking through the school's biome simulations with Katherine at recess, he felt like he was made of glass and would shatter if he took one false step. They were the "demiurgic couple," as Dr. Brown had gleefully labeled them one day, swinging his cosmetic eyeglasses around with two fingers; they were avoiding the other kids, as before, but now they were genuinely lost in their minds, separate even from each other.

He played along, feeling more and more like a machine, talking about their classes, books they were reading, essays they planned to write and submit to journals. (Both of them hoped to become famous scholars.) By Friday, he knew he had to act. As they walked through a Rocky Mountain pine forest, he kept one phrase perpetually spring-loaded in his head: "Hey, about *W & W* . . ." waiting, waiting some more. They followed a trail high above timberline and looked down on the aspens, which were bright gold in terror of the coming winter.

"Thirty seconds," said a female voice from the sky: the computer, warning that recess was almost over.

Katherine raised her voice to ask to be beamed offline. "Computer—"

"Wait—"

He had twenty-eight seconds, then the computer would beam them back automatically. Katherine twisted around, looking up for falling rocks. "What is it?" she said.

"Hey, about . . ." Twenty-five seconds. . . . How much time did he have? Not enough. No way he could say anything in twenty seconds. She was completely baffled, staring at him. "You want to do a meld-movie this weekend?" Blindly, stupidly, he settled for a backup plan, an idea so obviously bad he felt like he had just given up.

Katherine shaded her eyes with her hand, giving him a closer look. "I don't know. . . . I've got a lot of homework. . . . You know."

"Really, just a quick scan. It looks like an action movie, but it's supposed to be super-dramatic."

"Yeah, if you want to. Sure."

The computer beamed them back to school, cutting the conversation short. He didn't want to say another word. He would send her a message containing the name of the movie and the time to meet. The movie would do the rest, for good or bad. It contained a love scene. He had been careful to pick an obscure movie, something he had come across years before, shortly after hitting puberty, an action-romance with a decent plot and an incredibly detailed and erotic sex scene in a hot air balloon. His plan was to act surprised when it was over. They would both get pulled through the completely scripted, non-interactive scene, their brains passively receiving inputs, feeling the sensations of the actors, but they would know it was each other. Afterward, nothing physical would embarrass them; they would have done it all.

He imagined himself shrugging innocently and saying, "Kind of embarrassing, huh? I had no idea." Somehow his mind was able to fill in dialogue that went from this line to having real sex with Katherine. How easy it was to deceive yourself, he knew now, when you were determined to believe something.

She pulled out of the meld-movie before the leading man (a telepod mechanic with big, calloused hands) could finish unbuttoning her blouse. Clay had the computer route him to where she had gone. The telepod door slid open in her living room. Her mother ran past him, not even looking to see who had just beamed into her home. "What's wrong . . . ?" she called down the long parquet hallway, already receding.

Leaning around the corner of the compartment, he saw Katherine hurrying away, swinging her long, stiff arms but not quite running, morphed back to an ape but still wearing the tennis shoes. "Nothing," said Katherine, her voice steady and matter-of-fact, though she meanwhile sprang into her room, softly shut the door, and locked it.

Her mother tried the knob but was considerate enough not to tell the computer to unlock it.

"Katherine . . ." He could not hold back his voice. "Katherine . . ."

"Explain yourself, Katherine," said Mrs. Oliver to her daughter's door. "What happened?"

"Mrs. Oliver . . . Is she—?"

"Get him out! Out!" Muffled by the door, Katherine's voice nevertheless carried down the hall.

He fumbled with the hair in his eyes, the inadequate cover over his genitals, the fleshy lips so hard to control . . . "I'm sorry. . . . We were just online. I had no idea. . . ."

Mrs. Oliver kept her hand on the doorknob, visibly disconcerted, maybe by his ape morphology, though she had never seemed to mind before. "Well?" she said.

Clay waited for the door to open. "Katherine?" He waited. "I'll go," he said, when the instant came that he knew he would have to begin explaining everything to Katherine's mother.

Then he had beamed home and run into an old copy of his father. By the time he got a moment of privacy, Katherine had locked her comlink address. He left a message in the queue, not knowing if it would ever be viewed: "You know how we planned to go offline together? I'm going. Too bad about your comlink address. I would have said goodbye."

Every night, on shibboleth, this all came back, even worse than it had been, hallucinated, warped, magnified. He kept thinking he saw Katherine waving or smiling, or praying for him to return, but when he would call her name she would run or fade away. He was completely unable to join the mind games Joaquín and the others played on shibboleth, because he was always running off on his own, into the dense woods, sure that Katherine was there, that she had followed him. He would spend the night chasing her images and memories through the woods. Most of the time she was just a shadow, like a deer sprinting through the orange trees, but once in a while he would catch her gazing over her shoulder, or pausing to brush her hair, and she would be so beautiful, so sad and like an angel, all lit up by his imagination, that the forest would drop away, leaving a bedroom, or a part of *W & W*, or just light, and he would float to her, feeling totally unreal, like she was, made of light, then each of them would gradually, painfully vanish, like all hallucinations, himself finding leaves where before her gown had been floating, she finding . . . what? Him? Where was he, anyway?

Every night he chased her until his legs could go no further. Only after reaching complete exhaustion would he think of anything else, briefly, before sleeping. Lying on his back, gasping for air, he would have a moment of peace. He would watch the tall glass towers, majestic in the moonlight as the vacant temples of gods, and he would imagine the race of humans who had built them, the automatons driven by social machinery to produce wealth and more wealth, to pile it up to the sky. His drugged mind would create the roar of helicopters, hovercraft, trains; it would see lights everywhere, moving in the sky, illuminating long-gone roads, even brightening the awesome towers, now mostly vacant or preserved as museums, and for an instant the city would be alive, and he would be a part of its terrible energy, no longer alone. Everyone is here, he would think. We're all here together, working for each other. No one is lonely. No one has time to be lonely.

But the peace, like all shibboleth creations, would vanish. In a few seconds he would drift into sleep, where dreaming on shibboleth he would again swim in visions of Katherine, now frighteningly real, because there were no branches to prickle through her clothes, no tree trunks to petrify her limbs, no real world to penetrate his imagination.

He would wake up the next afternoon shaken, bruised from sleeping on the ground, his nose running, his stomach aching with hunger, and he would stink. The day would begin with a two-hour hike back to the vacant grade school (the gang's campsite), a shower (something, thanks to the hygiene programs on the Net, he had seldom before had to endure), and a studied effort to forget his dreams. After apologizing to the others for having wandered off again, he would bring a plate of food into the woods and again take stock. The conclusion would be the same. It was too late. As bad as everything was, he could never go back. His parents thought he had run away because of them, and when he got back their analysis of his emotional disorders would be continuous and mortifying. He would probably have to see another doctor. And Katherine—Oh, God, she would think he was the biggest coward on earth.

He had to accept the way things had turned out, move on. He had been lucky, actually, and should be thankful. Joaquín and the others had befriended him so quickly that he had not even missed a meal. A day offline and he had been sitting around a fire, a member of a gang of runaways, eating a T-bone steak that had been marinated in red wine. He was free and on his own. Through the group, he had access to an offline demiurge, which meant he would not starve.

And he was getting to do shibboleth. Joaquín, a 300-year-old from the Andes, morphed as a Mongol warrior, said to him, the instant they first saw each other, "I know you wouldn't be here if you didn't know what was going on." That night, Joaquín filled the pipes and delivered an impromptu sermon, mostly for the newcomer's benefit, Clay later realized.

"Shibboleth's illegal because they don't want you to see beauty where there should be ugliness. They don't want you to have feelings when there should be deadness. They want us all to see the same world, so that they can impose a single way of thinking. They don't want us slipping away into ourselves and each other."

Clay had heard this talk before. The main reason he and Katherine had wanted to go offline was to find out how much of it was true. Joaquín added, "Effects better than shibboleth could be made online, but they don't know enough about the brain. When they figure out how to read brain tissue, then it might happen, morphing of the mind—which is what we want, what shibboleth is about—but until then we have to use crude tools." With that, he smiled and placed a shibboleth stone in Clay's pipe: the real thing. Soon, within fifteen minutes, Clay would have his answer.

He wasn't expecting supreme enlightenment, but he had to find out what was so different about being on shibboleth that politicians spoke out against it, news shows gathered statistics on it, musicians sang about it, academics theorized about it . . . He dreamed about going back to his school (though he knew that would be impossible) and baffling everyone with his highly informed opinions. They were all groping for answers, trying to be part of the debate, to have opinions not just about the drug but everything—the music, morphing, the "artificial" laws that defined the modern family, the price controls used for limiting Net usage . . . Everything was falling into question. He often wondered where this doubt was coming from, after several uneventful centuries, this irresistible need to study and interpret the smallest details. Not from within, he guessed, but from the outside, as if the rapidly changing world, raising questions, was merely using people like him to get answers.

Unfortunately, shibboleth so far had brought only the strange visions of Katherine, no insights or anecdotes he could show off to his classmates, nothing harrowing or interesting at all. He was slipping away into himself, as Joaquín had said he would, but there was nothing there but a phantom of a girl. Even the lucid dreaming, the most unique part of the shibboleth experience, brought him nothing but more imaginings of Katherine. One dream in particular came again and again, making sleeping almost impossible. It was the meld-movie he and Katherine had done, only changed in terrible ways. They were still inside the bodies of the actors, unable to control their own actions, and they were still having sex in a hot air balloon, just having escaped from corporate terrorists who were trying to steal a new router technology from them (and whom they had left handcuffed, drenched in gasoline, and burning inside a wrecked hovercar), but the formerly romantic love of the man and woman had devolved into the sadistic relationship of a man to a simulated prostitute. The man (Clay) gave the woman orders, and she always did what he said. Angry, he seemed to derive more pleasure from giving orders than making love. Clay would call to the computer to stop, but the only computer running this simulation was his own mind, and it would not listen. Helpless, he would beg Katherine to forgive him and not listen to the man. "I didn't want this!" he would cry. "I didn't know what would happen."

Katherine's replies, even when she would be bent painfully over the side of the wicker basket, or tangled around the balloon's ropes, during some acrobatic, over-choreographed copulation, were bland and mindless, and he never knew if she were speaking or if it was the actress from the meld-movie. "I love you!" she would pant, or, "We did it! We beat the M-Plex agents!"

Other times—just as enigmatically—his mind would return to *Wizards & Warriors*, the early versions, which he had played alone. He would slay a monster or hordes of monsters, fill the heart of a maiden with gratitude and admiration, then, drenched in sweat and near exhaustion, make love to her. A man lived by his strength in *Wizards & Warriors* (unless he was a wizard), earning the pliant, grateful bodies of women with the power of his own body. True to this scheme, Katherine became a maiden, his adoring cheerleader, and they made love endlessly in an open, blood-soaked field, in the shadow of a slain hydra, their bodies sticky with drying blood, smelling like raw meat. As had been the case online, the exertion of battle led to unprecedented heights of physical arousal, yet he saw no similar emotion in Katherine's responses. It was her body he made love to, yet no recognition animated her eyes, no intimacy, not even the automatic delight of a simulation. He kept searching her blood-smeared face, but her eyes were always rolling, rolling, back into her head, where she could not see him.

It was out of one of these dreams that he lifted himself, heavily, the evening of the fourth day. He was finally breaking down. Sick to the stomach and trembling, he barely had the strength to sit up. It was freezing, even with the ape hide. There was no escape, he realized. Katherine was everywhere. He could close his eyes, but her image would remain, projected from every corner of his mind.

By degrees, he gave up. Katherine would laugh at his cowardly disappearance and sudden return, but he had to talk to her. It was time to go home.

Instead of returning to the gang's campsite, he started looking for a public telepod. Drearily, he navigated the ruins, no longer excited by the remnants of older civilizations, or by the cryptic psychedelic graffiti of various modern gangs, the filmy sky and bare palms curved sunward . . . He only felt annoyed at all the piles of rubble in the way, all the sharp twisted pieces of iron, the utter lack of roads or paths. Christ, what had he expected to find here? He had been lost in a dream.

He almost did not notice the woman, a runaway also, who would, remarkably, lead him to stay offline a while longer. A bird-morph, she was standing before the mirrored wall of a restored tower, stretching her lovely white and yellow wings as though seeing them for the first time. He blinked in astonishment. She actually had motor control over the wings; they were like added limbs, something he had never seen before. The

63

fashion was so new that he did not even need to see the human part of her body to be attracted. He hid in the woods, watching her furtively, like a savage who first sees an explorer from another race. Only with great caution and determination was he in time able to come out of hiding. Feeling naked and conspicuous on the trimmed lawn of the tower's museum grounds, he asked softly if she was new to Los Angeles.

He had surprised her. She refolded the wings hastily and with great difficulty, nodding. She said that, yes, this was her first time in L.A.

He helped her fold one of the wings down onto her back, admiring the style of morphing she had chosen, a very becoming gown of feathers that left her torso naked and human. She had kept all the best parts of a woman's body, he decided. Her face as well had remained human, sharp and proud with a tall comb of yellow-tipped feathers. The comb stiffened when he touched the wing, rising like an opened fan, whether out of discomfort or pleasure he did not know. "You can move them," he said inquisitively, referring to the wings.

She seemed to calm down, pleased with the compliment. "They're new," she said, stroking the wing nearest him with one hand. "It's a new thing they have, lower nerve splicing."

He asked about the technique and found that it was not quite as miraculous as he had thought. The wings simply listened to upper-body nerve pulses, opening and closing in sync with arm movements. A tiny jewel-like button behind her ear toggled the wings on and off. "So you can't fly," he said.

She looked back at the glass, saccade-like ticks of her head adding to the impression that she was a bird, perhaps a bird morphed into a human. She pressed the button behind her ear and spread the wings.

He stepped back, awed by the supple slow movements of the arms, the grand design of the wings, and the life trembling down to the tips of the feathers, all gilded by a setting sun. He felt stupid. He never knew what he was saying until it was too late.

"It's sort of pitiful, isn't it?" she said. He started to apologize but she continued, "The little costumes we wear. Ever since I was a girl I've wanted to be a bird, to fly and be part of the wilderness. I guess that's what I'm doing, pretending . . . make-believe."

"We're all pretending. So what? I'm pretending to be an ape." His mind did somersaults; he did not want her to get bored and ask him to leave. "A lot of people are tired of being what they're supposed to be. You should check out *Fly*. You morph into any bird you want and fly all over the world."

She smiled faintly, as though he had just said something very quaint. "No, I want to be a bird, a real bird. I'm waiting for science to catch up to me, and for the laws to change. Eventually everyone will want to lose consciousness, now and then, live as pure spirits, but it won't be for decades."

In a week or two Clay would be familiar with these stretches of her imagination, these futurist asides, but at the moment the technologies sounded far-fetched. "Maybe so," he said. "That would be weird. They would have to mess with people's brains."

She talked more about becoming a bird, about how light she would feel, in the sky, how changed. He was enchanted. What she described was impossible, but it was a beautiful fantasy, exactly what he had imagined was going on in people's heads offline. She had the same idea as Joaquín, the idea of morphing the mind. "Have you eaten?" he asked suddenly.

"Oranges," she said, wrinkling her nose.

He invited her to meet the rest of the gang. They walked to the school, talking intermittently and gathering branches, oranges, and flowers. The demiurge would remake what they gathered into any of over ten thousand meals. For the first time, he looked forward to eating outdoors. It would be romantic. Why had he wanted to return home? Stepping into a telepod would have ended everything; he would have spent the next two years restricted, by dataseals, to school, home, and approved educational simulations, where he would never have met a woman like this.

Christ, a moment before he had been on his way home. His mind was failing, he decided. He wasn't making decisions; he was living by whims. . . .

Around the fire, the woman introduced herself as Stella, and everyone loved her. She elicited the gang's sympathy at once by saying she was the victim of a scan-crime. "I don't know quite what happened," she said. "I think I'm an illegal copy." She told how she had tried to beam to Vancouver but had ended up in Arizona, how she had been "poached," and how she had been instantiated in London, in some creep's apartment. She had beamed directly from London to California, looking for a temporary hiding place. "I want to make sure no one followed me. Then maybe I'll go back online."

Everyone shared her sense of being an outlaw. Lynn, a red-haired ape-morph he disliked, was worried about the police, however. She told everyone what they already knew but were reluctant to admit: the police would be looking for Stella.

Clay, too, feared the police, but he wanted Stella to stay. "She was poached," he said hopefully. "Instantiated by someone else. We wouldn't be blamed for taking her in."

No one believed that any encounter with the police would end favorably, particularly since most of them were runaways. Yet the probability that Stella's data had been hijacked and put into prostitution software won a lot of hearts. They voted, and a majority elected to let her stay. "She's suffered enough," said Joaquín. "If we turn her away, we're no better than the people who stole her in the first place."

Stella became a member of the gang. That settled, they passed around the shibboleth rocks, getting ready for another weird night. Stella accepted a strobe-light necklace, seeming not to understand what it was for.

Filling his pipe, Clay asked Stella if she smoked.

"I never have."

"You would love it," he replied. "It's like stepping down into your mind and going for a stroll. If you fall asleep later, you'll remember your dreams, as clearly as if you had lived them."

She declined. In the news she had heard that the drug did horrible things to the mind, that one dose would make her legally insane, and that all of a sudden she might begin believing *all* of her dreams and end up going through the waking world like a zombie.

He informed her that those stories were spread by the government. "We're having a war of epistemologies right now," he said, taking up something Joaquín had said the other day. "The government wants you to think the world's concrete, you know, with laws and limits: organized, like with jobs, online resorts, tests, permission, the government always having to give you permission. But the world exists only in our minds—it's mutable and infinite. Shibboleth makes that obvious."

Eventually he managed to awaken Stella's curiosity. They smoked by the fireside, sharing a pipe, until faces of demons appeared in the coals, then they ran hand-in-hand to a silver mirror-tower, a hollowness of sound opening all around them. The mirrored wall was like the melted end of the world. Clay, at last enjoying the shibboleth experience, told Stella to watch her moonlit reflection and imagine that her body was a fluid.

They floated together down the wall, molten silver souls of long-lost bodies, and for several minutes Clay was in heaven, sharing one of the most important experiences of the modern world with a woman who was beginning to seem like a sylph, or a faerie, or some other magical creature of the wilderness. The fantasy ended, however, when they reached the edge of the building. Solid once again, Stella stopped laughing and faced a tall palm tree. "I get what this is about," she said.

Like a false waking in a dream, the world shed one of its layers, and Clay found himself talking to a woman whose changing face froze suddenly into the (very solid) face of a vulture. "What do you mean?"

"It's not what you think it is."

"You have to give it time. We haven't even used the strobe lights."

"I'll show you what I mean." With the pendant of her new necklace, she directed a red strobe at the palm tree. "Imagine that the tree is a serpent."

He concentrated. Soon enough the tree had eyes and fangs, the trunk was moving, and the leaves were a scaly diadem. His own body began to undulate and bend like that of a snake. He had seen enough serpents and dragons to do a realistic likeness. Soon he could even hear a throaty roar and feel a wet rotting wind on his face. "Whoa!"

Stella extinguished the light and the serpent vanished. "This drug is the most obvious little toy. All it does is project your imagination."

"That's what I said it did. It makes you feel like you're walking around in your mind. Wait 'till you see what happens when you fall asleep."

"You'll see. It'll play itself out. By the time you're an adult it won't be enough."

The condescension in her voice had a dispassionate, calculated feeling. "I *am* an—"

"It's not your fault." She sighed. "You're just like people have always been. You have the same mental organs as anyone of the species, going back a hundred thousand years—and the same disposition to believe in magic. You're like the Pre-Socratics, who imagined the entire world as a mind, and all material processes as the thinking of that mind."

"What?" Clay had lost the thread of her thought.

"You think the world exists in your mind, but that's not true. You just *want* it to be true. You want to be able to shape everything with your thoughts. That's what myth-making was about. That's what technology was about: shaping matter with the human mind, faster and with greater precision, until all we need is the spoken name of an object—the thought in our head—and we can have the object. Don't you see? All human wants feed the same need, the alloplastic instinct. We need an omnipotently ordered universe, and it's this need—this ideal—that directs all human striving, all history, all creation. Dreams and myths were the tools of the ancients. Invention was the tool of the primitives. Art, on the molecular level, is the tool of the moderns. And smoking shibboleth is your tool. But it's the cheapest of all possible instruments, the easiest to use, because just as it produces nothing—no systems of belief, no new inventions, no works of art—it also requires no skill or effort." Her many faces had frozen again: she was a statue, cold marble on a pedestal, a falcon eyeing him with hard, gray eyes.

"I—I'm sorry," he replied. "I thought you would like it."

"I'm not yelling at *you*." Another false layer fell from the world, melting away this time to reveal the living creature Stella had concealed, white and soft, still full of warmth. She made a pocket around his body with one of the wings. "It's just that I hate to see so many people so close . . . but not able to get where they're going."

Clay swallowed. His throat was dry and there was a howling in his ears—wind? Never having had such an involved conversation on shibboleth, he was finding it difficult to remember what had been said. He didn't want to look stupid. "It's not our fault. We—I mean, that's why we're here, right? To get away from all that."

She wrapped both wings around him, making a warm enclosure and pulling him against her bare chest. "I'm sorry. I'm not blaming anyone. I—it's silly. I get so angry about nothing. I've been going off about the world, which will never listen, anyway. So easy to lose track of your thoughts on this stuff . . ."

"Kind of hard to think . . ." Their thought-streams were running parallel again. The warmth of her skin came through his thin hide. His arms had encircled her waist and now—avidly—he watched the yellow-tipped feathers of the comb open like a fan.

She faced him, smiling, once again the lovely bird-morph he had invited to dinner. "I have a secret to tell you," she said. "Come closer."

He placed his cheek against hers so that she could speak into his ear.

She whispered, "Don't tell the others, but I know an anonymous way to go online. There's a place we could go, a secret place. It's the real way to dream: perfectly awake."

Her cool fingers were combing the hair of his shoulders and back. "Where?" he whispered.

She giggled and kissed him. Her features seemed to have transformed again. She had gone from appearing much older to being very young, like a teenaged girl. "It's a library of simulations, illegal simulations. New technology, new . . ."

He interrupted her with a kiss, unable to wait another second. He pulled her down on top of him, onto the cold grass. He briefly regretted that he had not found the same confidence that night in bed with Katherine, but the thought went away with the surge of pleasure from his body locking into Stella's, heaviness and strength, the sensation of his own trembling pressed into her and coming back. Multicolored strobes from all directions made him feel like he and Stella were floating in empty space, the barest forms of man and woman rendered in a void. Then he heard voices approaching. "The others might see," he protested suddenly.

With a sensual sneer she extended the giant wings as wide as they could stretch. "My little Leda . . ."

She was crazy, he decided, absolutely mad, but exactly what he had wanted from the L.A. ruins. Yes—exactly . . .

When he was an old man, he would remember this night, this vigorous, spastic love-making in the open forest, and more than anything he would remember this lovely bird—many birds: glowing, strobed like phantasms, now a swan, now an eagle, forms to match the movements of his emotions.

As though she could read his mind, she asked him to use the lucid-dream power of shibboleth. "Pretend that I'm an angel," she said. "Imagine you're God. Imagine you made me. Can you do that?"

He made her eyes black as gems, her feathers white as snow. "Sure," he said.

Chapter 7

I regret having to raise partisan issues in an address of this nature. Only the misunderstanding of this administration's critics could bring me to say what I am about to say. Bear with me.

Once again, warming up their voices for Election Year, the reformists claim that a world crisis looms, just after Election Day, if the people of the world make the wrong choice. This so-called "world crisis" is a campaign slogan, irresponsible and unfounded, spun from exaggerations of crime statistics, from questionable polls, and from—my reformist colleagues will excuse me—lies, absolute shamefaced lies. Though qualifying for a child remains a selective process, nearly one percent of childless couples continue to be granted child permits *every year*. The reward of having a family remains intact, balanced with the demands of population control. Similarly, the rising suicide rate, far from a symptom of popular despair, reflects instead a healthy awareness that a full life can be lived in a few hundred years. We should applaud our departed friends for letting the gift of life devolve, graciously, to new generations, not pity them. And last, we should recognize that we are not—as the reformists claim—experiencing a "crime wave." Aside from a few minor felonies on the increase, the Net is safe and will remain safe, thanks to the vigilance, ingenuity, and ever-expanding capabilities of the World Police. The Smile Crime Initiative is a success, probably this administration's greatest success, and we will not have it badmouthed by dissembling opportunists.

— World President Henry Smile, "State of the World Address," Jan. 20, 2997

Instead of Persia, the telepod door, sliding open, revealed the flat in London, where Banks and Spalding Morris, the director of Beijing's intelligence effort, had been waiting to break the news.

Dying again was no great trauma. He watched a condensed computer-edited holomovie of his copy's assignment, recorded by Stella's trans-mitter, and was caught up in no time. He paid close attention to the look on his copy's face as he went over the recordings (of Persia but also the ones from Phoenix and Tokyo), this time seeing what hadn't been there before.

So he was a philanderer. The big surprise was how easy it was to recognize the appetite on his copy's face at the bar. Not the periodic lust aroused by holomovies and simulations—or daydreams—easily satisfied with "gentleman's clubs" or by having Claire wear a new body. No, this was a definite appetite for another person, another life, something complex and mysterious. It was there. He believed that now.

Banks beamed to London early one morning and caught Paul staring at a still frame of himself talking to Stella at the bar in Persia. The Beijing agent was out for a jog, so they had a moment to talk. "Sometimes," Banks remarked, "you remind me of this guy on my college wrestling team; he was always watching videos of himself being pinned or thrown out of the ring. He was obsessed with failure."

"Did it help?"

"He always had new videos to watch. I think they taught him how to lose."

Paul stared at the mini-hologram above his lap. "Look at my face. I bought it all, all that cowgirl stuff." Not much better than spider elephants on Mars, he reflected.

"You were just kicking back, enjoying the assignment."

"No wonder he lost the stun gun; he was screwing around."

"You knew what happened to your original. I can't believe . . ."

"Yeah, he was kicking back. He completely forgot he was on assignment."

"Paul Cramer's always on assignment. Always."

Paul glanced at the main display above the coffee table, where Clay was sleeping in Stella's arms. Actually, right now, he could have cared less about any assignment. He wanted to get his son the hell out of California and away from Stella. He wanted to find the original. And he wanted to talk to Claire. She should not have had to deal with him running around, telling lies, getting copied and killed all the time. What he really wanted was to put his family back together. Put his life back together. "Yeah, always on assignment, and now my son, too. . . ."

"Spalding says we've got to let the scenario play out."

"Is that what you think?"

Banks sank into an easy chair and pulled up a display in his own lap. He began going through his messages, his morning routine. "Beijing wants progress."

Paul took a long look at Clay and Stella, still baffled by the coincidence. Though L.A. was the single most popular hangout for runaways, the odds were astronomical that two random people would meet in such a sprawling megalopolis. Stella had to be executing a deliberate counterattack, trying to get at him. But why? Why had she singled out his family?

Paul killed the display of Persia, wanting to talk about something else. Banks was supposed to be in Alaska right now, asleep, not coming in early to nose into other people's business.

They watched the sun rising over Los Angeles. The couple slept on, like criminals, thinking they could close their eyes and not be seen. But everyone could be seen. Hadn't he taught his son that much? Hadn't he explained, again and again, how even the smallest black mark could lock in your future? A shibboleth charge and the use of illegal simulations would, perhaps for the rest of his life, exclude Clay from government work—and therefore from having a family. There were too many applicants with perfectly clean records. Clay knew that. He knew exactly what he was doing to himself.

Spalding returned from his run, wet with drizzle and sweat, his non-prescription glasses beaded with moisture. He trailed a sour odor into the room. "Anything new?" he asked, eyeing the holodisplay on his way to the telepod. He paused to observe the sleeping couple and smiled mysteriously. "Ah, youth. I've got to freshen up." He stepped into the telepod.

Paul noted the agent's chilly voice, the voice of high authority, aloof, cerebral, relaxed. It reminded Paul how little Spalding—or Beijing, for that matter—would care if something happened to Clay. The edifice of government was not built to crack or shift for one person. If the investigation left Clay with no chance at all to live a normal life, it was tough luck for Clay.

Nevertheless, Paul had to hope that Spalding, who had taken over the investigation after the screw-up in Persia, could be brought to understand what the case was doing to his family.

During the few seconds it took the telepod to scan Spalding, destroy his sweaty body, and instantiate a clean one, Banks commented, "Why doesn't he just morph into a healthier body?"

"Said something about wanting to 'feel alive,'" said Paul.

"He should take up a real sport, like rock climbing or hunting."

Banks was an avid rock climber. When the agent reappeared, he said, "There are much more interesting ways to get exercise."

Spalding responded with his characteristically humorless smile. "Games . . . entertainment . . . not the same." He told the computer to instantiate a breakfast named "Mango and Beans," a meal he had written himself: bite-sized cubes of mango on a bed of green beans, accompanied by a tall glass of coconut milk.

"Fine—no games," pursued Banks. "If you have to run, run. But why do it here, at night, in the rain, in some old, ruined city? You could go to *Craters*; you could go running on the moon. Wouldn't that be better? Wouldn't a change of gravity and rocky terrain be more interesting? And wouldn't it be better not to sweat or gasp for breath the whole way?"

Arranging the food on a small tray, Spalding seated himself in a love seat. "Sure," he said, chewing. He looked at the holodisplay. "Good. They're waking up."

Banks dutifully looked at the holodisplay, taking the hint.

Paul thought, He's just kidding, for crissake, trying to make conversation. Spalding might have rank, but if they were going to work together, they were going to have to communicate, especially since Spalding wasn't a cop and didn't know a thing about field operations. Paul said, "We have to talk about getting an agent out there."

Spalding turned his eyes on Paul, eyebrows slanted as though to greet some inanity. "An agent is no longer necessary. She's going to take the boy online." He took a drink and looked back at the display. The couple was awake, blinking in the midday sun.

Paul placed a hand on his tie, a nervous habit. "He's just a boy. We've got to get him out of there."

"That would slow down the investigation."

"We should send someone anyway, as a backup," said Banks, seeing what Paul was after.

"Undercover cops make bad actors. We've got the real thing here, and the suspect is about to go online. At last we'll have something to report to Beijing."

"We don't know if they're really going online," said Paul. "It could be a set-up. Clay might step into the telepod and be dissolved."

"She said she was taking him to a library of simulations."

Paul watched his son guilelessly pet Stella's high comb of feathers. Bad actors. . . . He had so much to say that he was unable to translate any of it into professional language before his partner spoke for him.

"We can't really know if there's a library or not," said Banks.

"Murder is too simple. It would bore Stella. Whoever she is, she—or whoever employs her—has something more in mind. Why go to all the trouble to seduce your victims? Why not just send Jerome Wallses into the world?"

Paul saw the logic. He remembered, too, that the original had come back to see Claire. The original had beamed to a secret location and returned home. So something was out there, and they had to find it. Already anticipating the next unpleasant task, the interrogation of his wife, he said simply, "There's gotta be another way forward."

Spalding gave Paul a direct look. "You're his father," said the agent. "I realize how worried you must be. Beijing wants him out of there, too. Not out of sympathy, of course, but they hate bad press. Imagine how damaging this would be if it got out. You're a very public figure, you know, probably the one person average people think of when they think about the World Police."

"You don't see me making any speeches. If people remember something about me it's not a bunch of goons sitting around trying to score PR."

Inexplicably, the agent started smiling to himself, pushing his food around with his fork. "Imagine what the press would do with this. 'Cramer and Son: Fallen for the Same Fair Felon. Coincidence? Fate?'"

This banter was more than playful. It was sly, direct, provocative. Spalding hunched lower over his food, watching for a reaction. Paul declared, "You're out of line, Mr. Morris."

The agent chuckled, miffed it seemed that the joke wasn't registering with either one of his listeners, round eyeglasses flashing in light from the display. "Imagine the plot of the holomovie: 'detective sends mistress and troubled son on the run, both go to the obvious hideout, Southern California, they meet—Are they aspects of the detective's disturbed psyche? Are they symptoms of our own centrifugal emotions? Or are they just an allegory of the times, what we all fear is happening, to our children and to ourselves?' I guarantee you: Beijing fears the media almost as much as they fear holes in the Net. They don't want to look weak, especially now, with crime so prominent in the news."

"Where do you get off talking to me like that?"

"I—sorry. Just my imagination. Tends to get away from me."

"I am the lead detective on this case. I expect you to address me in a professional tone."

"Okay, okay . . ."

Paul had succeeded, at least, in wiping the smile off Spalding's face.

"But let's be objective," said Spalding, "Beijing lets dozens of people disappear every day. Thousands more have already vanished. We let this happen so that we can learn something about the security breach before whoever is using it knows we're on to them. Now we finally get a break, and you want to ignore it? I know how you must feel, but try to see things from the perspective of the World Police."

Paul was sufficiently chastised—and he had said all he could for now. He stared at the display over the coffee table.

"There's something else," added Spalding. "Those of us in intelligence are greatly disturbed by this crime. I personally requested fieldwork on this assignment because this case has implications far beyond Net security. You aren't intellectuals, but believe me when I say that this crime should be viewed as a symptom of a much larger disease, a disease that reaches down to the roots of our civilization. If my department is right about the library of simulations, they are a truly novel cultural development—and a threat to the existing order, perhaps the leading edge of something very big indeed. Naturally the government is concerned."

Spalding returned to his meal. Clay and Stella were walking hand-in-hand toward the runaways' campsite.

"Right . . . if you say so." Crooks are crooks, thought Paul. "I just wish Clay knew what was going on, what the danger might be."

76

"You can tell him soon enough. If we don't learn everything we need to know today—which I bet will be the case—we'll need Clay on our side." He gave Paul an important look. "You will have to talk to him."

Paul was unsure exactly what he was being asked to do. "Of course. I'm his father."

Clay and Stella started to chat with the kids sitting around the demiurge. Paul watched his son commit a felony by asking the offline demiurge for a waffle.

Banks interrupted. "What sort of threat do you mean, exactly?"

Spalding was absorbed in the kids' talk. "The ultimate threat. Total breakdown. It's a theory we've been working on about the inevitable uses of the Net. Wait—listen."

Banks asked no more questions.

Professionally, Paul had to support the current line of investigation, but he still worried about Clay. What really made him crazy was that Spalding was right. The police had no choice.

He got up and went to the room he was using as a bedroom. He had to see Claire. Though protocol forbade him from discussing the investigation with her, this involved their son. He would tell her everything.

However, he was still enough of a detective to collect his thoughts before beaming away. He needed to find out what she knew about the original. He could not waste an interview with her, because she was his only chance of finding a line of investigation not involving Clay.

To his surprise, the computer had discovered something. As instructed, it had quietly left a note in his box, so that he could talk to his wife before notifying the police. He had told the computer to cull through every bit of data recorded by his house, looking for inconsistencies. Everything from flushes of the toilet to climate control had been analyzed, and what the computer had discovered made him angry at Phoenix. Lazy bastards, he thought. They had trusted the teleportation daemon in Paris to record all of Claire's visitors, by habit treating Stella and the original like typical scan-criminals, who would have no ability to travel in secret, and they had presumed Claire would not lie about who she had spent time with. The slightest suspicion or deviation from standard procedure would have revealed that two weeks previous, though the telepod records showed no travel, his home's medical software had monitored the tissues, fluids, and organs of an unnamed male guest, a man who had appeared like a phantom inside the telepod and then disappeared a few hours later from the same place. A little suspicion would also have revealed a remarkable similarity between the man's molecular structure and Paul's own. Claire had been telling the truth: the original had come back to see her, and now Paul had the hard evidence to turn her in to the police—if it came to that.

He wasted no time. As soon as the computer located his wife at an online ski resort, he went into the living room and beamed onto the slope.

He joined her at the lip of a massive snow drift, a bowl-shaped drop-off of about fifty feet. A hissing wind, abrasive with blown snow, made him grit his teeth. She did not notice his appearance, intent instead on the arrangements of snow and stone below.

He said his wife's name, not knowing how to begin. "We have to talk," he said.

She gave a start, turning so that her ski tips extended beyond the drift. Fragments of a videoplastic jewelry ad were visible, flowing over the skis and up her outfit. She held herself in place with ski poles. "How did you get here? I told the computer . . ."

"Police business. Look, a million things have happened in the last few days. I—"

"Did the goon squad get our son?"

Paul winced. "We're not a goon squad."

"Did they find him?"

"Yes. He's . . ." Paul opened his mouth but held the words in. "He's fine," he said.

"He's in jail."

"No. Not yet."

"They let him go home?" She relaxed her stance momentarily.

"Not exactly. Look, I have a lot to say. You've got to believe me. It all happened while I was—while . . . I died again, you see, in Persia, and before the reinstantiation—"

"What the hell are you talking about?"

He took a deep breath.

He told her all about the transmitter, the episode in Persia, and what had followed in California. What the police were doing was pretty irregular, and it sounded worse the more he tried to rationalize it. "We're desperate," he said finally. "There's nothing I can do."

"Leave him alone."

"I talked to Sorenson, but everything happens in Beijing now. The case is too big. Even the central government is worried."

"He's a human being for chrissake."

"Claire—"

"Doesn't it make you sick, everyone watching your son? It's ugly. You're so used to treating people's lives like little holo-movies on your desk, things to be edited and examined, that you think people don't mind being watched now and then, but it's not true. People need to do things on their own. That's all Clay wants, a chance to make some decisions, a chance to be himself. Can't you give him that much? If you're not going to talk to him or bring him back home, you could at least leave him alone."

"Dammit, Claire." He was losing his grip on the mountain, sliding forward, stabbing his poles at the deep fluffy snow. "Dammit. You think I *enjoy* having movies of Clay all over my desk? If I hadn't been dead, maybe I could have gotten him out of there before all of this happened. But it's too late. They're going online in a few hours."

"Can't you talk to anyone? Make some kind of complaint? You could at least leave the case."

"An investigation this big . . . Challenging it would be treason."

"They can't make you spy on your own son."

"They brought me back to work on the case; it's my only reason for being here. If I quit, who am I? I'm a second copy of your husband, useless to them or to anyone else."

The tips of Claire's skis had slid gradually over the lip of the drop-off. She cast her eyes over the slope with expert scrutiny. "You always have a choice, Paul."

"I'll file a formal report, okay? But listen. Clay made his choices. He left home and he's been breaking the law. He brought this on himself. Whatever happens—" He broke off, because with a thrust of her poles, Claire had sent herself off the cliff.

She was running away, as she always did when she could not face something he was saying. That was her problem: she thought she could make things disappear by simply turning her head.

Paul was not going to disappear, however.

He watched her free-fall thirty or forty feet until the skis edged against steep powder. As always, when she took control of her fall, he was impressed and even proud. For some reason, her skiing ability contributed to his own feeling of self-worth. He was fond of telling people at work about her various feats and awards. In a way, her skill was a mark of his own professional success, one of the results of his working so many years, providing the money necessary for professional training and trips to the best resorts.

Following her would have been impossible, so he had the computer delete him and then reinstantiate him when Claire stopped to catch her breath. The intervening minutes passed in the blink of an eye, and he found himself balanced at the edge of another drop-off. He hated online ski resorts. The mountains had no bottoms; they just fell and fell and fell, on and on, forever.

Claire was breathing heavily, in complete control of her fatigue. Her face had become pink, and the ad on her ski outfit was now a steaming Phong-Universal-CodeOne salmon steak. Some corporate database must have informed the computer of his recent eating habits. He noticed that he was hungry.

His wife said, "If you don't leave me alone, I'm going to call the police."

"I haven't even told you why I'm here."

"I'm skiing."

"I have records of the original's visit two weeks ago." This got her attention. "And I know that you spent several hours with him." He waited for a response, but she just stared across the valley, at an irregular ridge of peaks, a fractal image mapped onto a flat polygon sky. "You can either tell me what happened," he said, assuming a professional tone of voice, "or someone else from the department will ask the questions. Either way, I will get the answers."

"Go ahead," she said. "Arrest me. Arrest me and Clay and the original, too; put us all in jail. See where that leaves you."

In real life, the three of them would not be put in the same cell, but that was how he saw it, how Claire had wanted him to see it: him locking the whole family in a metal cage, standing outside it, apart, not her husband, not Clay's father, not part of the family at all. "I don't intend to arrest you. I just want to know what happened. Why did he come back? Did he give you any idea where he was hiding?"

"You have to arrest me. I helped a felon."

"We can talk about that later. It's much more urgent that I find out where Stella takes her"—he searched for a word—"targets."

Thinking, Claire stamped the snow off her skis, revealing a cartoon parade of Phong-Universal-CodeOne burgers, two columns marching at attention. "He wanted me and Clay to go with him."

"Where?"

"I don't know."

"He must have said something. Is he online?"

"What are you going to do to him?"

"Just answer the question. Jesus Christ, do you have any idea what's going on? We don't want your husband"—he caught himself—"the original, I mean. We want the software that's hiding him, and we want the people who built it. It's a matter of global security."

"Yes, he's online." She moved her videoplastic goggles to the top of her head. "He says he wants to live there for the rest of his life."

"Where? In a simulation?"

Her eyes were clear blue, clear and intent on what she was about to say. (She always wore these blue eyes when she went skiing.) "He seemed to think he'd found some sort of paradise, a simulation run on stolen computer time. He wanted us to live there, like we used to talk about. Remember? He kept going on about how it was before we got married, about how we used to talk about saving up and buying a house online. He thought he'd found the perfect place."

"But he knew he would get caught. Right? He knew we would track down the simulation."

"I don't think so. I think he felt perfectly safe."

A blast of wind caught Paul from the side, making his face hurt. What was she saying? That the original, a cop, thought he could pull off a scan-crime? It was impossible. All scan-crimes, by nature crimes committed with computers, were solvable. There were always log files, here and there, that the criminal had overlooked. The original might think he could get away with a short spree of stealing, but to involve the whole family, to ask them to move into a stolen simulated house, to *emigrate* online—that was absurd. They would all go to jail. "Did he say anything else? The machine they're using? The company? Any details about the simulation itself?"

She tucked a loose piece of hair into her ski hat, her face pink from the cold, her nose and eyes a particularly dark pink, as though she had been rubbing them. "All he said was that we could live in Machine-Age London, when the city was still grimy and crowded. He said I would enjoy the theater and the city, and that he would support us by solving what he called 'real crimes.' It sounded horrible. He also said that for five days he had lived as a black slave chained up in the bottom of a big boat. Somehow that had been enlightening."

Paul felt ill. Why would his original risk going to prison for a couple of nasty historical simulations? "Anything else?"

"Yes," she said, solemn. "He said we could have another child."

The words were slow to sink in. "A real child?"

Claire nodded, looking away.

It was possible, he guessed. Fetuses were incubated online, and nothing said a fetus had to be beamed offline when it was ready to be born. It could become a simulated baby, data maintained with stolen computer time, rendered in full detail, growing and learning. It would be absolutely real, a new son or daughter, except that if the police discovered it, by law they would have to destroy it. Claire would not meet his gaze. He knew, without asking, that the idea of the child had lingered in her imagination.

He now had a sense of why so many people were disappearing with Stella. But who would offer such a deal—and why? "You didn't go. Why not?"

"It—" She broke off, shivering. "It was all too bizarre and sudden. He said he'd come back in a week, but he never did."

"Why didn't you tell the police? You knew they were looking for him."

"I hadn't made up my mind whether or not I wanted to go."

Paul understood. It was the same for everyone. All parents, given that one gift, which no one can understand until it is beamed into your home, and out of nowhere becomes so much of your life, wondered—what if? He did not need to hear more. "Did you tell Clay?"

She shook her head.

"Look," he said, wanting to move closer but not trusting his maneuverability so near the cliff. "I want you to go to the station and allow yourself to be questioned by someone other than myself, someone less personally involved. We need every detail you can remember, particularly having to do with how the original described the illegal simulations. It might help us guess who wrote them or where they might be running."

"Am I under arrest?"

"I would rather not make that determination."

"Will you visit me in jail?"

He said nothing.

"Great job it must be, rounding up your family. What are they going to do with you when we're all behind bars? Slap you on the back and send you to a telepod to be erased?"

"I believe they've given that decision to you."

Instead of replying, she stared at the ad on her skis. Then she told the computer to beam her to Phoenix and vanished.

She was right. It was a rotten job he had been given. His job at the police department was making him do things he would regret, and who would thank him? Probably not Claire, and she would decide his final reward, life or death.

*

Though department protocol required him to share what his wife had said with the rest of the team, he did not feel like discussing it. When Banks asked how Claire was, Paul just shrugged and said she was fine.

They didn't have time to talk, anyway. Clay and Stella were just stepping into a streetside telepod. Paul took a seat, alarmed that they were already on their way. "Where are they going?" he asked, sounding more worried than he had intended.

"We'll see," said Spalding.

The couple appeared online, both morphing rapidly into spiders. Since they were online, their movements were speeded up by a factor of five.

A spider web appeared in the center of the room. Clay, a small white spider, was moving ever so cautiously toward Stella, a black widow.

The detectives got to work. They warned OpenEye Systems that a foreign process was stealing time from their largest simulation, *Forgotten*

Planet: Spring, then they talked to various OpenEye technicians, none of whom could trace the exact origin of the invading code. All records indicated that the program had emerged, spontaneously, from the refraction pattern of sunlight through a honey bee's flapping wings, a split second of buzzing around a flower having generated just enough encrypted sunbeams to spin a web and two spiders.

They let the program run, looking for clues. Clay clambered underneath Stella and began to mate.

"A nature simulation. I don't get it," said Paul.

"It's a grade-school simulation," said Banks.

Spalding said, "There must be something more. Not exactly appropriate for schoolchildren."

"So they're having kinky sex," said Paul. "Big deal." It occurred to him that he, too, might have had sex with Stella in this way, but he could not see the attraction. Would his original have cheated on Claire for—*this*? This wasn't what Claire had described. She had talked about moving the whole family to London, and about having more children.

"We should assume that this program is somehow didactic," said Spalding. "That's how Stella presented it."

"Then what's being taught?" said Banks.

"Computer," said Spalding, "show me the neuronal map between the white spider and Clay Cramer." Two complex masses of labeled fibers, one human and one arachnid, appeared in front of the couch. Lines of light connected them. "Highlight the sexual organs in yellow."

"That's to be expected," said Banks. "They're having sex. They want to feel it."

"I know, but look at all these other connections. Stella—or whoever—is trying to teach much more than what it feels like for a spider to have sex. Let's see. . . . Computer, highlight proprioceptors in red."

Another web of connections appeared.

Meanwhile, intercourse having concluded, the black widow turned on her partner. Clay's chitin limbs began flailing about.

"Those are pain centers, aren't they?" said Paul.

Spalding nodded. "Stella said the simulations would be illegal. Pain must be the illegal element."

"Can he pull out? Can my son quit if he wants?"

"I don't know."

Soon Clay would be paralyzed, bound and dissolving in digestive acids. Would it go on? Would he have to watch Clay melt away and get sucked through a proboscis? "Is he going to die?"

"I don't know."

"His real body will survive, don't you think?"

Spalding and Banks were silent. Paul did not know what to do. Somewhere, unrendered and in great pain, was his son's true nervous system; it would be no more than a data structure, but the pain would be real, and the memories would be real. "We have to get him out of there."

"We can't," said Spalding. "We need the data."

Paralyzed, Clay was now being wrapped in secreted threads.

Despite the statement's coldness, Spalding was right. They had come too far to have OpenEye erase this portion of *Forgotten Planet: Spring*. They had to watch, because they had to figure out who would create such a monstrous simulation, and why.

The next few hours were agony for Paul. He watched a party of slave-traders hunt his son like an animal. They caught him in a net, bound him with chains, and stored him, like a sack of wheat, in the hold of a sailing ship, where he remained for over a day scan-time. This was the simulation the original had mentioned, but Paul did not say anything.

By sunfall, watching a malicious deck hand attach a thumb-screw to his son, Paul had had enough. "We can't let this go on," he said.

Spalding had been expecting the complaint. "You don't need to watch the whole time. Take a break. Let the computer run its traces."

"We've been running checks on fragments for hours. Whoever made these simulations knew what they were doing."

"We have to hope they were sloppy somewhere. All it takes is one mistake."

"How can you just sit there and watch him suffer like that?"

"Thousands just like him are suffering all over the Net. We have to go forward with the investigation."

Again, for professional reasons Paul had to agree, but he continued to grope for another way.

Maybe Banks, who had gone into the back room to take a nap, would have some ideas. Anything would be better than sitting in this dingy room around the clock, watching his son get tortured.

He drifted around the living room, watering plants, straightening tapestries, trying to ignore Clay, who just lay on his side, not daring to move a muscle. An hour passed. He was just about to beam back to Phoenix to work at his desk when a new line of investigation fell into his lap. His wife, quarantined to the house in France in lieu of a jail cell, called with very surprising news.

"I have a message for you," she said, her nose red and eyes puffy, the tears wiped away.

"A message? From who?"

"Your original is back. He wants to talk."

Chapter 8

President Smile, we understand your fear. Your one-party system is now a two-party system, and the tide has just begun to rise. Don't blink, Mr. Smile: the whole anachronism of hypercapitalism—not just your party's price controls—is coming down on your head, in a million pieces of broken sky. The people know what it costs to instantiate a meal—NOTHING! [*pounds podium*] They know what it costs for drones to maintain matter ducts, computers, antimatter reactors—NOTHING! [*pounds podium*] They know that copyright laws are a life-support system for a dying order. They know a copy is essentially free, and should be free. They know that the end of prices will not end creation, production, or invention. They know that real estate would be cheaper, more livable, and more secluded on the Net, which has multiplied our lands by a factor of thirty thousand. They know, also, that universal habitation online could mean a child for every couple—or two children! Or three! The time has come to crawl out from under the shadow of industrialism and accept the new order, that of the Information Age.

— Reformist Presidential Candidate Svetlana Chow, addressing the 2997 Reformist Convention.

He spotted the original at the agreed-upon rendezvous point, the outer deck of the Roald Amundsen Casino. For some reason (certainly not to gamble; Paul hated gambling) the original, unwelcome at home, had chosen as a residence a rusting slab of iron off the coast of Antarctica, a floating ruin of many levels, like a temple, typical of the time when telepods had made travel cheap but online resorts were still computationally expensive.

Even terror suspects were held in much less prison-like locations than this: dataseals could detect and prevent travel just as well as sea and ice. The original must have been looking for ways to seem penitent; he was pretty much at the mercy of the World Police.

As he descended the escalator to the outer deck, Paul crossed his arms against the wet Antarctic air and shuddered. The casino had all the worst flaws of the offline world. Between him and the original was a glaring expanse of white tiles, cracked by the weather, upset, and stained with rivulets of rust. Across the tiles aluminum janitorial robots raced around, clicking, bouncing, damaging themselves. Exposed pipes, losing their white paint, vandalized the otherwise elegant architecture. Two steps away from the foot of the escalator, Paul could already smell an unpleasant odor coming from a trash can. A trash can. The casino was out of a history book.

Leaning against the outermost railing, by the sea, the original—his collar up, head down, one side of his body inked out by a flagpole's shadow—looked cold and terribly alone, like a scrap of hardcopy newspaper blown against a fence, perhaps a lost fragment of the Jerome Walls story, which had first revealed Paul Cramer as a hero. "Keep your head, Cramer," Sorenson had said at the debriefing. "Don't forget that he's lied to us. Before you start in about personal matters, get him to open up. He can't expect us to believe he knows *nothing*. He must know how embarrassing it would be if we had to use X on one of our own people." Paul waved to his double and tried to smile. The pitiful creature, insubstantial as a hologram, looked up but did not make any gesture of recognition. This is what I became, Paul said to himself. The crumpled up remains of myself. Though Sorenson's questions were on his mind, they were rapidly being superseded by "personal matters." The original had nearly ruined both of their lives. Paul stepped up to the railing without offering to shake hands. "So?"

The original made a face, someone else's face, clenching and unclenching his jaw.

Paul waited. The original's expression, mildly defiant, was utterly impossible to read. What Paul had expected—he didn't know. Telepathy? "You'll be allowed to die," he said, "when the time comes."

"I'm not ready." The original, unshaven, impassive, fixed his eyes on a point far in the distance, behind the lambent blue of the Ross Ice Shelf, and his eyes stayed there, as though what he wanted to say lay deep within the ice. "But I'll do what they say, whatever Claire decides."

"They said you agreed to reset your timeline."

"I don't have a choice anymore, do I? Claire's the judge, and she gets to pass sentence—on both of us."

"I'm the one who's got to live your life. How about someone giving *me* a choice?"

"In name. You'll live it in name."

"Yeah? What'd I miss? Some kicks? Good piece of ass?"

"I've been gone nine months scan-time. Think you'd beam off to the Hot Tail for nine months?"

"We have recordings," said Paul, stretching the truth a little.

"All right. We hooked up. Is that what you want to hear? The opportunity was there. And don't look at me like that. You lived through Carmen. You remember Carmen."

The blood went to Paul's face. He remembered—and his thoughts went immediately to the transmitter, the officials tuning in. "Um . . ."

"You aren't a saint. You're about due, actually, and you know it. What's it been? Five years? You'll find a girl pretty soon. Doesn't matter who. For a week or two you'll sneak around like a fugitive. You'll feel dangerous, go on a few dates, then you'll calm down. You know how it goes, and you know how long it lasts. I was gone nine months."

"Let's save that for—"

"I had some time to think. If you're really going to take over my life and not screw it up, you're going to have to stop . . ."

"What?"

"Coasting along, like life is just a show that you can tune into for awhile and leave behind when you get bored."

"Me? You're the one who took off!"

"No, you are. The person I was when I left—that's you."

Paul's heart was hammering in his chest. He was light of breath. "We're being recorded," he said.

"Good, then you can play this back and listen to what I'm trying to say. Save yourself nine months."

"That why you came offline? Because you think you know something I don't?"

"I didn't know they'd already made you. No, it was just time. Stella—her system, whatever—was letting me make my own simulations, a house, a city . . . but I couldn't get Claire interested."

The original was holding back. He may have been homesick, but he would not have come offline without a plan for the authorities. "I think you came back because you knew you'd get caught sooner or later. You want to trade what you know about Stella for time."

"That would be brilliant, if I knew anything."

"Sorenson thinks you're lying. He thinks you can help them find whoever wrote the simulations. I think you're waiting for them to make an offer."

The original turned his back on the sea, for the first time cracking a smile. He leaned against the white guardrail and with great amusement let his eyes fall upon the upper deck's tethered hot air balloons, which, decorated with the faces of once famous explorers, carried curious hotel guests into the sky, from where the top of the ice field could be seen. "You have a very low regard for yourself. Would Paul Cramer bargain with world security?"

Paul didn't get to answer. A hologram of Banks appeared in front of them, projected by the regulation computer in Paul's tie clip. Banks said, "Paul. Got a moment? It's about to happen again."

A shot appeared of Clay staggering down a snow-filled alley, an image Paul was surprised the computer would allow to be projected in a public place. Apparently, nothing about his son or the alley was considered sensitive information.

Banks' voice continued, "His blood pressure has dropped through the floor. He won't last much longer."

"What the—" The surprise on the original's face was barely visible, a slight forward movement of the jaw, a pronounced blinking of the eyes. "You're actually going through with it. Is that Clay?"

"He's dying," said Paul, more tuned to the leverage this gave him over the original than to his son's suffering, which he was becoming accustomed to seeing. "We've let him die twice, and we're letting him die again. You've left us no choice. You were the only person to get anywhere in this investigation, and now . . ."

"Investigation? More like a bunch of talk while your software chases their software."

"And now you won't cooperate."

90

"I didn't learn a goddamn thing about the system. You're the ones with the camera in Stella's head."

Paul nodded toward the holodisplay. "Is this it? Is this what she does to people? What she did to you?"

An enormous detonation of water erupted at the foot of the high, calving wall of the ice shelf, hundreds of meters behind the original, but he didn't even blink. "Get him out of there. You're wasting your time."

Banks cut into the transmission. "Paul, the computer says he has about a minute. We're going through with it, on Agent Morris's authority."

Despite sharing Paul's aversion to Agent Morris, Banks reported this information in a perfectly level tone, back to business now that the approach was established.

The original said, "Beijing man? I'll talk to him. Put him on."

Spalding appeared, frowning with annoyance. "Yes, Cramer?"

"The death simulations lead nowhere," said the original. "I've already checked them out."

"We've just started getting data. What do you mean you've checked them out?"

"This is the original. I've examined them on stolen time. I don't have records, but—"

"Sorenson told me what you say you know. You don't expect the World Police to take your word for anything."

"Clay's a civilian. Do I need to quote the manual for you?"

"We're beyond parliamentary procedure, Mr. Cramer. This is a global emergency."

"Spying . . . on a child? Is this Beijing's idea of a joke?"

"Actually, it was your idea. Look, I don't have time to explain. Ask the copy if you have any questions." Spalding's image vanished, revealing Clay curled into a ball in the snow.

The original folded his arms over his chest, only now seeming to feel the cold. Meanwhile, Clay lay on his side and clutched his collar with black-tipped fingers.

Paul broke the silence. "It's not my decision. We're getting our first data samples. We can't stop. The only one who could have done anything about this was you, before you left. You spent a year in these things—" Paul tossed a hand at the display—"and now your son's in them. Are you surprised?"

The original turned back to the sea. "Shut it off," he said abruptly. "Kill the display."

"A year. You must have liked something about these simulations, to stay so long. Are they good enough for you and not for Clay—is that it?"

The scene in the alley vanished. In its place was David Banks. "He's dead. We're waiting for the next simulation to begin."

"Great, David," said Paul. "Why don't you get back to me when something new happens, something besides the death games."

"Sure." David held the connection, looking expectant, then abruptly he signed off. "I'll get back to you later."

The display switched off. Paul stared at the original, waiting for him to speak. A man could survive maybe two hours in the black water of the ocean, after which he would bob along like a piece of ice. How easy it would be to take the situation into his own hands, like sailors in previous millennia, who eliminated dissent by casting it into the sea. Why not? Get rid of that ugly part of himself so visible in the original, his other face, turning in the water and spotted with rime . . . if only they were not under surveillance.

Paul continued, "So this is what happened? You just went from one program to another, dying over and over?"

"She'll let him go pretty soon. This is just the beginning."

"You stayed for a year. Why?"

The original looked up at the balloon, which was moving toward the ice with a shift in the wind. He let his eyes drift with it. "I didn't care for dying," he said. "The pain . . . it was very real."

Paul waited.

"Stella would show up now and then, in the woods where I slept between . . . lessons. She talked in this voice like a religious teacher. Very prescriptive."

"A religious cult. Great."

"It was like a religion, yeah . . . a religion of life."

The original had the soft, urgent whisper of a patient in an "art therapy" commercial, one of those alternately happy and despairing patients running around in a paint program, finger-painting playhouses and puppy dogs and giant flowers, crying to be children again. He had the same fragile look about him. Paul said, "A religion of a fantasy life, you mean. A religion of the fake worlds she put you through."

A hologram of Spalding appeared. "All right, Cramer. He's out. We need you to talk to him."

"What?"

"Clay. He's out."

"What's going on? Is he okay?"

"He's fine."

"Where is he?"

"I said he's fine. Here—" He moved out of view.

The display showed a green hill and some trees. It took Paul a second to see Clay and Stella; they were sleeping side-by-side on the well-manicured bank of a small pond, naked, their private parts tactfully smudged by the computer into low resolution.

"Okay?" said Spalding. "We need him to do two things."

"Yes, let me talk to him. He should know what's going on."

"Two things. First—First we have to tell *you* what's going on. The Beijing lab has a lead. We need someone close to Stella to ask a few questions. She'll probably lie, but maybe we'll get lucky. She might mention a morph artist, or she might just react funny. Anything would be more than what we're getting under X."

Paul asked about the lead, and Spalding explained. Stella's hair, though made of molecules, was a fractal, which meant that it had been generated online. Moreover, the fractal, simplified to the level of wires and springs, exactly matched the hair of Bendetta Beautifica, a simulated prostitute popular in romance simulations of the previous decade. The police were currently trying to make a link either to the programmers of Bendetta Beautifica, to a cut-and-paste morph artist, or to someone who might have stolen her data. Spalding added, "The people in the lab also want Clay to get her to go offline. They say they need the log-off sequence to understand the log-on sequence."

Paul was going to lose this one. He could see that. But there was a window here—a chance to get something for Clay. "I want him coming offline in France. He's my son," said Paul.

"Understood. But first get him to talk to Stella. We can't wait for another agent."

"He's not an agent!"

"Another anything. We've got to keep moving."

"Give me something to bargain with. If Clay cooperates, can the department allow him to reset his timeline, clear his record?"

Spalding, who had the power to authorize such a bargain, gave Paul a pleased, accommodating smile.

The original had been quiet during this exchange. When Spalding vanished, he allowed himself to speak. "Tell Clay he doesn't need Stella, not yet."

"Yet? I have a hard time believing anyone *needs* this woman."

"I just can't imagine how it would affect . . . a child."

"Simulations are regulated for a reason. Perhaps you should have remembered your oath as an officer of the World Police."

"Please, no moral high-horses. I know why you became a cop."

The transmitter . . . Was the original crazy? "I . . ."

"One hundred percent economics. Amazing you've been such a success. You've lucked into a perfect life for yourself, and you know it. I invited you here because I thought you could use some perspective—on every-thing, including yourself."

"All I want from you is the facts required for this investigation."

"To be sure. Detective Cramer always keeps matters well in hand. Guess that means we split up. Mind if I'm the one who patches things up with Claire? It could mean you'll be the one who has to step into a telepod when this is all over."

"Do . . . what?"

"Well, she can't go back to . . ." The original took a good look at Paul, for the first time showing the mixture of wonder, fear, and distaste one would expect a person to feel in the presence of an exact double. ". . . back to you."

"You're in detention. You can't leave the casino."

"I can make comlinks."

"Do what you like." Paul wasn't sure exactly what the original planned, but he refused to cower in the face of a direct challenge. "Meanwhile, I'm going to request that you be questioned under X. I think you're putting on an act."

"I'm already scheduled to go under tomorrow, and I have no worries."

Paul left, abstractedly considering the legal consequences of pulling out his stun gun, cranking up the voltage to a lethal level, and pumping a few jolts between the original's ears. Unfortunately—he realized quickly—the law would favor the original in any dispute over their life, and a backup would exist, from when the original had beamed to the casino. His only hope was to win votes, mostly Claire's vote, if the police were really going to listen to her—to be "better" than the original, somehow. But as he rode the escalator to the upper deck and watched the receding form of his double, still married to the sea, he knew that anything could happen, despite his best intentions—that Paul Cramer, the copy, might indeed be capable of anything the original had done, maybe more.

Chapter 9

You are a cave-dweller and you worship the spirit world. Your mind resists these terms, but they describe the latent structure of your thoughts. Biologically, your brain is the brain of every savage who ever gave sentience to rocks and trees. Even the most coldly rational advances in your culture's technology flow from this same brain, inflicting mental organization on the physical world. The world *must make sense* to the human mind, whether as totemic spirits, omnipotent gods, Matter, or merchandise. It always has and always will. We might say we've been preprogrammed to believe that some overmind or logical system or that *something*, anyway, subsumes everything we see, makes sense of it all, when really—and this is the key insight—everything *is* subsumed, but by our own minds; we wield the material world the way we wield language, as mental information.

My arguments will show that this "alloplastic" instinct (the appetite for ordering and manipulating the material world as language) determines a common structure for all human activity, past or present, all artistic creation, all systematizations of religious or philosophical thought, all science and technology. If you follow my arguments, you will come to believe, for instance, that when you tell your demiurge to make dinner you are casting a spell (i.e. you speak the word "dinner" and, wah-lah, there it appears). This will become clear later.

> — Claude Bouchet, *The Instantiated Apple: What the Demiurge Appliance Says About Language, Spellcasting, and Technology*, 2655.

Clay, naked, unmorphed, and lying on his stomach beside a mirror-smooth simulated pool, was lifting and turning a mossy stone with his hand, for the first time in his life contemplating the mechanism of bones and muscles grasping, lifting, and turning beneath the skin. Stella had warned him that he would experience the Age of Machinery, and that there would be pain, but never had he imagined that in the Age of Machinery he, too, would be a machine, working, running down, being broken. Around his neck he could still feel the iron collar from the slave simulation, in which his skin had been black and he had lived for a day in the fusty hold of an ancient seagoing vessel, chained to the necks and ankles of other black men and women.

Stella, stretched out beside him, her breasts cool from the grass and pressed against his arm, giggled and petted his head when he told her these thoughts. "What did you think the body was?"

"I don't know." He had always imagined that it was putty, soft, monotonic, ageless putty that could assume any form.

"You're growing wise, bit by bit," she said, rising to massage his back. Instead of feathers, soft red hair brushed across his shoulder, part of a new morphology. "Unspoiled. Curious. You will grow into a great man; already you share the oldest memories of the human race."

A tingle ran through his body, modulated to movements of her fingers and vibrations of her voice, the red curls licking his ribs. Some piece of software was feeding subdermal inputs to his nervous system. "This is all free? They can't track us?"

"We can stay here as long as you like, or we can go to another simulation."

"Is this where you live? Online, stealing computer time?"

"Sometimes."

Her officious tone gave him the impression that she brought people here often, strangers perhaps, like him. "How did you know about this place? I mean, all of this, the simulations, the security leak, all the software. Who built it all?"

"I don't know . . . but it's been here a long time. I've been using it since I was a girl."

"Why haven't the police found it?"

"We keep it secret. We share it only with people we trust, people who might appreciate the experience, and traces are never left behind."

"We?"

"Those of us who know."

"How many of you—are there?"

With hands thrumming with electric energy, she touched the side of his body, prompting him to roll over. She drew the feathery red hair behind her back, unhooding her face, and began kissing his stomach. "You're full of questions today."

"It just seems strange that all of this just—*exists*. Why was it built? There must be a reason." He was getting a hardon, coaxed by an invisible touch that was conducted—telepathically, it seemed—through the warm afternoon air.

"Simulations have been misused for centuries." She spoke haltingly, in between electric starburst kisses. "They've been designed, by corporations . . . for common people. . . . The corporate studios . . . warp history and reality . . . to make vacation lands . . . for people with no appetite for history *or* reality. . . . We understand the true function of simulation . . . which is to transmit the memories . . . the wisdom . . . the horror . . . the traumas and revelations . . . of all humans and all creatures . . . that have ever existed." Crouched at a right angle to his body, she was now too engaged to speak. He closed his eyes and though not yet satisfied with her answers abandoned himself to her caresses. They could talk later.

He gave up asking questions, happy to spend the afternoon here. When the white and blue suns of *Forgotten Planet: Spring* were both setting behind a low ridge of hills, he went for a swim, moving slow as a shadow through the water. With dusk descending, cool and silent, upon the small hollow, he was reluctant to make any loud or sudden movements. He crossed the pool with the smallest possible strokes, floating on his stomach, and when a small channel appeared, beneath a bower of fictional trees' violet branches, he slipped into it with all the soundless grace of a crocodile. He was just beginning to hit a head current when a voice broke the spell. "Clay, it's your father."

He stood up, the water's surface touching his ribs. The voice had been his father's all right, but no one was standing on the bank.

"I'm down here, the yellow flower."

Clay turned his head just in time to see the flower's petals trembling. A futile desire seized him to swim back down the channel, or to dash into the woods, but he knew that the little yellow flower—a cloaking program of some sort—would just reappear somewhere else, and that the police, if all else failed, would simply instantiate a cage around his simulated body. "How'd you find me?"

"This is going to be hard to explain."

Clay sunk down to his neck in the water. This is it, he thought. The end. All I can do is wait and listen to what they're going to do to me.

"Clay," his father began, his voice low and foreboding, "the police have been trailing Stella for several days, and you just happened to fall into the net. As you know, she's a scan-criminal, and you're an accomplice, technically. What you don't know is the scope of her crimes."

Clay swallowed hard. The police would have recordings of everything that had happened online, maybe more. "They've been following her for several days, real-time?"

The flower bowed its head. "There's a transmitter in the floor of her mouth. A lot has been recorded, more than we wanted or ever needed. I'm sorry. You're in the archives. You can be charged with aiding a criminal, drug use, and the use of an offline demiurge. All the evidence is legal, incidental to a legal investigation."

The flower seemed to have straightened, seemed to have assumed a smug posture. Had the cloaking program been listening to his father's voice, analyzing the tone, mapping the overall mood to a flower graphic? It seemed so.

"It's not as bad as it seems," continued his father. "I've gotten you a very generous plea bargain. You shouldn't even have been there, when Stella got to California—I should have tracked you down myself. We all know you didn't mean to get mixed up with a scan-criminal, and you shouldn't have that following you. The police understand and are willing to make a deal. They're going to let you reset your timeline with all charges dropped. It will be like none of this ever happened."

His father had a knack for making the most absurd proposition sound perfectly logical; without a hint of empathy, he was asking Clay to delete himself. "Let's make a new version," he might have said. "This one hasn't turned out all that well." Clay replied, "I did exactly what I wanted, and I want to remember it."

"Oh, Clay . . ." The flower touched two of its leaves together, like hands—a pointless, goofy animation; the flower construct must have come from a children's simulation. "I hate to be the one to tell you this, but all Stella wants is to put you through those simulations. Some sort of indoctrination, like a cult."

"I don't want to be reset. I haven't been injured; I haven't lost part of my brain or anything."

"It's hard—I know, but there are other reasons why you might want to reset your timeline. Frankly, I think you should look on it as a fresh start. Not many people in your position have a chance to completely undo the crimes they've committed, and you've done a lot of embarrassing things since you beamed away. They will follow you."

Again, his pulse surging in his throat, Clay thought of dashing into the woods, but there was no escape. He was a digital file, online, a data structure in the hands of the police, and so were the records of his crimes. He was defeated, yet his father's solution came from one erroneous assumption: that nothing would change in all the thousands of years Clay could expect to live, that the World Police—and society at large—would always shun him because of a drug record and a few petty security breaches. But when Clay looked to his future, he didn't see the World Police at all, or the world government, or many of the laws that seemed so absolute now; he saw them all crumbling away. And every day more people came around to his opinion. Just last month he and Katherine had gone to an online concert for two-hundred million people—a "reformist" music festival—and there were millions of old people there, too, mostly from the oldest two or three generations. Reformism was for real. To-gether, filling a crater of *Habitable Moon III*, the very old and very young had raised their fists, shouted the refrain of Sound Evasion's most famous anthem,

> *divide your fortunes, your world of waste,*
> *run your money one last race,*
> *the old can see the birth is coming,*
> *the young can see the end is coming,*

and sent up an unequivocal howl of defiance to the blue planet above. A new era was coming, in which shibboleth and simulated death would be as acceptable as taking a swim on *Forgotten Planet: Spring*. "I don't care. If what I do is illegal, fine. Lock me up, put me on unemployment for eternity, disown me."

The flower was silent for some time.

Clay added, "It's not right that a person can have a job and a kid only if he does exactly what the government says every day of his life. It's . . . totalitarian." Clay stared at the little cloaking construct until it said something.

"But that's the way it is." The flower, tense, swiveled left and then right. "Listen, I'm not going to ask you to go offline right now. I just want you to look at the last few days and decide what to do. I'm here and the police are here, on your side, if you want to reset your timeline. And to make everything easier, they're giving you a way to send a message to the authorities, a gesture signifying your cooperation and respect for the law."

Clay listened quietly while his father explained the trace that had been run on Stella's hair, the impossibility of overt interrogation, the impossibility of tracing Stella's worms, and the gratitude the authorities would show for his willingness to ask a few questions. The flower was now a dim gray ghost, barely distinguishable from the stones and white plums on the bank, and it gave Clay the impression that his father's voice was hovering, disembodied, enfeebled but everywhere, like the voice of a careless god.

"But most importantly, in my opinion, they want you to convince her to come offline so that they can record the log-off sequence."

"I don't have a choice, do I?"

"You have no choice about coming offline, no. Whether or not you help us, we will beam you offline. We have to."

"What if I side with Stella?"

"What if you—what?"

"What if I believe in what she's doing?"

His father held back for a time, thinking, calculating something, the flower dim and inscrutable. "You need time. Take a few hours. Watch how she acts. She's not who you think she is." His father added, "You don't want to find out what this woman does to her victims. I wasn't going to say anything, but I saw my original today. A few months with Stella didn't exactly do him a lot of good."

"Your—who?"

Paul reminded Clay about the undercover assignment, telling him how Stella had lured Paul Cramer online for a year. "The man's given up on everything. He'd go back. If they'd let him, he'd go back to those—those programs."

Clay didn't know what to say. So his father had left for the death simulations. Interesting. "He stayed for a full year? I'd like to talk to him."

"You can do that when you come offline."

"How can you blame me for hanging out with Stella, if even you—you just admitted it—a copy of you ran off with her, too."

"I'm not blaming anybody. It's just a matter of understanding the consequences. That's right. You make a choice, and you face the consequences. Had the same conversation with myself an hour ago."

Clay decided to let the conversation end, because he had already made up his mind. He thanked his father and said he would think about helping the police.

The flower vanished, and Clay swam back to the pool. Before leaving the water he paused to admire Stella's lovely figure. She was breathing softly on the grassy bank, her skin shining like gold in the light of Forgotten Planet's several ringed moons. Everything was peaceful and quiet, the wind still, the sound of crickets very soft. Stella, asleep and comfortable, made this huge empty planet seem like a cozy, private game-world. She might have been manipulating him, she might even have had some diabolical plan up her sleeve, but he liked surprises, and she was full of surprises. Since he knew he would never delete the past few days from his life, and that consequently a drug record would turn him into a second-class citizen, he decided to make a break for it.

With wet hands he shook her body. "Stella, are you awake?"

Confused, she wiped at the water on her shoulder. "Yeah."

"Listen." He lifted her by the elbows so that she was in a sitting position. As softly as he could manage, he whispered into her ear. "The police have a bug on you. We're being recorded. Can you get rid of it?"

Her big blue eyes searched the animated wind, insects, leaves . . . the specks of detail, any of which could contain recording devices, invisible observers . . . "I—I don't know."

"Can you get us out of here?"

At that moment a cage materialized around them, and they were suddenly dressed in white robes. A mysterious light illuminated the area, such that Clay was able to see his father appear with two other men outside the bars. His father, arms behind his back, looked distracted. "I was wrong," he said to someone Clay did not know. "I'm sorry."

"You did what you could," replied the man tersely.

To Clay, his father said, "God, I can't believe this is happening. Jesus. I'm sorry, Clay."

Stella had rushed to the bars and was now gazing up at the sky. "I'm bugged. What do I do?"

One of the police officers joined her in looking at the sky. "Computer, beam these two to the Phoenix holding facility."

A blast of wind, coming out of nowhere, slammed into the cage, knocking Clay to his knees. For several seconds they were caught in a violent whirlwind, then suddenly the cage and the three investigators vanished. He and Stella found themselves hovering in a featureless void, naked once again. "What happened?" said Clay. "Are we safe?"

"I don't know."

"Where are we? Is this one of your simulations?"

"I don't know."

"Did the bug get removed?"

"I . . . I don't know."

Chapter 10

. . . The critical philosophy of science became as it were negatively metaphysical—in other words, materialistic—on the basis of an error in judgment; matter was assumed to be a tangible and recognizable reality. Yet this is a thoroughly metaphysical concept hypostatized by uncritical minds. Matter is an hypothesis. When you say "matter," you are really creating a symbol for something unknown, which may just as well be "spirit" or anything else; it may even be God . . . Scientific materialism has merely introduced a new hypostasis . . . It has given another name to the supreme principle of reality and has assumed that this created a new thing and destroyed an old thing. Whether you call the principle of existence "God," "matter," "energy," or anything else you like, you have created nothing; you have simply changed a symbol.

— Carl Gustav Yung, "The Difference Between Eastern and Western Thinking," 1939.

An iconographic map of OpenEye's system lay before Paul. One by one, 3D icons, like houses in a tiny village of advertisements, were highlighting themselves, as Net security proceeded to scan for Stella and Clay. *Ikibana Warrior. The Bold and the Breathless. Deathscan 3020.* It was taking forever. Paul told the computer to hurry up, but the highlighting of simulations continued slowly.

"I said 'Top Priority,' goddammit. This is an emergency. I'm Detective Paul Cramer of the Arizona Precinct." What was he saying? The computer knew who he was.

"Every available processor allocated," said the computer.

Paul held his tongue; he had nothing useful to say. Once again his hands were all but tied by legislative feature-tweak. No matter what he said, OpenEye's system would keep rendering karate chops, lovers mooning at each other, interstellar spaceships, the shivering leaves of trees in a hundred vacation paradises . . . while the security search would be relegated to 'available processors.' A real Net OS would have given him full control during emergencies like this. Like much of the Smile Crime Initiative, such tools had been killed by the liberal legislature.

Screw it, he thought. Several seconds had passed; Clay and Stella would already be on some other system. "Get me the police computers in Phoenix."

A cubical blue holographic space opened up to the right. Meanwhile, Spalding came up the grassy slope behind him.

Spalding said, "I contacted Beijing. Their computers are no help either. The transmitter is dead. Even the other Stellas—there were others, by the way, instantiated after your initial success—even the others have stopped transmitting. It looks like we lost this round."

Spalding gave Paul a serious look, his face all one color in the morning light, like a graphical model without textures. He just stood there, observing *Forgotten Planet's* proto-romantic Red Dawn through his sunglasses. The smoldering red giant—reflected twice in his lenses, ray-traced, running like a movie—was far from romantic now; it was just fire, two balls of fire like demons' eyes, burning away trillions more clock cycles, any of which could be hiding something. Spalding turned sideways to join Paul in watching the search.

Forms appeared in the cubical display: a yellow sphere, variegated blocks and pins adhering to the sphere, a zodiac of graphs. This was how the police made sense of the worldwide Net: Clay and Stella skipping away across a globe, when anyone with Paul's experience knew that in reality they were lost in an incomprehensible non-Euclidean mush-ball, huge as a star and more convoluted than the brain. "Find my son. Computer, find my son. Clay Cramer. Top priority."

"They're gone," said Spalding. "We won't find them again until they want to be found."

Paul watched the white patches sprouting here and there on the globe as the search began. There was no sound, just spreading color.

"I don't blame the boy," said Spalding. "I would be afraid of the police, too, if I was his age."

"He grew up with the police."

"So he's had time to form an opinion." Spalding smiled, removing the sunglasses. He chuckled to himself. "My daughter was the same way."

With a salutary bell sound, a comlink opened to Phoenix. Sorenson was at his desk, red in the face as though he had been holding his breath. "For crying out loud, Paul. What the hell's going on? Do you have to tie up every computer in the building?"

"This will just take a second." He told the chief what was going on.

The chief pinched at his chin, where the previous year he had had a beard. "Great. That's just great. Your son? Think he's all right?"

"He's fine, I'm sure. Sorry I didn't register the search. I'm not all here right now."

"Procedure, Cramer. Procedure is our friend." After a pause, Sorenson said, "Let us know if you need assistance."

Paul said he would keep Phoenix briefed, then he killed the comlink. To Spalding he said, "I'm sorry. What were you saying? You have a daughter?"

"Never mind. It was nothing."

"I imagine almost everyone in Beijing has a child."

Spalding gave Paul a curious look. "Most of us are pretty old; we've had time to qualify. Yes, about a hundred years ago I had a daughter. We wanted her to be a scholar, like her mother and father, but getting her to study was like getting a cat to fetch a ball. She wouldn't even apply to college when the time came."

In the simulated twilight Spalding had a faraway, melancholic look about him. Out of nervousness, perhaps, he poked at his palm.

"That must have been a letdown. Did she ever come around?"

Spalding scanned the abstract, colorful globe structure, where the search had picked up speed and was making visible progress. "Not that I know of."

"What do you mean? What does she do now?"

"We haven't spoken in half a century. She left home . . . Well, we had a fight. Silly stuff. My ex-wife Toril and I published a book . . . a study about children and their development."

"You wrote a book about her?"

"Look, it doesn't matter. I don't know why I brought it up."

Paul backed off. Not the best time for a heart-to-heart, he decided.

The white color spread all through California County's teleportation routers. Either Stella and Clay had not returned there, or they were indeed untraceable.

Spalding said, "We used the data of thousands of children, which made Regina statistically insignificant. She just had some sort of complex about having famous parents."

"Are you famous?"

The agent replaced the sunglasses, leaving them low enough on his nose such that his eyes were not quite covered. "Not as famous as you, but famous enough, in some circles. Famous enough to give Regina identity-defense issues, according to our analyst."

"Sorry to hear it. That's really tough, I bet. So you were saying you think that's what's wrong with Clay? Is that how this got started?"

"Well . . . think what it must be like. Everywhere he looks, there's his father, on holovision, in the news, in history class. Did he have a Detective Cramer doll?"

The Beijing agent was openly smiling. Paul turned to face him, beginning to suspect he was being set up for a joke. "So he's . . . identity-defensive? I've never heard of it."

"Just talking about a 'reference count,' what they call it, the number of images pushing your kid in that direction."

"He never had one of the dolls."

"You never bought one of your own dolls?"

"No."

"He probably saw the commercials, in any case. That sort of thing, to a lesser degree, bothered my daughter. She got in a hurry to be her own separate person—and finally left. For Clay to be separate from you, he would have to leave behind the whole world."

"A kid can be himself at home. There's no such thing as complete isolation and being one hundred percent your own person. Everyone's got a family and everyone's part of society."

"Oh, the breakup comes eventually. The government designed families to do just that, in fact. You come together for a while, then you raise a child, then what do you do? Not specified. No goals, achievements. Nothing that requires partnership. Circumstance pulls you apart."

"Everyone these days wants to blame their problems on the government."

"Isolation—it comes. It's built into the immortality laws."

Spalding took a comlink from Beijing, walking down the side of the hill. Paul stared at the displays. Where now? Would he get a hotel room again?

He could not exactly hold up his own marriage as a counterexample to Spalding's theory. From all appearances, he and Claire were flying away from each other as well, inexorably, inexplicably. His son, too, was drifting away, much earlier than most people's children. Meanwhile, parents were vanishing into the Arizona desert, in ever increasing numbers, and all over the planet illegal children were being born, without futures, to parents without futures. Did anyone have a future? He felt utterly helpless against—what? Circumstance? Was it really the laws, as Spalding claimed? When Spalding walked back up the hill to central control, Paul said, "You're quite the cynic."

"Forgive me. I didn't want to meddle."

"So you go through life thinking people are doomed to get bored with each other, to forget their relatives? You go around expecting . . . what was it the other day? 'Total breakdown?'"

"One's personal behavior cannot transcend the rule systems established by a civilization. That's all I wanted to say. You can't expect to have complete control of a relationship when the parameters of the relationship are defined by the legislature. You're in a system. You're doing just what you're supposed to at your age, what I did a century ago." Spalding laughed unexpectedly. "For twenty years I did nothing but wonder how I had made Toril and Regina leave, but it wasn't my fault; it was just time for us to go our separate ways. I mean, realistically, how long would Toril and I have had anything in common? Or Regina and I? Five hundred years? There comes a point when you have to let go."

"You can't just forget about your wife. Or your daughter. You don't communicate at all? The computer could tell you where they are."

"We lead separate lives. I don't think families were meant to last hundreds of years."

"You don't have to completely lose track of each other."

"Oh, you do. You'll see."

Paul scanned the immediate environment. Online, even the hair growing on their heads—not to mention the conversation—might be getting archived somewhere. "Does Beijing know your—do they know how you feel about this?"

"I'm a theorist, a big-picture type. That's my job. They were interested in my theory of the ideoplasm."

Paul nodded, though he had never heard of the ideoplasm.

"I published the theory a century ago. It managed to predict many current social problems, including the security leaks on the Net."

Paul was surprised. There was more to the Beijing agent than he had suspected. "What's it about?"

Banks interrupted, appearing with a soft chiming noise beside Spalding. "The technicians have their heads up their asses," he said. "They don't even know what a context-switch is."

"Never had much luck with OpenEye technicians," said Paul.

Banks shrugged. "What's this?" He pointed to the Phoenix link. "Have they left the system?"

The yellow planet was now a white planet with a few yellow splotches.

"They're gone," said Spalding. "We've got to start over."

"I think they slipped away," said Paul.

Spalding stepped in front of the Phoenix display. "Why don't you guys beam into *Dream Summer* with me."

(*Dream Summer* was the simulation Stella's hair had come from.)

Banks eyed Spalding. "You're beaming in?"

Paul had the same reaction. There was nothing to see. Opticon, the simulation's producer, had kept no archives of clients' visits. There would be no informational footprints or fingerprints.

"I've had a copy beamed to my home. Why don't you two come over. My great-great-grandmother is staying with me, and I've got to get back. She would enjoy some additional company."

Few private citizens owned simulator-sized computers. Paul said, "You have a—"

"The latest. I usually work at home. What do you say? Let's move operations to my place for a few days. I have a feeling there's something special about the mistress with Stella's hair. She will help us get to know our criminal."

Paul said, "Billions of men like red hair."

"The hair won't be the only clue, nor will *Dream Summer* be the only simulation we're led to. I hope. For now, it's all we have."

It was true. With the transmitter neutralized, they were starting over. Watching the last spot of yellow vanish from the globe in front of him, Paul agreed; he would beam into *Dream Summer*.

Chapter 11

ideoplasm: *n.* 1. the set of all matter and energy the human imagination can manipulate with precision. 2. *in modern cultural theory*, the material scope of human endeavor during a given historical period: the combined feats of architecture, technology, art; etc.

— *Webster's Dictionary*, 2905.

The story of human history is the story of the ideoplasm. During the three great societal transformations—agriculture, industry, and nanotechnology (the three fundamental enlargements of the ideoplasm)—human beings remade themselves in the image of a newfound power. Agricultural man, learning to control organisms, sunk roots into the ground, became fenced-in and territorial, a slave-owner of plants, animals, and other men, a slave in turn to the seasons and nature's vicissitudes. Industrial man became a wheel in a machine, wearing time on his wrist, keeping it in his breast pocket near the staccato of his heart, turning a few degrees when it was time to turn. The crudeness of his philosophy and social organization mirrored the low resolution of his ideoplasm, the crude masses of material he hacked from the earth, the sloppy smashing and pounding of metals into useful forms, the machinery this labor required, and the children's toys this labor produced. Nanotech man is an archived copy of himself, a datafile, able to be copied, transmitted, and preserved indefinitely. Though he fashions his life and his society with great precision, like a demiurge building Bouchet's famous apple, only gradually has he been moving toward genuine freedom and power over what he can become. He is waiting for the ideoplasm to make its final, most difficult annexation: the human body in all its complexity.

We are nearing the end of the nanotech age. What is coming might be termed the "information age." Within two or three centuries, we will move beyond the mere ability to instantiate molecular data to a true power to draft, comprehend, and transform complex material structures. Everything will be expressible as information. By mid-century, radical cosmetic morphing of the human body should be common; personal identity will separate itself from the human organism. Much later, perhaps centuries from now, tools for representing and transforming the human brain should begin to appear; thought will separate itself from the

113

human mind. On the Net, we may see developments like telepathy, group minds, and non-human or supra-human morphologies of consciousness. What it means to be a sentient being, to have a self, etc., will entirely remake itself in the image of this new and ultimate plasticity. The ideoplasm at last will be coextensive with all earthly matter, energy, and complexity of organization. We will be able to amplify or diminish ourselves in ways we cannot even imagine.

> — Spalding Morris, *Tremors in the Ideoplasm: The Coming of the Fourth Rupture*, published in 2901.

Dream Summer was what Paul had expected. The concept, a candlelit dinner on an old wood pier, was fine—romantic, elegant, and tactfully rustic—but somehow everything was just a little too perfect, the languid breeze off the ocean just a little too rich with the smell of brine, the full moon just a bit too large and yellow, like a cardboard set piece, the waiters and busboys just a bit too efficient, materializing and dematerializing like ghosts at all the right moments, and Bendetta, the woman, too overtly sexual: nipples artificially hard, pricking the chiffon of her blouse, a quick, adorable smile, full of affection, and of course the wild red hair. For ten minutes Paul played the part of a young bachelor, enduring Bendetta's crooning and giggles, which continued to erupt at predictable intervals even during his description of a childhood spearfishing accident, then he lost interest. Her personality seemed to be caught in an infinite loop.

"I'm not learning anything," he said.

"Oh?" Bendetta's painted eyebrows lifted and shaped themselves into precise crescents. "What do you want to know?"

"I want to know what the hell I'm doing here."

"Oh?"

"I'm wasting my time. Someone stole the data for your hair; they didn't steal *you*. They didn't tell you what they were doing."

"Someone took my hair? I'm flattered." Very pleased, she twirled a finger through her bangs so that she could admire what had been stolen.

He logged out. Not knowing what else to do, he went straight to the third-story loggia, which overlooked Spalding's tropical garden. David Banks was already there, pale and drawn and watching the rain.

"Pretty pitiful, huh?" said Paul. "I don't know what the hell Spalding thinks he's going to learn from Ms. Beautifica."

"It's a dead end. I knew that before I beamed in."

Banks placed his hands on the balustrade's pink marble and looked down into the garden. "Been awhile. A couple of years? I think the last place I went was the Hot Tail."

"You do her?" Paul could be as juvenile as he liked around Banks, and his old married friend would play along like they were buddies in college—but this time David didn't parry. He just watched the water dripping from the trees, rapped his knuckles absently on the marble, and sighed. Paul said, "Don't tell me. . . . You didn't."

Banks shrugged. "Relieve tension. I don't know why. . . . I just felt like it."

"You and Amy on the rocks?"

"You could say that."

Once again, Paul had been kidding—but now he was caught short. A mosquito stung the back of his hand, but he didn't move to swat it or even remove his hand from the balustrade. Banks continued to stare at the leaves of the banana trees, sagging from the periodic rain. "You mean—are you serious?"

"Oh, not really. I'm exaggerating. There just seems to be these flashpoints, and when one of them goes off—whooom! Man, did we go at it tonight."

The mosquito flew away, leaving a pinprick between Paul's knuckles.

"I'd grounded Heather. Amy let her go out . . . not worth going into. We've just been having these spats."

"You and Amy? You guys?"

"It's funny . . . I'm not mad. I'm not unhappy. But I get home and . . . there she is, waiting, and . . . Just by talking, we get so aggravated. It's friction just having the other person there. I say I'm going to open something to read, she asks what I just said, and I want to yell at the top of my lungs. Repeating myself seems like the most agonizing chore. Where's *that* coming from?"

"Pretty typical. Bad moods."

"It's a question of degree."

Bank stared at Paul for a second then looked back at the forest. Paul and his old partner watched the rain grow more heavy until it drummed like thunder against the broad leaves of the garden. When Paul spoke again, he had to raise his voice. "You aren't getting divorced, are you?"

Banks was standing with his hands in his pockets. "Maybe. I don't know. Not 'till Heather leaves for college."

Paul could not believe his ears. Banks—shallow, changeless David Banks—even he was running up against a "second childhood"—the supposedly inevitable disorientation of the post-family years; the last genuinely content man Paul knew was turning out just like everyone else. Paul had a flash: Banks and Amy becoming versions of those very old couples he saw in restaurants, those people so old you could guess their ages at a glance, regardless of their morphological ages: tired old folks sitting still as figures in 3D photographs, consumed by long lives, emptied but beautiful people, eating in silence, nothing to talk about. Was this what happened to you? Was it inevitable?

"I never would have brought you back if I'd known what I was doing. Your reincarnation . . . I just wanted to believe these things could be patched back together."

Paul checked his watch—5:22 in Alaska, about time for Banks to leave work. "Why don't you take some time off. You could work out of your home this week. We need to do a lot of interviews at Opticon—just comlinks."

"Yeah, a vacation . . . but a real vacation. No interviews."

"Okay, sure. Except . . . Hell, I'd hate to lose you completely."

"I'm almost lost already. Two months . . . and now we're back to guesswork. I don't know how much longer . . ."

"We're talking the worst security breach in a hundred years. You bailing out? You're the one who wanted me reinstantiated and put on the case."

"Either we give up, or we think of a new approach, something whoever wrote Stella's software would never anticipate."

"I doubt our scan-criminal would ever expect us to go through his old porn library."

"Yeah, or maybe that's the whole point: he wants everybody to check out his porn collection. What's Stella, anyway? Probably his favorite lay. I think Spalding's studying *Dream Summer* out of some general academic curiosity, not to learn what we need—who, what, when. Who cares what fetishes the criminal has?"

"We're still waiting for lab results. There will be other leads."

"You haven't been on the case as long as I have. There won't be any leads, or if there are, they will be ten-year-old simulations like this one."

"Okay, fine—a real vacation. Spend a few days with Amy. But don't leave me alone with these Beijing people. I'm going to need backup."

"Sure." Banks smiled faintly. He took a deep breath. He surveyed the garden as though he were seeing the world for the first time, the real world, seeing it, nodding at it, and finding that it was exactly what he had imagined.

Banks agreed to beam back to Alaska. He went back into the house to find a telepod.

Paul was left with a few hours to kill, since Spalding would be busy with *Dream Summer*. He got a cup of coffee and pulled up a chair to where he could see the forest. When the rain finally stopped, tiny sounds filled the misty, dark woods: chirping, dripping water, the rustling of small tree-climbing animals. Unseen macaws croaked warnings of nightfall. A giant butterfly landed on the balustrade, showed off the eye-like markings on its wings, then left again, having seen, apparently, what it had come to see. Paul unbuttoned his shirt, hoping to dry the perspiration that had collected on his chest, then he kicked his feet up onto the balustrade.

It was hard to believe that beyond this ancient biome, which was more primitive and thriving than it had been since prehistory, a society existed that was almost the complete opposite, stranger than anything Nature could have concocted, fragmented, interconnected, always changing. He did not understand it. When he imagined his future—out there beyond the trees—he saw a loud, very bright place filled with lights and motion and perpetually laughing people, doorways leading to every possible location. But all this vastness meant nothing and went nowhere, and he did not know what he wanted to do, really, about Claire, his home, about anything that had been thrown at him since the reincarnation.

He couldn't stop thinking about Spalding's and Banks' stories of divorce. Everyone he knew was yellowing at the edges and waiting to fall from the tree. Then there were the logoffs, those awful people he had arrested in Arizona, who had risked everything just to have a few children, children they knew would have to be erased, eventually. Were they any better off? Was anyone? He lived in a world where entire continents could be repopulated with forests and long-extinct species, down to the level of the blood-drinking insects he had been squashing against his neck (reincarnated, he presumed, to satisfy some modern guilt complex about primitive man's destructiveness), but all of this technology, all of this life-creating force, could not maintain a community of people that was happy and stable.

He did not ask the computer for light when darkness came, preferring his thoughts. For a time he flipped through a hologram of Spalding's seminal study, *Tremors in the Ideoplasm*, but he soon lost interest. A honey bear came out, shocked its paws on the electric concertina wire that topped the outer wall, then returned to the forest's dark understory. Night had long fallen when Spalding finally returned from the simulation.

"I'd forgotten how horrible those programs are," Paul said in greeting.

Spalding pulled up a chair and told the computer to turn on the lights. "Horrible? It was charming. The service was excellent, the food was delicious, and the sex was—how can you deny it?—outrageous. Come on, an antigravity bed?" Spalding sat down, a bowl of grapefruit cubes in his lap. He was eating breakfast, having spent a night of scan-time in *Dream Summer*.

"I didn't go to the cabin," said Paul, referring to the cabin on the hill where Bendetta would take her dates.

"Didn't make it through the dinner conversation, huh?" Spalding chuckled. "Pretty simple personality construct, I admit, but you've got to overlook the small faults. The important material was inside the cabin."

It might have been because he had just been thinking about the state of the world, or maybe because his meditations had been so suddenly interrupted, but Paul found Spalding's bright manner inappropriate. They were detectives working on the most important criminal investigation of the century, and here was the central investigator lounging about a private estate, joking about a porn simulation. Maybe Banks was right. Spalding was more interested in feeding his own curiosity than solving crimes. "My partner checked it out. He didn't find anything."

"Where is he, by the way?"

"Alaska. Listen, we don't see the point of going through this old porn simulation. It didn't tell us anything. We need to make some concrete progress, and we need to make it soon."

"Sexual fantasies say a lot about a person. They're like fingerprints. We all have them, and they're all slightly different."

"You can't fingerprint a fantasy."

"You can make statistically relevant distinctions."

"Billions of people would find *Dream Summer* perfectly enjoyable."

"I don't think so. Besides, we aren't looking for those who would find *Dream Summer* acceptable, we're looking for the few who would love *Dream Summer*, who would want to save pieces of it, like Bendetta's hair."

"I don't see how we could ever make a connection."

"You wouldn't be saying that if you'd gone into the cabin."

Spalding awaited Paul's question with a self-satisfied smile. Paul said, "What could possibly have been in the cabin?"

"For one—" With a flourish of his fork Spalding speared a cube of grapefruit—"the inside of the building was five or ten times as large as the outside." He raised his eyebrows, as though waiting for Paul to do the same.

"So?"

"The same light was ambient everywhere, even under the covers. You could take a painting off the wall, pull it over your head, and suddenly the room would look like a Persian harem, an oriental palace, a castle in the Alps—whatever had been in the painting." He put the cube of grapefruit into his mouth, chewing ferociously. "You could switch camera angles and watch yourself from an arbitrary eyepoint. You could even switch bodies, make love to Bendetta as a woman, an ape-morph, or any of several wild animals. And the bed had an antigravity switch."

"Every gimmick in the book."

"Everything was non-Euclidean and non-Newtonian. The list of vagina effects was endless: squeezing, kneading, peristalsis, clonic massage, vaginas full of mouths, vaginas full of snakes. Bendetta was like a carnival ride. This is the porn simulation of someone who prefers the Net to the real world."

"Who doesn't?" said Paul, only half-joking.

"It's our first glimpse into the mind of an individual. I wouldn't be surprised if the person who picked out Stella's hair also organized the crime."

Spalding had the didactic air of a detective in the holomovies revealing a murderer's identity to a room full of suspects. If he was right, Stella—as opposed to her male and morphed counterparts—was the key to unlocking the case. "You can't be sure about something like that."

"I don't see any alternative. The kind of person who would enjoy *Dream Summer* is someone excited about the future. Someone who would welcome the spread of morphing, of alternative neural mappings, of online experience in general. Perhaps even someone who would want to push simulated experience to the next level. I wouldn't be surprised if one of Opticon's own developers were behind the crimes."

"You got all of this out of a porn simulation?"

With smug confidence, Spalding said, "I can see a lot in a fantasy. I wrote three books on online eroticism. You might have come across the more famous one, *Cathectic Coordinates: Remapping the Instinct to Reproduce*. It made it out to the general public, I believe."

Paul shrugged.

"Anyway, I've had a lot of experience with this sort of thing. It's given me a sort of intuition about people who use and design these programs."

"Never trust intuition. Intuition is the enemy of good police work."

"It all comes down to the evidence, I suppose. But we can use a broader definition of evidence—until we have specific suspects, at least. Crimes are culture like anything else and open to the same interpretations. The fact that they involve real people and real events makes no difference. We're all constructs, continually writing ourselves, and everything we do or say can be analyzed as though it were imagined, especially in a world where even our bodies change with our sense of style."

"Tell you what. I'll grill the suspects for evidence. You do the analysis. Good cop, bad cop."

"We may have to build a profile first and run some database queries before we have any suspects at all. It's always best to pretend that the suspect is a fictional character, self-created or otherwise, because at heart so is everyone, or so they strive to be."

"So what kind of construct am I? Who made me?"

"I'm serious. You are no exception."

"Well, run some queries. What am I trying to say—by being me?"

"Oddly put, but I do have an interest in your story. You really want to hear my interpretation?

Of course not, thought Paul. How'd we get started on this?

"You're a very important person semantically. If this were a play—" With his free hand, Spalding indicated world society—"you'd be Hamlet or maybe Malvolio."

"Who's Malvolio?"

"Never mind. The point is that a great number of forces are coming to bear upon you, pure lines of force, corresponding to the stresses and fault lines of the current order. I'm not boring you, am I?"

"Go ahead. Let's hear it."

"Well, we're losing our conviction in the current system, as you well know. Our leaders are becoming caricatures of themselves, increasingly lampooned and ignored, respect for laws and regard for once universal dreams, like serving the government and earning a baby, are declining, and as a consequence our idea of the hero, woven from our most basic values, is unraveling, like morality itself. You're this hero, iconified, universally respected, distilled down to a parable for children; you, too, are unraveling, both publicly—in the average person's regard for you—and privately, in the particulars of your own life. In your personal problems I see a stage for the political, moral, and intellectual turbulence of our time. You're being reconstructed, and you're reconstructing yourself, grasping for the next moral system, for a justification for the way you live your life."

"Is that so?"

"I'm very interested in what's happening to public figures like yourself. Why don't you stay here a few days? I'd like to pick your brain—for a book I'm doing, on the moral crisis."

"You want me to spend the night?"

"Heard you were on the hotel circuit. Just stay for a night or two, long enough for some interviews. You might enjoy the visit—you never know. I have someone staying with me whom you might like to meet, someone who survived the last moral crisis. A conversation between you two would be fascinating material for my book."

"Your grandmother?"

"My great-great-grandmother. Stay for dinner, at least. What do you say?"

Spalding's face shined with perspiration and apparent bonhomie.

Good grief, thought Paul. No wonder we can't solve this crime. Beijing has replaced its intelligence officers with socialite intellectuals. "Sure," he said. "I can't go home."

"Wonderful. You'll love the forest. I'll have Jenny take you on a hike."

They talked some more about the investigation. Spalding was sure a designer of *outré* porn simulations was behind the crimes. The exegesis of *Dream Summer*, however, remained incomplete in Paul's mind. He would give Spalding's approach a try, by building a search-profile for the criminal, but he had no faith in it. There had to be something they had overlooked.

*

Spalding's great-great-grandmother, Jenny Morris, naturally did not look old. She was sexy and young and—in fact—she dressed like a teenaged girl making a first attempt at showing off her body, her dress divided into pieces and stretched together with large brass rings, her skin polished, fragrant with some sweet lotion, her hair black and marcelled like folds of silk—an impossible hairdo for a tropical climate. She had an excuse, he guessed. She had been born before scanning and therefore had aged, physically. She had been a hundred fifteen before morphing could make her immortal and a hundred fifty before she could look beautiful and young again. He guessed she was still compensating for having been an old prune.

"What was it like? A lot of pain?" He had never talked to someone so old.

"You were never old, Grandma. Were you?" Spalding was on the opposite side of the fondue pot, his back to the forest. With miniature forks, they were dipping squares of bread and raw vegetables into the melted cheese.

"Oh, not really. By the time I got old they had so many little machines in my blood that there weren't many ways I could get sick. No viruses, bacteria, cancers . . . The only trouble I had was with my heart, large-scale problems. I was always out of breath, and my legs got cold. My joints hurt—oh, and my lower back. I guess they never got good at repairing the big stuff until people could be scanned. Something about coordinating the nanites."

"Did you have wrinkles?" Paul was trying to imagine the woman's lovely face all shriveled and bruised, like the faces of old people he had seen in books.

"I wasn't the sort of person to go to a cosmetic surgeon. You'd come out all pinch-faced and smiley-looking, like a plastic doll."

"It must have been awful, knowing you were dying."

"It's been three hundred years. I've had time to get over it." Her eyes sparkled in the flickering light that came from below the fondue pot. In three hundred years—well, evidently, her ordeal had become a light topic of conversation.

Spalding stood to distribute more bread and vegetables from a large serving plate. He wore a wristband computer that was recording the conversation. The dinner was to be a "found dialogue" for his next book. "I wanted to interject—pardon the moderation—a specific topic. The detective and I—you'll find this amusing, Grandma—have found simulations online that have death in them. People are scanning in and finding out what it's like to die."

"Oh, I believe it," said Jenny. With the little fork, Jenny was separating the bread and vegetables into two piles, some kind of nervous tic.

"We really shouldn't discuss the case," said Paul.

"I'll be discreet." Spalding took his seat. "The book won't be done until next year, at the earliest."

"You do this a lot? Write about operations?"

"They keep me on a tight leash, but—yes—when information becomes declassified, I can publish. Very good for sales."

Jenny finished her sorting routine. "I suppose there's value to the whole thing, but I don't see how you could simulate death. You'd have to really believe you were going to die."

"Paul's son seems to like it," said Spalding. "Despite the painful physical effects."

Paul gave up keeping the investigation out of the discussion. It was Spalding's call, after all.

"Son?" said Jenny.

"His name's Clay. He's gotten hooked into the system—whatever it is. A copy of myself, too."

"That's right," said Jenny. "There are two of you."

"You know about—my original?"

"She's been briefed," said Spalding. "Just the essentials."

"Okay. Fine." Spalding was running the show, clearly. He obviously trusted his grandmother the way most agents trusted their more immediate family. "They can't get enough of it," continued Paul. "Death—they want these death-simulations more than they want their normal lives."

"I liked living through it, I suppose. I can see that. The change, you know, changing slowly every day. You forget the little pains. I don't want to do it again—no way—but I can't imagine what I'd be if I'd never been old. I'd still be a face in the mirror. The thing about your body breaking down, you start to realize who *you* are apart from the face and the body. Know what I mean?"

"Sure—but these simulations only last a few days. You don't age at all."

"Simulations—well, I wouldn't expect to learn anything from a simulation."

Spalding smiled to himself, apparently imagining something for the book. The discussion continued through dinner, Spalding interrupting only to laugh at something witty passing through his mind, something reserved for the scholarly press. Paul was relieved when the agent set a pot of chocolate boiling and declared the session to be over.

"You hardly asked anything at all," said Paul.

"That's my method: I bring the voices together and let them talk. The dramatic artist—and those who study his so-called "primary" source material—deal in stylized imitations of voices, and therefore dialogues that belong inside one person's head, not in real life. I study society directly."

"You aren't having dessert?" Jenny had noticed that Spalding had fixed only two plates of fruit.

"I'm stuffed. You two go ahead. I'm going to read awhile and then turn in."

"Okay, study-bum. Give Grandma a hug."

As Jenny straightened her back for the hug, the tight dress creaked with the changing stresses. Grandma . . . ? Paul shook his head, staring at the shameless outfit. Jenny's long legs, crossed under the table, were bare to the tops of her thighs. A brass ring framed the bare profile of one of her breasts, two others showed off the hard declensions of her hips, a fourth encircled her bejeweled naval, and in between black, thin-sheeted rubber deformed itself over her lean, hard-muscled figure. Spalding kissed her cheek. "G'night! And thanks, you guys. Good material. I'll be adding it to the corpus."

Spalding went inside. Paul listened to his footsteps ascend the marble staircase. He turned to Jenny. "Corpus?"

"Oh—his database of interviews. He calls it a corpus."

"You don't mind all this—being recorded?"

"Spalding's my great-grandson. I can begrudge an interview or two."

"You must have a lot of descendants."

"Probably. I haven't tried to find them all. Spalding did a family tree in gradeschool—*he* found *me*, you know. Turns out he was descended from one of the oldest human beings that ever lived."

She did a little pose, giving him a pretty, girlish smile. He watched her small young mouth as she licked the melted chocolate from a strawberry.

"You really enjoy being young, don't you? Despite everything you said . . ."

"Oh, this . . ." She waved her hand down the length of her body. "I just wanted to dress up. I don't go to many dinner parties."

"Sorry I didn't do likewise."

"Oh, you're fine."

He pointed to her plate. "That any good?"

"Try one." With her fingers, she put a chocolate-covered slice of kiwi in his mouth. He pressed the soft fruit with his tongue, openly running his eyes over her body. He liked this. Whatever kick Spalding's grandmother was on—he was ready to go with the flow.

You're about due, actually, and you know it. Well, that's two points for the original, he thought. Is this all it takes? An invitation? Paul fed Jenny a strawberry and she held his fingers in her mouth, licking and kissing them. He slipped his sticky hand between her knees slid it along her thigh, her legs parting, opening . . .

125

She took his hand and led him down the steps to the garden. Without undressing, he thrust himself into her and carried her on his hips to the stone perimeter wall, behind a tree. They were loud as boars, his belt still fastened, Jenny in the dress, her panties stretched between her ankles. If Claire found out . . . oh . . . oh . . . he would be . . . dead.

. . . dead . . .

He would be dead.

He collapsed against Jenny, the orgasm subsiding, this skeleton of a girl, five hundred years old, panting in his ear . . . a brand-new machine, instantiated today maybe, and an old, old brain, like something dug from a grave, looking out at him through two grateful young eyes.

They disengaged, restored their clothing, and went to lie in a hammock between two palm trees. He felt the full weight of her body against his chest, her chin on his shoulder, her legs crossed with his at the ankles. She felt like Claire. Closing his eyes, he pulled her closer. He had not even hugged his wife since the reinstantiation. "Funny . . . all this talk about death, and I'm the only one who might actually face it."

"Oh?"

He started to tell her about Banks' bright idea for saving his marriage.

"Spalding explained. Don't worry. I'm an adult."

"Then you knew I was married."

She gave him a soft kiss on his shoulder and snuggled closer.

"Well, anyway, she already has plenty of reasons to have me deleted."

"Like I said, I'm an adult. You want to be alone?"

His turn not to reply. He held her and watched the strange, silky palm leaves floating on the breeze. Jenny no longer reminded him of his wife, now that they had spoiled everything by talking. He was relieved when she kissed him on the forehead, after a long silence, and went to bed.

Somewhere on the other side of the world Claire was in bed. Morning was an hour away. The house was empty, her son gone, her husband having an affair. He pictured her lying there, curled into a corner of the king-sized bed. Innocent—the only one of them who was innocent. She didn't really want to be alone. Whatever she had said . . . she wanted her family back. He knew that much.

In an hour, he would call her, help with the aftermath of the Phoenix interrogation. The situation could be repaired. It wasn't too late.

He tried to rest, but it was hopeless. In bed, he dictated a profile of a "non-Euclidian porn designer" to the computer, figuring he might as well do some work. He ran a query, filtered it for time zone, put his shirt and tie back on, and started making calls.

The first suspect, porn designer Vince Shan-Loc, appeared scaled-down on the desk where Paul was working. Paul introduced himself and explained the general nature of the investigation.

Shan-Loc was petting a douc langur monkey, hugging it to his body as though it were a teddy bear and could protect him. The shy little creature, clinging to its master's neck, avoided Paul's gaze. "Why me?" said Shan-Loc. "*BFL* is soft compared to most menageries."

BFL was *Barnyard Fantastic Lover*, the underground smash that had made Shan-Loc wealthy. "We have just a few questions. You aren't suspected of any crimes."

"You wouldn't be asking questions if you didn't suspect something."

Paul sighed. "You aren't a suspect. We just need your help in locating someone."

The man scratched the monkey's ribs with a trembling hand. "Who?"

"Someone capable of breaching Net security. We believe a porn designer has committed some very serious scan-crimes. You've worked a little in software security. Do you have any acquaintances capable of cracking a simulation host?"

Shan-Loc did not reply. He petted the monkey's ribs with his fingers.

"Do *you* have such skills?"

"Of course not." The monkey was startled by his keeper's suddenly raised voice. "I spent a hundred years designing locks for Phong-Universal-CodeOne. We plugged the last known hole back in the 'seventies."

"There are other holes. Ever watch the news? For five years the Net's been in the middle of a crime wave."

"Hey, hey, it's been decades since I did security. For all I know, the new OS is impenetrable."

Paul pretended to read from a report projected above the desk. "What about people you know or people you've heard about?"

"There are people I used to work with at Phong-Universal-CodeOne. If anyone could crack a system—"

"What about in the porn industry?"

The monkey must have been getting bored. It laid its yellow head on Shan-Loc's chest and closed its eyes. "No one I can think of. Most of us are the creative type, you know, not too good with the technology."

Paul asked only a few more questions before he had to let the man go. The porn designer, ranked number one by the computer, was guilty of something, but it was probably small-time, a theft from an online petting zoo, perhaps. The computer had recorded the conversation, so if there was a reason to dig further the man would reappear on the short list of suspects.

The second suspect, a man who had morphed into a tall, slender woman, refused to say anything about his work on *Against Their Will: Lesbian Fantasies for Male Heterosexuals* until he could consult a lawyer.

The interviews went on.

This was going to be difficult. There did not seem to be a way to distinguish between the thousands of non-Euclidean porn designers. Maybe Spalding would have a clever idea how to narrow the profile.

He lost interest in doing interviews. The only person he wanted to talk to was his wife, who would still be asleep. He sat at the desk counting down the minutes to when he knew she would get up, but impatience got the best of him. He finally just told the computer to wake her up.

The computer informed him that no one was sleeping at the house in France, then it brought up a comlink. Claire was up and about, wearing an outfit he had never seen, an elegant black dress with crisscrossing spaghetti straps, long shining silver earrings, a short feathered hairdo parted to one side. "Going out?" he said.

"Just getting back."

"Were you online?" He could hear a man's voice in the background. The voice sounded familiar. "It's six a.m. your time. Where were you?"

Claire did not reply.

"Who's that? It sounds like—" He gasped—

Paul's original strolled into range of the holographic sensors, holding a bottle of wine. "The chardonnay," he said, smiling at Claire.

"You!"

"What do you want?" said Claire icily.

Paul addressed his original. "You . . ."

Demiurge

"We just had dinner in Antarctica," said the original. "Don't overreact."

"Your detention—you can't leave the casino!"

"I was questioned under X yesterday. The department has granted me limited freedom to travel while they sort out this mess—as has Claire."

Paul watched, helplessly, as the original rested a hand casually on Claire's shoulder. "How—what did you tell them? You're an accomplice."

"They know where I stand about this case."

"He's cooperating," said Claire.

"Why wasn't I informed?" said Paul. "I specifically requested a transcript of the interrogation."

The original produced a corkscrew and began to apply it to the neck of the wine bottle. "By the way, don't get too comfortable in Phoenix. I filed a request to get my office back." The original faced Claire. "I'll meet you on the veranda. The sun is rising." He turned and vanished from view.

"Office!" called Paul. "You?!"

"I don't have time to talk right now," said Claire. "I'll call you tomorrow."

"What's going on? Is he living there?"

"He's not living here." Her silver earrings flashed as she threw a look toward the veranda.

"Why's he there at all?"

"We had dinner. Listen, can't this wait until tomorrow?"

"First you tell me—You tell me what you're doing with my original, after everything he did to us. Claire . . ."

Claire took a deep breath. "Oh, Paul, let go. Just try to let go. You're an illegal copy."

"But—but . . ." But I'm Paul Cramer! he wanted to yell.

"The police broke the law when they made you. They've acknowledged that."

"You're going to have me erased?"

"Really, I want you to leave me alone. I can't be here and two months in the past at the same time."

"I . . ." Paul groped for a reply, remembering Jenny, trying to recall what he had felt there, in the hammock, holding her. "All I know is—I miss you, Claire."

"Woo-hoo," called the original from off-screen.

129

"Good night, Paul."

The connection broke.

Paul was gooseflesh from head to toe. He continued gripping the sides of the desk and stared at the empty place where his life had been, in excerpted form, just a second before: his real life, on the other side of the world, unfolding lazily without him. Drinks on the veranda, an easy hand on his wife's arm, a long, careful talk, followed by silence, waiting, what? Making love at sunrise, no words necessary . . . They would say nothing. They would go to bed and forget themselves. Forget . . .

Forget him as well. He was an illegal copy. (His wife had used the right term.) A memory . . . As real as he felt, he was the translucent face on a holodisplay, miles away, the interruption, the annoyance, something to be ignored, excluded, petitioned against, erased. He and everything he felt was already dust, nanite dust. Banks had been foolish and wrong. . . .

He went outside. The tropical air, still warm and humid, calmed him. He followed a winding brick pathway through the garden, half hoping a poisonous snake would get him. It was entirely by chance and without interest that he found himself standing below Spalding's window.

The lights were on. The scholar, naked from the waist up, was standing close enough to the window to be seen. A woman with dark black hair was tickling him with a huge pink feather.

It was Jenny, his great-great-grandmother.

Paul was amazed. She was not just visiting; she lived with Spalding. They were lovers. He watched only for a few seconds, then he turned away.

This is one screwed-up twisted world, he said to himself. And I'm a complete fool. What am I doing here, with this lonely intellectual and his incestuous grandmother? I should be in France. If Claire wants me dead, I'm going to die today. She's going to decide. I'm going to make her listen to me—or kill me.

Chapter 12

Does *your* relationship look like *this*? [*Man and woman wear white boxes on their heads, upon which are drawn vacant, bored cartoon faces.*] Are you the same people you've always been, boxed-in by habit, afraid you'll never change? [*Couple nods forlornly; spiral-wipe to Stephanie's Online Boutique. Couple's faces are drawn bright and happy.*] Maybe it's time you beamed into Stephanie's. We'll put a whole new face on the love of your life. Choose from a full selection of features. [*Woman takes blond hair off of mannequin, puts on head, pulls it longer and curls it with fingers. Man sinks two blue eyes into the white surface of his box-face.*] Or try one of Stephanie's unique and acclaimed facial designs, including likenesses of your favorite celebrities. Come to Stephanie's and be all that you can imagine. [*Close with beautiful couple holding hands and boarding a roller coaster.*]

> — Holovision Commercial for Stephanie's Online Boutique, January 2997.

Once again Claire found herself on the beach, drawing in the sand with her toes, the elevated house crouched behind, plain as a child's toy against the wool-gray sky. It was cold down here, near the waves and mistral crosswinds, but another hour in that little dollhouse and she would have gone mad.

After Katherine had left, the house once again became deathly still, all systems suspended, the computer expecting Clay to return from school, Paul from work, perhaps wondering why the schedule had changed, why the house had not been informed, perhaps guessing that Paul and Clay had moved away, that the family had split, or simply matured, that maybe this was the beginning of a long wait for a new family.

Katherine hadn't noticed a thing, self-conscious, checking her reflection on every polished surface available, never looking at any one thing for more than an instant. "I know Clay went to California. He talked about it a lot. One of his romantic fantasies," she had said, too preoccupied to drink the tea Claire had set on the end table, her fine features surprisingly expressive underneath the ape hair. "I think I can help find him."

At first Claire offered only a businesslike exchange of facts regarding her son. She had never met Katherine, though she had heard, from Dr. Brown, that the girl was a good friend of Clay's.

Katherine was surprised to hear he was probably online. "That means he's back. They ran a trace, right?"

"Apparently not. He's using some sort of cloaking software."

"But the police can crack that stuff, right? They know where he is."

Claire conveyed what she knew about the investigation. She would not have said anything—Paul had sworn her to secrecy, for the sake of avoiding public hysteria—but it hardly mattered now, with Clay gone and the police growing more and more ineffective.

Katherine had predictable problems with the police's designation of Clay as a "victim." "So he just beamed away with her?"

"She's the one with the software."

"Does he *know* her?"

"Well—what do you mean? They picked up with each other in L.A."

"So it's like a fling?"

"Well, at sixteen . . ." Claire stopped herself. She knew what Katherine wanted to know. "Um, yes . . . from what I understand."

Katherine paused to think, twisting her hairy blonde finger into a tassel of one of the couch's decorative pillows. Claire thought the girl was about to say something deeply personal, some sentiment very difficult to articulate. Instead, she said, "I bet I know exactly where he is."

"I'm sure it's—what was that?"

"He's so predictable. There's only one place—he *has* to go there."

"He could be anywhere," said Claire. "The police have been searching all the places he used to go. So far they haven't found anything."

"This place we went only once. He loves sword and sorcery. That's exactly where he would take her."

Claire cautioned Katherine not to get carried away, but the girl was convinced Clay would want to relive a particular episode of Medieval romance the two of them had shared. Her sincerity was touching, the unblemished optimism of a child. "You two were close, huh?"

"He never mentioned me?" Katherine dragged the pillow into her lap, holding it against her belly.

Claire shrugged. Dr. Brown had told her a great deal about Katherine. Clay, however, kept almost everything to himself. "Clay and I—well, he's growing up, getting more independent."

Katherine seemed to accept the response. "Well, we went out for a while, I guess."

Claire was warming to the strange girl, who with less body hair would have made a lovely maiden in that sword and sorcery simulation. "It's good to meet you. I'm glad you came over," she told her. "We're not with him that much anymore—Paul and I—when he's out there living his life." Since Katherine knew only half the story, Claire summarized the night of the copy's return, the fight which ended in Clay's vidmail farewell.

"Wow," said the girl, with sincerity, "I had no idea it was so intense."

"I never understood why he wanted to look like an ape, but it wasn't a big deal, to me. It's his own body, right? Paul can't stand morphing, though."

"My father's the same way. He says I look ugly as an ape."

Claire patted the girl's freshly brushed forearm with reassurance. "You don't look ugly."

"Even if I do, that's the point. I don't want to be their little designer princess."

"Well, it's none of my business, I guess." Where Katherine—and other kids her age—got this sort of anger, Claire did not know. There was nothing wrong with good genes and good looks. She added, "It isn't pleasant, though, to see your child change form after you've put so much into a gene profile. It's like being disowned."

"That's their fault for wasting their money on a custom-designed face. The easiest thing to morph."

"I'm sure your parents put a lot of thought into your genes. All parents do."

"No, they just let themselves get talked into all this boutique shit and then could only afford an off-the-shelf Remington-4 brain. They just wanted a pretty face in the family album."

Remingtons were the creme of generic plug-and-chug brains. "It sounds to me like your parents gave you the best morphology they could."

"But who are they to design a face? It's *my* face."

Since instinctively Claire had known she could make no headway against Katherine's mindset, she had changed the subject, offering to tell the police about the sword and sorcery simulation. Katherine, however, had insisted that they avoid the police, not wanting to upset Clay.

A wave took a bite out of Claire's toe-scratchings. The tide was coming in. In an hour she would be meeting Katherine at a small town in *Wizards and Warriors VII*, the simulation where Clay might be hiding. After the last few weeks, she was more than willing to circumvent the police for a while. The problems she wanted to solve were not the same as theirs.

She would have been satisfied just to get the size of her family back down to three—and to know that all three of them were safe. Having two copies of her husband around—and no copies of her son—had made her feel like the subject of some goofy psychological experiment.

When she noticed a figure coming down the back steps she didn't even care if it was Paul or the copy. Whoever it was seemed surprised to find her out here. She had always hated the gray days of January. "You look cold," he said.

She quit drawing with her toes, wishing she had put a dataseal on the house's telepod. He was the copy. "I asked Phoenix to have you erased."

The man did not reply. She knew he was the copy because he kept a respectful distance. The other Paul would have kissed her.

"Please leave," she said.

"Hear me out."

Nothing he could say would change her mind. He might be human, he might even be her husband, but he belonged to another time, another world. "It's best for both of us."

"But—why *him*? He pops in one day and—what's the connection?"

"He's the real you." She gave him a go-figure look.

"*I'm* the real me. Look at me. *I'm Paul Cramer just as much as he is.*"

He looked different. Young, it seemed, perhaps because she was expecting signs of age, of all in him that had changed over the years. She was being foolish, since his features were the same as they had always been, but somehow he looked younger. "You're no one. You're a freak experiment of the police department. An accident. I have every right—"

"Listen—"

The copy raised his finger to make a point, but she stopped him. "I have every right to demand that you do not disrupt my life."

"Disrupt?" The copy came toward her. She backed away, stumbling on the uneven sand. "Disrupt? Since when did we stop living the same life?"

"Just understand! Why don't you understand?"

He ended up staring down the long, straight beach, where in the distance the Baxters were walking hand-in-hand. The Baxters were new to the area, young, both working part-time, and both still in love. Their child, nearing the end of its online incubation period, would get beamed into their home soon, and they would be a family. Paul watched them a long time, until they disappeared down the forest path that led to their house. "It's all over, isn't it?"

"What is?"

"Us. This life. David brought me back to fix something that doesn't even exist anymore."

The copy was getting the message. Yes, he was going to die. He might as well face it.

"I see why you want me to leave," he continued. "The old Claire and Paul are already dead. I'm the old Paul."

His face was so stricken—so full of apparent bewilderment and horror, like nothing she had ever seen in him—that perhaps out of an old, marital instinct she took hold of his hand. When he came forward, however, gray with despair, and hugged her, she felt nauseated and off-balance, losing her footing on the sand, her muscles bunching up, her skin feeling unclean where he pressed against her. He was right: he was not a man with whom she could become intimate again, not the gentle, older Paul, who seemed to have aged so many years, who had discovered a dark corner of himself and come to understand and control it; he was someone else, who had never made that journey. "Paul—" She pulled away, stepping out of the circle of drawings she had made. "Yes, I want you to leave. You're from another period of my life, a period I want to forget."

"How about this? One more thing. Do you remember the cliff at Vyostok?"

She didn't know what he was talking about.

"Remember the sky, how dark and low it was, the cliff, the other tourists thinking we were nuts. Remember your hair then? The long ponytail? I watched it twist like a ribbon as you fell. Then there was an instant, a bare second before you hit the water, when I realized you hadn't been timestamped since we'd met, and that if you got hurt and had to be reinstantiated, you wouldn't know me—that we might never . . ."

The cliffs in Russia. He was talking about the singles' raft trip that had brought them together. Claire laughed. "That's ridiculous."

"I never told you, but when you came to the surface, laughing, and called me a coward, I breathed the most overwhelming sigh of relief."

This was not like Paul, either Paul. Paul Cramer did not linger on details from the past. He started every day fresh and oblivious to the one that had come before.

"You see, Claire, I can remember everything that ever happened to us, the smallest details. It's all inside me. I may be a mistake, an out-of-date copy of myself, but you have to understand why it's hard. I'll leave— you're right, I should be erased—but it won't be easy." He remained standing in the center of her scribbles, deliberately, it seemed, waiting for a response.

He was making her feel sorry for him, making her see him as a real Paul Cramer, exactly what she did not want to happen. "Go, before you make it just as hard on me."

"Let me ask one favor first, a last request, something to make the end a little easier."

"What?"

"Just let me say goodbye to the old house, sit in my old chair one last time, take one last walk through the woods, watch the sea—"

"I don't think so. Your original and I—"

"I know, I know. Just give me a few hours. I'll be gone by sunset. He doesn't live here, does he?"

"Not yet." She felt anxious about letting the copy stay; if the original came back, there would be trouble. But he wasn't asking for much, and he looked so sad and sincere, standing where she had left him, in her circle of confused scribbles. She said he could stay until the sun went down or until she got back, whichever came first. When he asked who she was going to see, she did not answer. Clay was no longer his concern.

Chapter 13

I'll be your bonsai, your beautiful bonsai,
Your black-eye bonsai, erotically rotting.
Will my tiny feet fit your desire?
Warped and tied I walk on fire.
Burn me out, twist my wrists,
I promise not to shout, beat me with your fists.
Squeeze me, squeeze me, make me feel,
In my red high-heels I'm an easy kill.
Tease me, tease me, make me see,
You're the only one, I need to be me.

— Crass, "Bata Motel," *Penis Envy*, 1981.

It was good to be King. Good to rule. Good to wage war. Good to live in a high, many-tiered castle, where he owned everything the eye could see, walls, flag-bearing towers, the river valley, the violet mountain tops. And it was good to have his pick of the villagers' daughters, who were beautiful, coarse, often dirty, and strong as wild animals. He owned all of these things—and a winged horse—and they all had been given to him by Stella, his lovely and obedient Queen.

His only wish was that his Queen was more of an adventure, a puzzle, someone with at least one state variable—happy/sad—anything. Just once he wished she would come to the Royal Chamber with a headache, or with a smoldering resentment about something he had done or had ordered her to do, a little sidequest. But she never complained. She was here to please him, and to create whatever worlds he desired. In bed, she was the most loyal of servants, open to every fetish or perversion. He had tried to find her limits, making her perform for him, with other women, with various props—making her do things that could bring pleasure only to a voyeur— and still she loved him, or pretended to love him, remaining absolutely loyal to whatever power had put her here.

137

Once, hoping to provoke an admission, after what he had thought was a particularly outrageous night of performance and love-making, he had asked why she always did what he said. They were stretched out on the sticky silk of their canopied bed, limp as rags, watching two simulated peasant girls gather up their clothes in preparation for the cold walk back to the village.

The response was typically sweet and elliptic. "I want you free to explore the full potential of your mind."

"A straight answer this time."

"Your mind is the author of your destiny. A small perturbation today can yield a great transformation tomorrow."

"I'm serious—" He was amazed how easily she could continue on like this, even when caught in a lie. "Who hired you?"

"Hired me?" She gave him a surprised laugh. "To do what?"

"To be my slave."

She smiled. "I'm not your slave, Clay. I'm your friend."

"You're one of thousands of copies; you do what *they* do. You let me be a king, you instantiate anything I want, you do anything I order. You're my slave."

"I could take it all away, any time, with a snap of my fingers." She snapped her fingers.

Nothing happened.

This was the first time he had mentioned the copies. It was like she did not even hear the question. "But you won't take it away. As long as I beam into one of your simulations every week, you'll do anything I want. Why?"

She was giggling, snapping her fingers again and again in the air, with gay waves of her arm. The two peasant girls halted in the doorway, thinking the Queen was signaling them.

"Go on," said Clay testily. "The Queen's drunk." The girls hurried into the dark antechamber, fearful as mice. He paused to watch them, surprised how real they seemed, how easily they aroused his compassion. Especially Melinda, the blue-eyed girl whom he had disgraced in front of her father, having her give him a blowjob in the tailor's shop, just to make her cry, while the rest of her family pretended to look at bolts of material hung on the wall. How strange that he could feel so strongly for a couple of simulations—mere threads of stolen computer time—while Stella aroused

138

little if anything in him. "You know, I thought I was going to like you, Stella."

Quiet now, attentive, perfectly composed and waiting for him to finish, she resembled a gymnast before a performance.

"You seemed . . . strange, dangerous . . . Whatever. But now I can't stand you."

He wanted to hurt her. He wanted to believe she could feel something besides pleasure.

But instead of pain she showed only mild concern that she was no longer interesting. She offered to change morphology, asked if he needed a new venue—sex in zero G, sex with hot oil, sex in the town square, with everyone watching—and she asked, as she always asked when relations between them were at a low, whether he had some deep hidden fantasy, however bizarre or disturbing, that she might fulfill. She operated his body as if it were a complete interface to his feelings.

So he gave up discovering her motives, and agreed to some exhibitionism in the village square. He would learn her secrets someday; he just did not know how or when.

In the meantime, he lived like a king. Days passed, filled with adventures into goblin lairs, flights on his Pegasus out to the nymph-rich islands of the Fogbow Sea, hours of profound, ennobling struggle within Stella's simulations, and petty squabbles with the other lords and barons of the Elfhorn Mountains, who had not yet accepted the sudden materialization of this new and apparently invincible kingdom.

He might have lived this way for months, bored and content, if the outside world had not finally sent an ambassador. An unusual pair of travelers appeared one day, while he was on the throne arbitrating the week's legal disputes. "Last, my Lord," began some court official, whose title he could never remember, "we have two travelers, from the Fiefdom of Tymalion and the dark plains of Oran."

The travelers came forward. Despite the chain mail and leather armor, he recognized them immediately.

"Clay? Is that you?"

He blushed. In a fantasy simulation there was nothing wrong with glazed muscles and jewelry on a man, but they made him self-conscious in front of his mother and Katherine. "How'd you find me?"

He could see the laughter in Katherine's eyes. "I knew you'd come here," she said, triumphant.

The log cabin, still gathering dust . . . somewhere. Had he left a clue? How had she found him?

His mother, apparently wanting to hug him, came too close to the dais. She was forcibly returned to the center of the room. "You insult the Court," said one of his henchmen, driving her backward with the stock of a halberd.

This was no place for a family reunion. "Let her be," said Clay, cracking his scepter's ferrule against the marble of the dais. Millennium 4 Systems, it seemed, allocated very little computer time to the henchman constructs. "The court of King Cramer is adjourned. The foreigners and I will have counsel. French—" He pointed the bejeweled crown of the scepter at the porter. "Bring a fruit basket and a flagon of iced tea to the East Tower."

"Yes, my Lord."

He told the scepter, a magic item Stella had programmed, to take them to the tower, and they were there. A blast of sunlight hurt his eyes. Small puffy clouds were everywhere, above and below. The royal park gleamed, small as a model from this height, sunlit, walled-in beside the castle, green and speckled with spring flowers. The Pegasus was grazing there, as it was fond of doing.

He commanded the scepter to return his morphology to that of non-simian Clay Cramer, and his mother breathed a sigh of relief. "That's much better. You looked like Thor." She crushed him with a studded-leather hug.

"How 'bout I leave you two alone? I can come back in a few minutes."

He got his first long look at Katherine. He saw nothing in her face but the reserved dignity of the ambassador she had pretended to be. She had come . . . Why?

Too much to think about. . . . "I'll send for you?" he said.

She nodded. Nothing more needed to be said. He lifted the scepter and sent her down to the royal park. They would talk as soon as he got rid of his mom, who, meanwhile, continued to hug him. She would not let go. "Oh, Clay, you're in so much trouble."

"Are you being traced?"

"I'm *your mother*, Clay. What? I'm supposed to forget all about you so you don't get caught?"

The police would be searching, of course. But their list of his favorite simulations would be ranked by hours of attendance.

His mother finally withdrew, retaining an empathic hold on his shoulders. "It's awful, Clay. You didn't want to break the law. You're sixteen. We know how it is, your father and I. Believe it or not."

Her sympathy felt overplayed, maybe because he was used to the universal fear and reverence of his subjects. He was King Cramer, ruler of twelve mountains. He did not evoke pity. "Everything's fine, Mom. I never wanted to end up online, but it's okay. I'm a king. I live in a castle."

"Your father thinks they'll go easy on you, if you turn yourself in."

"It's too late. I'm already here. But I can go anywhere on the Net, and no one can trace me."

"You can't run for the rest of your life. They'll catch up."

"Maybe."

"Clay, you're stealing computer time. Stealing. You could go to jail."

"They could put me in jail for a lot of things."

"Don't you care? What about going to college? The computer told me this morning—you got into La Sorbonne."

"You mean . . . already?"

"There's a personal message from a dean or somebody, the head of the Philosophy Course."

Philosophy . . . La Sorbonne. They wanted him. They really wanted him! He hadn't known whether they would take him seriously, the famous scholars . . . with him not having any publications. But they recognized who he was, who he was going to become.

However, he was stuck in here, at least until he turned eighteen. He would have to defer a year, maybe two. He wondered what the policy was but didn't feel like hashing it out with his mother. "Oh," he said. "Well, that's not until fall."

"You have to clear your record before you can accept."

"Yeah. . . ." His mother was right: the police could stop him. They could lock him up and ruin his whole record. Fine, he thought. Let them try. I'll get where I'm going, one way or another. If some barbaric code of laws keeps me out of school, then that's a loss for society, and by leaving out the best people society just bleeds itself, and before long it will die. "Well, I don't really want an offline life. If you want to know the truth."

"What do you mean? Offline? We aren't logoffs. A few weeks ago you didn't want to be 'online' your whole life and thought people who went 'offline' knew something we don't."

"I didn't get it until now. Everyone's offline. That's why nobody can do anything without permission from Beijing. The government uses economics to keep people offline, even though it costs almost nothing to live on the Net. They can't have it both ways; either you're online or you're not; either you're free or you're still stuck in a material age."

"You can't spend your whole life online."

"In a few years, everyone will live online."

She wiped at her cheek with a black-gloved hand, perhaps removing a tear, though she did not appear to be crying. "Are you really happy, Clay? You don't look happy."

"I was going to move out *eventually*—and what's the difference? I was already spending most of my time online."

"But it's all make-believe."

He shrugged. "The queen's real. I met her in California."

The porter was standing at the top of the stairs, a perplexed look on his face. The conversation would be mumbo-jumbo to his simulated brain. "Thanks, French. Carry on."

"My Lord." The servant bowed and departed, leaving the tray of fruit and the flagon of iced tea. There were chairs set around a table, but Clay and his mother ignored them.

"You're not happy here," said his mother. "You just don't know where else to go."

"I was going to grow up sooner or later, Mom. Might as well be now."

"Not this way, Clay. Not as a thief. Not as a king. An adult doesn't live his whole life in a fantasy simulation. Come home. Your father's promised not to interfere with your morphology."

His father . . . always the negotiator. "Sure. I'll think about it."

"I'm talking about your real father, not the copy."

"Who?"

"The original."

"You talked to him?"

"He's going to move back to France at the end of the month, if all goes well."

"What about . . . the other one?"

"He's going to be erased today or tomorrow. The original and I—we've worked out some things. He and you and I, we're going to get to know each other again."

His mother had a way with optimism. Everything was always fine, or going to be fine. If only the world had listened to her pleas, he might never have left home. "That's great that you and Dad are getting back together, but what's the point? I graduate this year. I can't live at home forever."

"I'm not talking about forever, Clay. I'm talking about the next eight months, time you're supposed to spend at home with your mother and father, time you're supposed to go to school, high school, which has more to teach you than you think. You're the one talking about forever. Forever running from the police."

"I'm not resetting my timeline. I didn't do anything wrong."

"Well, you might not have a choice. That's up to the police."

"It was Dad's idea. They probably wouldn't even have thought of it."

"You're lucky, Clay Cramer. You have a father who is in a position to help you."

"That's all he wants: to wipe everything out and pretend like it didn't happen. I'm not changing *anything*."

"It's not about the last few days; it's about the rest of your life. I'm sorry, you're still a child and need some decisions made for you. I'm going to have to turn you in. Keep running if you want, but I'm your mother. I can't let you ruin your life."

Mention of the police did not frighten him. He already planned to beam to another simulation after Katherine and his mother beamed out. Their travels would have left records on hundreds of machines. Fortunately, Stella had given him the scepter, which she said would save him if anyone attempted to capture his data. "Do what you must," he said.

For his mother's sake, he gave her a long hug and said that he would think about going back. He even wanted to go back, for a moment, for the time that she held him. He had not run away from her, or anything she had done.

For some reason, he could reveal none of what he was thinking to his mother. He managed only the vaguest of apologies and assurances before zapping her down to the park. Maybe Stella would have a way to copy his data, so that he could send a copy of himself home. Then everyone would be happy. His mother would not know the difference.

He began pacing the flagstones. Now he had to face Katherine, Katharine. . . . Where to start?

Screw it, he said a minute later, knowing that he could pace the flagstones for an hour and not get anywhere. Let's see what she has to say for herself.

He beamed her up.

She gasped and lifted her arms, thrown off-balance by the sudden translation of x-y-z coordinates.

"Sorry to startle you."

She was quick to regain her poise. "That's quite a little toy you have there."

Though he knew she could care less about his scepter, he was relieved to have something to talk about. "It's cool. If I get hungry, I just make some food. If I have to go somewhere, I just say the coordinates. I'm like a superuser, not just for *W&W* but the whole Net."

"Is that above wizard?"

She knew what a superuser was. He glared at her.

The wind was gathering strength, auguring a change in the weather. When Katherine removed her helmet, it swept up her hair in wild, flame-like arcs. Though by any standard her beauty was no greater than Stella's or the peasant girls' of the village, she looked lovely. He could not get enough of looking at her.

"Quite a disappearing act," she said.

"Magic," he said. "Poof."

Perhaps to fit the game, she was in human form. It was like talking to an image in his mind, a memory. "Wanna sit?" He motioned to the table.

She tore loose a bundle of grapes and took a seat, abrupt, sloppy, oblivious to the grapes that fell from the bundle and rolled under the table. Yes, a memory, he thought, her face bent forward, eyes looking up at him, full of the bemusement and calculation with which she had always watched him, even when she was just another face in his algebra class, watching him graph polynomials at his desk and explain to the class what the images appearing on the central holodisplay signified.

"Okay . . ." He remained standing, leaning with both hands on the scepter. "So?"

"So—what?"

"Last time I saw you—at your house—you slammed the door in my face."

She leaned back on two legs of the chair. "A piece of advice, about how to treat a woman. When you want me . . . just reach out." More grapes were falling, as she gestured with her hands. "Just reach out with your own hands and do what you want. I'll stop you if I have other ideas."

Clay swallowed. He turned and placed both hands on one of the crenels that encircled the tower, blushing hotly. *Now* she tells him this, rudely, condescendingly, when it's too late.

"Quite a place," she said. "I don't blame you. Free simulation time, a castle . . . Wow."

She knew—of course she knew what guys did in simulations. Still, he said, "You just don't like fantasy."

"I certainly wouldn't want to spend my whole life in one of these things."

He went forward, gesturing with the scepter. "This is just where I live. There are other simulations. My dad told you, right?"

"In *any* of these things. Not every day of my life. That's a little psycho, don't you think?"

"These are totally different. I know—you think it's just a bunch of games, but they're *real*. They're totally illegal. I got stabbed!" He pointed between two ribs. "I got shot. I froze. My fingers were black. I died a couple of times and I felt it. Not just wireframe tingles. I felt the pain."

"You're starting to freak me out."

"Really. . . ." There she was, a few feet away, casually leaning back, neck arched while she pulled a grape loose with her mouth. He wanted—again—something. To get around the huge oak table, put a hand on her shoulder . . . No. . . . Instead, he continued talking. Talking. Not the time, no . . . "Everyone talks about going offline, but that's nothing. The stuff online is what's really mind-blowing. I'll show you. Just hang out awhile."

"State-owned media conglomerates." Katherine let the chair fall back onto all fours. She threw the grapes on the table. "You're right. I don't like fantasy. It's stupid crap." She tried to smile—then gave up. "They just feed it to you, whatever you want. It's not real."

"You don't get it. Look—" He pressed a short-cut gem on the scepter to bring up the Ice Age.

Katherine, being in a seated position, fell into the snow. "Agh!"

Clay helped her up, snow crystals stinging their clasped hands. Their breaths collided as steam-puffs and then vanished. Dry trails of snow hissed past their *Wizards & Warriors* sandals. His feet already burned.

"Oh my God! Clay!"

"See? Ah-h-h-h . . ." He threw out his arms and stomped around in a circle. "It's real. . . ."

"My feet!"

"No thresholds . . . Come on!" He ran to the top of a small rise, duck-walking through the deep snow. A pack of hunchbacked human beings had surrounded a woolly mammoth with their spears. The mammoth had smeared blood in a spiral down the sides of a wide depression, to a dark place at the bottom, where it now limped, dragging its tusks toward its spry, cautious attackers. Clay yelled, "Computer—spears!" A wooden spear with a stone head appeared in his hand. Katherine used hers for help on the hill. "Ow! Ow!"

Clay's feet were aching, too. He'd proved his point. "Computer—furry boots!"

Their feet were now wrapped in cowhide and rabbit fur. "See?" said Clay. "They make it as realistic as possible."

Katherine clutched her spear with both hands, gaping at the mammoth.

"Come on! Let's go!" Clay took a couple of steps down the hill, but Katherine stopped where she was. "What's wrong?"

She was staring at the sky, the rheumy yellow sun, the thin white clouds. She inhaled and blew steam into the air, again, again. "Oh . . ."

"See what I mean. You don't realize how fake most simulations are until . . ."

Katherine's eyes were closed as though she was savoring a sip of coffee.

"Watch." He pressed another gem. Now they stood in their cowhide boots in a steel mill in Machine-Age Pittsburgh. A huge iron ladle passed overhead, tracking toward the volcanic Bessemer thirty yards away. Clay watched as two workers in bulky clothes helped fit it into a metal frame between them. Clay grabbed Katherine's hand and pulled her forward.

He had to shout to be heard over the twin steam engines running the blowers. His face burned. What he found interesting about the heat was that it wasn't the air but some invisible radiation from the furnace that seemed to cook every surface of his body.

"I can't—I can't breathe!" Katherine let herself be dragged to where the Bessemer was being lowered.

"This is really what it was like!" hollered Clay. "They dug up rocks from the ground and then melted them down. Look!"

The white-hot steel was pouring from the giant, gourd-shaped Bessemer into the ladle, giving off enough heat to blister their faces.

"Hey, get out of there!" One of the workers, soot-faced and wearing two wool hats for protection, waved at them to move.

"People spent their whole lives in places like this. Six days a week."

"Okay, let's go back," said Katherine. "It's too hot."

"Hey, John," called the worker, standing on a catwalk above the ladle, now glowing with steel, "get these two outta here!"

Clay continued, "If you want to, you can live in one of these things for weeks, see what it was really like. The worlds are huge. The constructs are totally life-like. Look out!" A big man in a grimy coat was approaching. Clay grabbed Katherine and started pulling her again. He hoped to stir up a little mayhem to see how the constructs reacted. Katherine got going too fast, though, and tripped on a loose piece of metal. She fell face-first into a wheelbarrow a man was pushing and smashed her nose. She rolled on her back with her hand over her face. Blood streamed down her cheek. "Oh! Oh! Oh!"

"Computer!" cried Clay, lifting the scepter, "Back to *Wizards & Warriors*."

The computer put Katherine on the oak table that held the fruit and wine, perhaps favoring some heuristic about injured people and operating tables. On Stella's instructions, minor injuries were not repaired automatically by the simulation host.

"Computer, no blood!" cried Katherine, sitting up.

The blood vanished.

"Sorry . . ."

She still held her nose. "Ouch," she said quietly.

"Computer," he said, "full repairs, all injuries."

The order was executed instantly. Katherine pressed her nose from different angles, searching for pain.

"Well," said Clay. "I guess you get the picture. I went offline, you know—I went to L.A. I did shibboleth and everything, but shibboleth just makes you imagine stuff. These simulations make things that are completely real."

She stared at him, a little afraid, he noticed, just enough so that he knew she understood why he was here, why he had stayed. "This woman," she began, "who is she? How long can she get away with stealing time?"

"I met her in California. It's nothing. I'm not in love with her or anything."

"There's something really creepy about this. It's all too easy."

"I asked her about it. She won't say anything."

"To have this kind of access . . . she must be pretty high up. And the detail . . . You can't just throw together simulations like that. It would take a full studio, hundreds of people. Clay, you're in the middle of a pretty major operation."

Katherine was sitting on the edge of the table, centimeters away. He laid his hand beside hers, not quite touching her. "I know. . . . But I can leave. Nothing stops me."

He wanted to make an excuse for the sex, but Katherine continued on, apparently indifferent. "It's like you're being brainwashed." She pushed off from the table. "I'm getting out of here."

"Wait—Hey, it's perfectly safe. Even my dad went through these things, and when he was ready to go, he just beamed out."

Katherine kissed him on the cheek, something that despite the eternity they had spent with each other she had never done. "The police aren't going to torture you if you come offline. Neither will I, and neither will your parents."

"My timeline . . ."

"You'll have to figure something out, or you really are trapped here." She told the computer to beam her home. Looking him in the eyes, the fear not yet gone from her expression, she vanished.

He grabbed the corner of the table to throw it end-over-end, but he wasn't wearing the King Cramer morphology and just ended up hurting his wrist. "Dammit!" he cried. Aggravated, he just told the computer to get rid of the pain, and then he floated down to the garden to say goodbye to his mother. She pleaded with him again to come home, but he told her he had things to do. "I'm not leaving until I know what this place is all about," he said. He told the computer to beam her home, an OS privilege Stella had given him.

Then he put on the King Cramer morphology and went back to the castle. He was going to get some answers from his Queen, and this time she wasn't going to slip through his fingers.

He found her in the royal parlor, seated, as usual, in a tall throne-like easy chair, completely still and staring out the vast west window. She was like an automaton that came alive only in his presence. She seemed particularly mechanical today, perhaps because he had been affected by the less predictable behavior of his mother and Katherine. The ebullience which carried her up out of the chair and into his arms seemed thoroughly contrived.

"My liege, you look exhausted. I know how the court vexes you so."

"Yeah." He kissed her on the forehead and groaned as though he were unwinding. "More llama trouble. Now McGregor thinks that Carmichael is stealing his roans. Llamas, llamas, llamas."

"You need a break from being King."

"Stella, I'm about to ask some questions. You've heard them before, but this time I want answers."

"You've never been to the Dark Ages, Europe. You could see what it's like to be a real King."

"The only thing keeping me here is my curiosity about what you're plotting. So? What is it?"

"Don't be silly. All of this—the simulations, the time online—all of it is just a flapping of a moth's wings, a tiny widening of possibility, which only in the far distant future will you—"

"No more crap. I want to know exactly who you are and who you work for." He grabbed her by the shoulders. "Tell me, goddammit."

He had shouted this in his booming throne voice, but her face remained as untroubled as the pond on *Forgotten Planet: Spring*. "No one knows who built the simulations. Their presence has been spread by word of mouth."

This time, he was going to shake the truth out of her. He knew it was in there somewhere, somewhere behind those sweet blank eyes. If he could just make her talk, force her. With thick muscle-man fingers he tightened the hold on her shoulders. She was trying to pull away, collapsing under his grip, yet still she refused to talk. He slapped her across the face, sending her shrieking over an end table.

Instead of cursing or crying or fighting back, she turned to him on her knees, plaintive and beseeching. "What's wrong, baby?"

He slapped her again. "You know what I'm talking about. I want to know why the hell you're here, why you do exactly what I say, what it's all about."

Her eyes were addled and staring. He slapped her again, and again. And each time she did not move but took the blow willingly, meekly, then she began to cry and to hug his giant legs. "Oh, baby. Don't hit me. Why? Why are you hurting me? What did I do?"

He began to weaken. He could feel the beating of her heart against his legs, the convulsions of her crying, the tears smeared against his thigh. He felt sick, seeing her like this, the lovely bird-morph that had attracted him, the woman who had once seemed like a goddess, now down on her knees, allowing herself to be beaten. She just would not hate him, no matter how much he hurt her. So convincing was her performance that he almost believed that she loved him. But he knew—as impossible as it seemed— that she was operating under some inhuman fealty to a person or power he might never encounter. No woman with a free will would grovel before him like this. His mother, Katherine . . . they would have hit him back. Yet he was sure Stella had a breaking point, and he was determined to find it. He yanked her head back by the hair, spit in her face, and threw her by the hair onto the floor. "Do you love me, Stella?"

"Yes!" she cried, desperately. "Yes! Of course."

He kicked her twice in the ribs, so that she curled into a ball. Her moans were feeble, probably because the computer was attenuating her pain, not rendering the full experience. Frustrated, he kicked her square in the teeth. "Goddammit, then stand up and tell me the truth. Stand up!"

She rose and came to him, bleeding from the corner of one eye, tears streaming down her face. She kissed him. She kissed him again and again on his cheeks, his nose. "Baby, I love you so much. Don't do this."

"Something is wrong with you. I don't know what it is, but I can't stay here not knowing. I'll give you one last chance to tell me what's going on."

She was silent for a moment, watching him with eyes that he thought betrayed, at last, something, a secret desire to express maybe. But then her features hardened, and she gave him the most passionate of kisses, driving her tongue into his mouth, frantically, violently. "I don't want you to go, Clay. Please stay, just a little while." She licked the blood from a split lip. "Do you like this? Do you like the blood?" She offered him the bloody tip of her tongue. "Does it turn you on?"

"You can't be human."

"Do you want to beat me? Is that it?"

"You can't possibly be human." He told the scepter to beam him home.

Chapter 14

We must consider the copying of the self to be the gravest of all scan-crimes. Far more than an infringement of a copyright, it is a violence against the very foundation of human existence. The person who takes more than the one life the state (not to mention Nature) has given him feeds on his fellow man's blood; he is a vampire whose heart should be run through with a wooden stake.

> — Agent Maria Batacharia, "Stopping the Plague of Illegal Incarnations," Get Tough on Crime Symposium, March 2996.

Though computer-operated lights came on as Claire walked through the house, she advanced cautiously, examining the darker rooms before entering. She had a funny feeling that one of the Pauls was near.

His snoring soon led her toward the balcony, where he was flopped back in the lawn chair like a suit of clothes. It was the copy, breaking his promise to disappear by sunfall. She went outside, causing the computer to switch on the balcony lights.

If he were aware that he had broken his promise, he did not show it. He yawned leisurely, squinted, scratched his whiskers, and asked what time it was.

"It's dark," she said. She stood watching him, hipshot, one arm akimbo.

The sleep fell out of her husband's eyes. He sat up. "Claire—listen. I can't do it."

"Computer." She walked back inside. "Get me the police."

The copy leaped out of the chair. "No! Computer, stop. Ignore that last command."

"No, continue. I want to talk to Sorenson."

"Pardon me," said the computer. "There has been an error. I cannot execute either your command, Mr. Cramer, or your command, Mrs. Cramer."

"Just do as I say," said Claire. "This man is a copy—he's an illegal copy of my husband. He has no rights and no authority in this house."

"Wait," said the copy. "Just hold off, just a minute. Claire, you've got to give me a minute to explain, just a—"

"Pardon me," said the computer. "There has been an error. I cannot execute either your command, Mr. Cramer, or your command, Mrs. Cramer."

Claire went inside and gestured to the telepod. "I want you out of here right now."

He followed her, looking off-balance and taking scissor-steps, then he fell on his knees and grabbed her hand as if he was about to propose. "There's one more memory I have. Remember when we moved in? Remember when we sent the order for Clay? Watching the first cell divide . . . the hologram of the fetus in the living room, seeing it get bigger . . . the day the demiurge panel slid open . . . There he was, wrapped in that little blue blanket, his tiny red face . . . just yesterday . . . I—I'm not trying to prove anything."

He smelled like bourbon. He'd fallen into some swamp of memories, and now a slimy green hand had her by the ankle. She pulled away. "You've made your point. You're Paul, okay? I believe you. Now get out."

He sank against the side of the couch, draping an arm over the armrest like it was the shoulder of an old drinking buddy.

Yes, she believed him. Facing death—she could only imagine—would make anyone a little crazy. He looked old. His head hung forward, like an overripe piece of fruit about to fall to the ground. She guessed that it must be very real for him, their marriage slipping away, the knowledge that no matter how difficult he made it for her, she was going to get rid of him. "I wish you could see the present as clearly as you see the past," she said.

"I do," he said. "I do."

She pointed to the telepod again. "Go."

"You want me to *kill* myself."

"The police will take care of everything."

She waited, her husband slouched down in wretched silence. She gave him several seconds to accept that this was indeed the end, then she asked the computer to contact the police.

He pulled himself up into a kneeling position. "No! Not yet! Computer, stop."

"Pardon me," began the computer, repeating the same error message.

"I don't have to die," he continued. "I could just go off to some island and never bother you again."

"There aren't any loopholes, dear. Either you or your original must die. It's the law."

Another evasive suggestion was on the tip of the copy's tongue when the telepod began thrumming. The computer, faithfully executing an old, old command, said, "Your son is home."

For a moment, listening to her son's body being constructed, she was surprised and somewhat overwhelmed to hear the old machine's walls purring again, as they had used to do several times a day, when Clay would return from school, when Paul would return from work. The house filled with sound, with the pneumatic wheezing of matter ducts, with the sigh of nanites being flushed out of the assembly chamber; it was like the place's heart had started beating again. She worried that Clay would come offline as Thor, or the ape, or whatever was cool now . . . a teenager. God. Exactly what post-parenting counselors warned about. *Even your son, Mrs. Cramer, even the baby you adore, who loves you dearly, will become Play-Do in the hands of the world. When he no longer needs you, let go, because you can't save him. He's gone. He's like everyone else, gone, gone, gone.* Why was that a rite of passage? Trading yourself for outside personalities . . .

When the doors popped open, and Clay stepped, unmorphed, into the room, she gave him a big hug. "I knew you'd come back," she said. It was all she could think to say. "I knew it."

There was something perfunctory about the way he hugged her, a rigidity. Strangely, he still held the scepter from the fantasy simulation; he set it against the wall.

Meanwhile, the copy leaned heavily on the armrest and got to his feet.

"I need to talk to Dad," said Clay, stepping back, his eyes bright and animated. "I think I've figured out what's going on."

"Figured out—what?"

"I know what's wrong with Stella."

While she was trying to understand what her son was talking about, the copy came between them, ghost-white and staring. He shook his son's hand with the stooped posture of someone in great, mortal pain. Then he did something Claire had not seen him do for many years. He gave Clay a hug. "I thought I'd never see you again," he said.

Bewildered, Clay was looking at her over the copy's shoulder.

"He's the copy," she said. "He's about to be destroyed."

Clay nodded and gave the copy a pat on the back.

The copy continued, ignoring her. "You came home. That's great, son. That's a great place to start."

Clay stepped back with a defiant, teenaged swagger. "Yeah, I'm back." He tried to pull away.

The copy retained a grip on his shoulders. "That ape stuff . . . *nothing*. Caught me by surprise . . . It's nothing. Do what you want. Hey, it's the right to life, body, and mind. It's in the Bill of Rights."

Claire stood to one side, utterly baffled. What would happen next. . . ? She hadn't wanted *this*. . . .

"That's nice, Dad," said Clay. "But there's no time. We can talk later."

Dad . . . ? Claire stepped up beside them. "This is the *copy*," she said.

"I have something to talk to him about."

"You can talk to the original. He'll be here in a few hours."

"I've got to talk to someone now. Dad, are you still on the case?"

"The case?"

"The Net security case. It's still open, right?"

"Yeah. . . ." The copy gave his head a hard tilt. "It's breaking my neck."

"I think I know what's going on."

Right then, Claire could have cared less about any investigation. She barely listened to what her son had said. "Then tell the police. The *police*. This is the copy, Clay. He's going to be deleted. Come on, let's all beam to the station. The original is taking over. That's right, Paul, I've made my decision. Sorenson agreed to erase you as soon as I made up my mind. It's over."

The copy whirled around like he was going to punch her. The muscles of his face were taut and bunched together, his eyebrows bent into upside-down V's. "Can't you wait one goddamn minute while I talk to my son? If you want me dead that bad, why don't you make a knife and cut my throat?"

"You'd tell the computer to stop," she said.

"I give you my word. Go ahead, do it. Computer, make a hunting knife." The demiurge began to hum. "That's what you need. You need to do the killing yourself. Here—" He removed his gun from its shoulder-holster, changed the setting from "stun" to "goo," and handed it to her.

The panel of the demiurge was sliding open just a couple of steps to her right. She was suddenly surrounded by weapons. The metal of the gun was cold and heavy, foreign; it was the official weapon of the World Police, a gun; private citizens were forbidden to hold or possess guns. She let it drop to the floor. "You're scaring me, Paul."

Both Paul Cramers now seemed so real that they were blurring in her mind. She was unsure which of her husband's personalities had just gone haywire.

"You can't do it, can you?" He picked up the gun and handed it to her. "You don't want to kill me. You just want to wave your dainty little hand at the computer, give a command, and have me—and all your problems—deleted."

"All right," she said. She backed up a step, lifting the gun to sight down the barrel.

"Come on. Shoot."

"Is this the safety?" She tapped her thumb.

"It's off." He stared at her, shifting his weight from foot to foot. He cleared his throat.

"Jeez, Mom."

The copy closed his eyes and bunched his shoulders together, waiting for the impact of the goo pellets.

"Step inside the telepod," she said.

"You want me dead, just pull the trigger."

"Don't make me count to three."

"Do it! Freeze your heart and kill me!"

"No. Use your brain and leave."

"Dad! What are you doing? Mom!" Clay backed away. He reached behind himself until he had a firm grip on the head of the scepter.

"Freeze my heart?" said Claire. "Freeze my heart?" She took aim at the philodendron that grew along the sill of the big window facing the sea. One small squeeze and she put a pellet into a tangle of vines inside the pot. Immediately, a gray color spread down the vines, hissing, running like a fuse. Sections of the vine detached and fell to the floor, breaking apart like mud.

Paul's eyes were wide open now, arms stiff at his sides, but he stood his ground.

"The telepod. Now!" she cried.

Paul visibly relaxed. He breathed a heavy sigh and spread his arms. He closed his eyes and tilted his head back. "I'm sorry. I'm sorry, Claire. Go ahead. I'm ready."

She had the gun barrel pointed straight at his stomach. *Yes*, she thought. It would be so easy. . . .

"*Mom*! No!" Clay was holding the scepter against his chest with both hands.

There was terror on his strangely bare face, a wild incomprehension. Gradually, she came to her senses. She wasn't going to murder anyone. To the copy, she said, "I don't need to break the law to get rid of you. For heaven's sake."

She went to the bedroom and shut the door.

"I knew it!" yelled Paul.

"Dad . . . are you *drunk*?" she heard her son say.

She told the computer to lock the door, ignoring the voices coming from outside. She called the police, hoping they would arrive before the copy did too much damage. Finally, she went back to listen at the door.

She heard the copy sigh. "Oh, Clay," he was saying in a surprisingly soft tone. "Your mother's right. I'm not your father. I better go."

"I don't care which of you is which right now. Could you just listen for a second?"

"All right—what? What is it?"

"The online version of Stella is a simulation."

Claire heard Paul chuckle, faintly. "What gives you that idea?"

"I always know what she's going to do. She never does anything for herself. It's not natural. She's got to be some sort of program or construct."

The copy's voice rose. "Welcome to adulthood, son. People aren't always who they appear to be. I'm just glad you wised up as soon as you did."

"She's not a con-artist. She really believes everything she says and everything she does."

"Clay . . . there isn't a teenage boy in the world who wouldn't fall for Stella."

"That's not what I'm talking about. I'm positive about this. I was with her for over a week. She's not a person. Once she beams online, her body is replaced with a construct."

The police should be here by now, thought Claire. It's been almost a minute. . . .

"Okay. You have a theory. I get it, but I've been a detective for twenty-five years. I know a thing or two about scan-crimes, and I've been working on Stella's case for days. She's not a simulation."

"She is."

"I'm sorry, Clay, but you're wrong."

More supercilious lecturing . . . No, she wasn't going to let the copy start yet another shouting match. She went into the living room. "Paul Cramer," she said, jerking the gun toward the veranda with a flick of her wrist. "Outside. I've called the police. They'll be here any second."

Paul and Clay stared at her, as though waiting for something, then the copy, making an ugly face, moved toward the veranda.

He still had the nerve to throw a few words at his son. "We know that she's not a simulation because we ran a scan of her online body. It's not splines or anything like that. It's made of molecules, and the molecules exactly match those of her real body."

Clay watched his father turn and leave the room. His lips formed the beginning of a word, but he said nothing. Finally, he snatched up the scepter, took one last look at his father through the window to the veranda, then stepped into the telepod.

Claire told the computer not to let her son leave, but Clay managed to beam away anyway.

Chapter 15

As the last embers of industrial society cool and fall dark, the spiritual crisis of our age burns white-hot in our hearts, threatening to consume us all. We no longer merely take matter for granted, we doubt and even *deny* its presence. If an object does not immediately bend to our imagination (by "object," I include people we know and socialization in general), we stand amazed, or bemused, as factory owners once must have regarded the tributes to dismantled gods scrawled all over the currency feeding their machines and laboratories. We stand between worlds. We cannot yet give our faith entirely to Mind, yet our worship of Matter cannot endure the plasticity of the age. As during every great social transformation, we yearn for a new synthesis of belief, knowing that no synthesis is possible. Knowing, too, that we will yearn and wonder and wait for it regardless, for decades, perhaps for centuries, until the new age at last crystallizes, first in the world and then in our hearts.

— Dr. John Brooding, Professor of Theology, Beijing University, speaking during a holovised panel discussion entitled "Subliminal Belief: Our Unconscious Religious Dilemma," November 2996.

This time Clay told the scepter to cover his tracks. He didn't want to run into any cops. If his dad was right, they weren't going to be very appreciative or even receptive to his hunch about Stella, even though—and he was positive about this—*something* was wrong with her. He had never heard of neural programming that could take direct control of a person's speech and behavior, but a piece of software might be involved, a meld-movie-like program, something that would turn her into a puppet online, moving her muscles and deciding what she would say.

He would have plenty of opportunity to investigate Stella—very soon, when he went back online. He would stay at Katherine's house only a few minutes, because the scepter was dead in his hands unless he was on the Net.

When he appeared, anonymously, in Katherine's living room, which he found vacant, he stayed within a step of the telepod until he was sure her parents were not around. Then, hearing Katherine at her desk dictating commands to the computer, he made his way to the end of the hallway, where Katherine's mother had stared at him, imploringly, wanting to know what had upset her daughter. He was careful to hold the scepter off of the floor so that it wouldn't tap against the parquet.

Katherine heard him anyway, or maybe she had heard the telepod and then noticed that the computer had been prevented from announcing his arrival. She was already turning in her swivel chair to face him when he entered her bedroom. "That was quick," she said.

"I can't stay long."

"I figured you'd think about it for a few days, consult an oracle or something." Holograms of typed pages and photographs, pieces of the essay she had been dictating, hovered behind her head.

"Where are your parents?"

"Out to dinner. For crying out loud, sit down." She motioned to the bed. "Relax. You look like you've just seen a ghost."

"I *am* a ghost." He tossed the scepter onto the foot of the bed and sat down near where she was working. Next to Katherine's lovely blonde ape morphology, his default body made him look like a dork. He wished he had remembered to change. "My old life, anyway. It's gone. I shouldn't even be here. If I get caught—"

"Old life? You've only got one life, Clay."

"I was gonna make a deal with the police—or at least give them a tip. I think the woman's a simulation, or some kind of software, except my dad—well, he said she's made of matter, even online. That would pretty much kill my theory."

"Slow down. Who's a simulation?"

He recounted his interrogation of Stella, skipping nothing. He told how he had kicked and slapped her, not the least bit ashamed. On some basic level he had known that she was a simulation.

"My God," said Katherine.

"She isn't real. I know it. It's like she didn't feel a thing."

Katherine sat down next to him, warm, furry like a teddy bear, putting an arm around him. "I don't think it matters. Whatever she is—you can't trust her, it, whatever, if you don't know what it is."

"The police'll lock me up. That's something you can be sure of. Online—well, I can do anything with the scepter now, but it only works online."

"You and your scepter." She began combing her nails through his hair, treating him—as she often did—like a simple, lovable pet animal. It relaxed him.

"I can bring you with me. With the scepter, we don't need Stella at all."

"You're Makoto," she said suddenly. "Did you ever read that?"

He said he had no idea what she was talking about.

"It's an old Japanese fairy tale, from the 2300's. We read it in school." She stared at him, petting his hair. "This little boy is watching holovision, some little kids' show (there were lots of kids then), and his dog Makoto, this cute little Maltese, wants to play catch. The dog tries everything to get the boy to play. He drops the ball in the kid's lap, he jumps around, he whines, he tries to drag the boy away by the shirtsleeve—but the boy keeps watching the show. The boy hides the ball, holds the dog's jaws shut with his hand, spanks the dog; he's mean as hell. I don't know why Makoto doesn't just bite him. But he doesn't. He wants to be at the center of the boy's attention. He ends up jumping around and barking where the show is being projected. The boy throws a tantrum. He starts beating the dog with a plastic baseball bat."

"Jesus."

"The kid's an ugly little brat. They draw him to look like a weasel. Anyway, finally the dog just disappears. The only way he can get away from the boy is to fade out and fade back in on the holodisplay, as a character in the show."

"A media tie-in." Once again, remembering those sleepless hours staring at her shoulder blades beneath her diaphanous maiden's nightgown, he flushed, wondering how he could have been such a fool when he knew exactly what to do—and feeling it about to happen again, the moment here but his hands flexed and frozen at his sides. Once again he was afraid to move them a centimeter. Not again. . . .

He put a hand on her shoulder and tentatively ran his fingers through her hair. Why was this hard? He'd been getting laid with simulations for two years. This girl—this one girl was terrifying simply because she could comprehend what was going on. It was ridiculous.

She kept talking as though his touch was a perfectly routine event. "It's a fairy tale. Shut up. The rest of the story is about how the kid misses the dog. It's really sad, actually. He and Makoto just sit there, staring at each other, Makoto whimpering, the boy slapping his legs and calling, 'Makoto! Makoto!', the people on the show all confused. It doesn't matter what episode the boy brings up, Makoto is always there, and he can't get out."

"What a morbid story. I think I get the point."

"Then the dog wanders out of the show—not onto the Net (I don't think they had computers then), but somewhere, anyway, where he can get to other shows. The boy sees his dog run up and lick the news anchorman, fight with other dogs on a beach in a cola commercial, take a pee on the lawn of some famous holovision family, but the dog can't even hear him anymore. He just wanders along, sniffing, trying to pick up the boy's scent. Eventually the boy stops seeing Makoto all together. He spends a week alone in his room with the blinds closed. Then some workmen show up to change the billboard outside his window. He hears them working and opens the blinds. They replace a woman in a bikini drinking a Coke with a happy picture of Makoto panting beside a giant can of his favorite dog food. Makoto is finally dead. The story ends with the boy placing a tiny bouquet of lilies at the base of the billboard, as though on a grave."

"That's terrible."

"It's a children's book. We're studying how people in different time periods taught their kids to understand the world."

"And I'm Makoto?"

"Makoto when he became a transmission. You're pasted up on a billboard somewhere, and no one can tear you down."

Actually, he said to himself, I'm the boy, and everyone else is Makoto. I've beaten them all flat into pictures. "Then who's the boy?"

"You are."

He stared at her.

"No one's been batting you over the head except yourself. In my journal at school, I said it was me, but you're the one, Clay. You're the whole story, beating yourself with a bat until you disappear. You've got to stop."

Making a fist, she gently rapped her knuckles against the side of his head. She'd been thinking about him, writing about him in her school assignments. Thinking up these elaborate analyses of him. "I'd like to stay offline," he said. "I wish I could. Really."

"Maybe I can make you." Her brown upper lip curled with mischief. "All I have to do is steal your magic wand, right? Then you can't run away."

"That wouldn't be nice." He was being playful, but he was also afraid Katherine was making more than an idle threat. He shifted his leg so that the heavy oak scepter was pinned under his knee.

"It's too big for a demiurge, but I could put it in the telepod and have the computer—"

"You're not funny."

"Computer, open the telepod doors." A muffled clatter came from the direction of the living room. The computer said, "Telepod doors open."

Clay felt an elbow dig into his abdomen, and the next thing he knew he had been toppled backward onto the bed. Laughing gleefully, Katherine had snatched up the scepter and was presently bounding toward the bedroom door.

"No!" He launched himself across the room, managing to pin her against the door before she could open it.

"You'll thank me someday," she cried, grunting, trying to wrestle the scepter away from him.

"No," he said sternly. "Quit fooling around."

Her eyes lit up and she started laughing. "I was just kidding. Come on." She let go of the scepter. "Jesus Christ." Her eyes glittered.

Having won, he already missed this game Katherine was playing. He kept holding her against the door, feeling her breasts touching him. He moved his chest side-to-side, slowly, bashfully, trying to part the hair and expose them. Dropping the scepter on the floor, he touched her glistening brown lips with his fingers, finding nothing to say, then he kissed her, very gently.

An awful, menacing silence hung about the room. No music started when they kissed, none of the lights cooled or changed tint, their movements remained clumsy, frantic, uncoordinated. When Katherine pulled off his T-shirt, the stark, haphazard illumination made his chest shine far too brightly, white, ungraceful, marked all over with odd-looking hairs. Her bedroom was entirely unsuited for intimacy. Everything jarred the senses, fought with itself, undermined any sense of *mood*: the ranks of stuffed animals presiding over the bed, shelves and shelves of bright, cheery hold-overs from childhood, the sober fragments of homework hovering over the desk, the trophies and awards here and there, the countless videoplastic posters—all at once the wall beside the bed was displaying Slovenly Gruel's fierce nipple-ringed lead singer, a fly-over of a pile of fractal-forested hills, and a giant chocolate-chip cookie, made of gleaming silver and gold, being mined and urbanized by steel ladybugs. Every part of the room was a window into its own separate world.

It was almost obscene, having sex in such wide-open unsympathetic surroundings, but he enjoyed the feeling of nakedness—of being naked offline, with another person. It was like having sex in public. Katherine was watching him with bright, earnest eyes that seemed to wonder if they would ever see him again. They would, he came to realize. He was going to stay, because he needed to be with her.

He would try the police—or the original. Someone would believe what he had learned about Stella, and maybe his discovery would win some gratitude from the authorities. He could only hope.

Chapter 16

God said, "Let there be light," and there was light. . . .

BEIJING - Researchers at the Beijing Laboratory of Noetics announced this month that a general procedure has been devised for deciphering Broca's area (the brain's speech center). "We no longer depend on prolonged experimentation to uncover isolated semantic elements in Broca's area," said Dr. Linus Maugham, addressing the press. "This new technique—partly discovered, by accident, by the computers in our lab—takes greater advantage of organizational commonalties between brains; that is, it first uncovers the broad strokes of a person's internalization of language, the way a sketch artist begins a portrait, then the details simply reveal themselves, like texture."

What this means to the rest of us is a new era in user-interface friendliness. "In two or three decades," said Maugham, "computers may be able to 'listen' to the verbal activity of online users, which would make *thinking* (in the form of direct, verbal demands) a practical input device."

. . .

When asked if users would be able to "dream" objects like food or imaginary landscapes into existence, Maugham smiled dryly and said, "User-interface technology, I'm afraid, will remain somewhat more primitive for a few centuries. Untangling memory and non-verbal thinking will take at least that long, maybe longer. Sorry to disappoint. . . ."

— "God said . . .," *OMNI*, January, 2997.

To the scepter, Clay had said, "Tell the computers in Phoenix that I'm coming to see the original—my father—and that I'm going to turn myself in." No guards intercepted him at the telepod. His data was instantiated, quietly, and he was allowed to make the short walk down the hall to his father's office.

Nevertheless, he was certain that numerous software entities were watching him. One of these entities apparently notified the original, because the door came open before Clay could knock.

"I'm here to turn myself in," he said, before his father could speak. "Guess you get to make the arrest."

"You think you can just walk in here and get arrested? It doesn't work that way. Have a seat." The original shut the door behind them, his face in shadow, watching the tops of his shoes as he went behind the desk, taking long, slow strides. "No, first comes the interrogation. The arresting officer is the one who decides who is and who isn't a suspect."

"I'm serious. I'm turning myself in."

His father was extinguishing documents with touches of his fingers on the surface of the desk. "Just a little cop humor."

There was something genuinely carefree in his father's manner: his hands danced around the desk, magician's hands, making things happen with grace and showmanship, but Clay was not fooled. The spare formality of the office dispelled any illusions his father might have been trying to create: his father's nameplate, the Police Academy diploma framed in gold and hung on the wall, the brass eyeball on the corner of his desk (a trophy for his guess about Jerome Walls), the fourteen silver crosses—marking the times he had gotten himself killed, three more since Clay's last visit here (Career Day, two years ago)—arranged with military precision beneath the diploma . . . Even the personal touches evinced the familiar purposefulness, stability, authority . . . three small holograms at the side of the desk, one of Claire, one of Clay, and one of the whole family—all at least five years out of date. His father could joke about an interrogation, but if the police had really given his job back to him, he would not hesitate to do his duty. Clay knew that much.

"You back on the 'Force? I asked the computer, but it didn't know."

"I'm on suspension."

"So why do they let you use your office?"

"They don't quite know what to do with me. They distrust me enough to use dataseals, but they don't want to lock me away. I guess I'm still useful to them, or at least they think so."

"Did they really let Mom decide? Are they going to keep you and get rid of the other one?"

His father shrugged. "I think all of that's on hold. They have the copy downstairs, in some high-level meeting. There's been a development in the case."

"Mom said he was going to be deleted immediately."

"They want him involved. I'm going over his notes, preparing for—I don't know what, exactly—but they definitely want to use the copy. He's going to be around a little while longer."

"Both of you—on the case? Don't they have any other detectives?"

"They figure I can't say no. They've got me on just about anything they want, and so they keep hinting at a deal, knowing I've got to be a good sport until they decide."

"The computer's probably listening, you know."

"Beijing and I understand each other. We don't have a choice but to play this game. The one thing working to my advantage is that I actually want to solve the case this time." His father lifted his hands high above his head and cracked his knuckles. He groaned as though he had indigestion. "I wasn't in love with that woman, Clay. You must know that. You went through the same process."

Clay took pains not to repeat his father's fidgeting, steadying his grip on the armrests of the swivel chair, one of his legs akimbo, with the ankle resting on the thigh of his other leg. He had no reason to be anything except perfectly at ease. "Process?"

"The simulations . . . I don't know. I was in a mood that day, a mood . . . and then I was online. Once I saw all of that, the real-life simulations . . . I had to stay. I had to know what it was all about."

"For evidence."

"Well . . . I came back with something. I can say that much. Not log files or anything, but at least I have an idea who we're dealing with."

"She's a simulation. I don't care if it's her real brain when she's online, they did something to her. She's not real."

"I wouldn't go that far. She's playing a part—she works for somebody. I'm convinced a very large underground organization is responsible for constructing the illegal software." His father cracked his knuckles again, this time in reverse and over the desk. "I've talked with your mother, Clay. I can't write this thing off as an undercover assignment. I had an affair. There it is—I said it. A senseless affair with a woman more interested in turning me on to illegal software than anything else. And it absorbed me. I forgot your mother—and you, too. It was the real world, and you and your mom were the fantasy. Then I missed the fantasy. I thought I could get your mom to come with me—and get her to bring you . . . find a refuge in that other network . . . whatever it is. A refuge from what—I don't know. Gradually I've put one piece after another back. Put my head back together. Now I want everything to be as much like it was as possible, including us—you, me, your mother. I hope you'll come home when this is all over, whatever happens."

Clay listened to his father, more receptive than he had intended to be, ready to be back at home himself. He was beginning to see why his mother had picked this copy of his father despite everything he had done. "Guess that's up to the police," said Clay.

"I suppose so. Fair enough. More reason to cooperate, if you have anything to tell them."

"That's why I'm here. I'm telling the truth: Stella's not a person." He explained about the fight, the way she kept springing back up, even after he kicked her in the teeth. "She's just graphics—nothing inside."

"You hit her?"

"She's a construct. It was so obvious when I thought about it. I had to make sure."

"When I was with her, I saw no indication—"

"She lies under X. She doesn't mess up, no matter how many copies get made. She's got to be some kind of machine."

"Well, if you're saying they reprogrammed her brain . . ."

Clay knew his theory was pretty outlandish. Stella's bird morphology—with wings she could move with her mind—was about the cutting edge of neuroscience. "They did *something* to her. I'm positive of that."

His father wasn't even listening. No . . . actually, he was thinking, eyes lidded, averted. Clay was getting through.

His father's friend, David Banks, pushed the door open, rapping his knuckles on the wood in a lazy apology for not knocking. "Sorry to butt in. There've been some developments."

"Can it wait?" said Clay's father.

Banks continued, "I hate to be the one to say it, Paul, but you're being sent home. The copy was more cooperative than we expected."

"My mother made up her mind," said Clay. "The copy is supposed to be deleted."

Banks had backed into a corner beside a miniature synthetic olive tree, currently in post-bloom, its pretty white flowers closing in on themselves, asymmetrically, allowing their matter to be reformed into roots, stems, and leaves. Banks could have been one of these flowers, the way he slumped up against the wall, soft as putty, the straight lines of his face sagging, curving in strange places. Idly, Clay wondered what Banks would be turning into if he were a synthetic organism. An old man? "He probably won't be alive for long. He has a specific assignment, and when it's complete, if Claire hasn't changed her mind, he will be destroyed."

"What's going on?" said Clay's father. "I thought I was being reassigned to the case."

"You were the backup plan, in case the copy refused to participate."

"What happens to me now?"

"With Claire's permission, you will be quarantined to your home in France, as will you, Clay."

"I'm here to turn myself in," said Clay.

"Your case will be considered alongside your father's, at a later date."

"I'm with my son. I'd like to know where we stand."

"I haven't heard much—just the formal charges; they finally wrote them up. You still face fifteen for aiding and abetting and for treason. Clay faces a year for shibboleth possession and five years for aiding and abetting. They've postponed the trials indefinitely, probably because Beijing has plans for you, but also because they want to pick when the story breaks."

"They have nothing to worry about," said the original. "I committed some crimes, and I turned myself in. No one has to take the rap but me."

"They don't see it that way." Banks made a lazy semicircle with one hand, by which Clay assumed the whole office complex was being included. "Your name's practically synonymous with the World Police. Beijing's holding out for some miraculous turn of events that would let them pass off your crimes as part of some clever plan."

"I'm working on it," said the original.

"Take as much time as they give you—that's my advice," said Banks.

"I just want to get it over with," said Clay.

"Yes, David, the sooner we clear up this mess, the sooner I can get on with my life. But I can't very well do that from France."

"We have to wait on Beijing. Everything's been way out of my hands since I gave Batacharia the idea to bring you back. Right now, they're betting on the copy. He's a little low on morale and a pain to work with, but they're giving him a chance. The fate of the investigation is in his hands."

"Are you going to tell us what his mission is?" asked Clay.

"I would be shot on the spot."

"What happens when the assignment is over?" said the original. "You said Claire has to approve his death. Does that mean he gets to make another appeal?"

Banks shrugged. "Well, like I said, Beijing's betting on the copy. If he succeeds—who knows? I have to be honest. They might want him to stick around."

Clay's father shook his head. "No appeal. David, I understand how little say you might have, and I don't blame you for what's already happened. You had good intentions in bringing me back, a good idea which backfired. However, I don't want my copy anywhere near Claire. You have the authority to make sure dataseals are placed around Claire and the house. If you care about me and my family, you'll do this much, and you'll double-check that the software has been installed properly."

Being given a task seemed to brighten Banks' spirits. "Sure, no problem. Something like that is in the works already, I think. I could push it through today."

"Wonderful. I want his movements contained. The state created him, and now it has to watch over him. He's no longer a part of my family."

Chapter 17

Anchorwoman: Our top story tonight: the Network security leak has been verified. Curiously, the police have yet to provide an official verification, but since the posting of the noon news, seventy-six subscribers have called to corroborate sightings of a tall, red-haired female believed to be copying herself on a global scale. [*hologram of Stella appears beside anchorwoman*]. Though she is unarmed, there is widespread fear of another Jerome Walls disaster, in which 1.2 million people died from laser wounds. . . .

— *Kay-Tell Evening News*, Feb. 1, 2997.

The copy entered the conference room fearing the worst, noting that the meeting was beginning at the precise moment he had been scheduled to die. He suspected they were going to put him back on the case, but it made no sense, considering that the original was upstairs right now, in the old office, finalizing the transition. Clay was even there, talking to him, getting to know his new father. Why didn't they use the original?

"Great. We can begin." It was Agent Batacharia, of Beijing, nodding briefly to Paul as he sat down. "Most of you know why we're here, but let me review for the others. We've been investigating a list of suspects, compiled against a profile developed by Spalding Morris. So far, leads have been minimal, but there is one suspect, ranked very high on the list, whom we have yet to question."

Paul glanced around the room, looking for others who shared his surprise, but he found only calm attention. To his knowledge, each of the top 150 suspects had been interviewed either by himself, Banks, or an official from Beijing.

"This individual was prudently removed from the list by the computer, so as not to alert him."

Paul watched Banks for a sign, but his friend merely nodded to Batacharia approvingly.

"I'm talking of course about Mr. Morris, the person who until now has been directing the investigation. We're here to decide how to proceed."

"Spalding?" Aware that this was old news to everyone around the table, Paul nonetheless had to continue. "Do you actually think—how could he have anything to do with it?"

"The computer ranks him number one," said Batacharia. "He has the technical training, from his university work in Paris and his years in Beijing. He has the computing power, at his estate. And he has a long-running interest in porn simulations and morphing technologies. We're required, by operating procedure, to investigate."

"Spalding wrote the suspect's profile," said Paul. "Why would he lead us right to himself?"

"That's the mystery," said Batacharia. "He didn't have to volunteer to head the case, nor did he have to pursue it the way he has. If he's guilty, he must want to get caught."

"It doesn't make sense," said Paul.

"We're open to second opinions, but you won't have any, when you see what we've discovered. The man is definitely hiding something." Batacharia brought up a holographic map of what looked like an apartment building but which gradually showed itself to be the estate. There were three underground levels Paul had not known existed. "The place is a fortress. He has an unknown—and very effective—dataseal on all of the Network connections, making most forms of espionage impossible." The conference room computer, eavesdropping on what Batacharia was saying, highlighted several antenna-like structures in red, all in the basement. "The outer wall conceals an array of autonomous weapons—Yeltsin guns, pulse lasers, goo guns—and a complete umbrella of surveillance scanners." All these devices appeared in red. "He also has a radiation screen"—a translucent blue sheet appeared—"which has made scanning difficult. The lower three levels are a solid block of metal, like a steel submarine. The only entrance is a hatchway at the far end of the south wing. You pass through two security doors before you reach the main hallway." The doors and hallway glowed red. "We don't know what's going on down there, but it would seem to be illegal."

Paul gaped at the holodisplay. He had been sitting right in the lap of the crime of the century, oblivious as a housecat.

"We've also detected the heat of several human beings on those levels, but the molecular structures are unreadable, because of the radiation shield. We can't identify them, their equipment, what they say, or even very many of their movements. We can tell when one beams online, however, which is quite often. Unfortunately, they keep their actions hidden by staying on the lab's local network. Spalding pays a visit to the area once or twice a day."

The room was silent. The estate hovered before them like a castle awaiting a siege. "What do we do now?" asked Banks.

"We have nothing to gain by confronting Spalding directly," said a Beijing man Paul had not met. "My group created a temporary copy from Life Insurance data—the Spalding who beamed back from London. We're sure he was aware of the laboratory in the basement, but like Stella he beat Exegesis. His mind—barring illegal forms of interrogation—is closed to us. The only accessible information is in the computer system."

Banks pursued the point. "Those defenses wouldn't hold up against a full-scale raid."

Batacharia said, "A raid would trip the alarm. We need a peek at those systems before they can be wiped."

"We have to try from the inside," replied the Beijing man. "The press are asking questions, and two months into this thing we still don't know what we're up against. We must find a way to use Mr. Cramer. He's the closest to the facility and would arouse the least suspicion."

"Tell us what you know about the inhabitants of the estate," said Batacharia. "We've noticed a third occupant."

Paul tried to read Banks' expression, but his partner was staring at his hands. They know, thought Paul; they know everything. "Well, that would be Spalding's great-great-grandmother. She's visiting for a week or so."

A parlando of glances traveled around the table. "We've noticed that you've spent some time with her," said Batacharia.

"You know, it would be really great if we could work out a signal for when I'm on camera. Seriously."

Batacharia blinked her eyes but kept looking right at Paul. "Then you have a relationship that could prove useful to the investigation."

"I can help you," said Paul, recognizing his new value to the police and wondering what it might buy him, "on one condition."

The six officials listened.

"I want to see my wife again, in person." Batacharia drew her arms together and straightened in her seat, but Paul did not let her speak. "Without at least a chance to talk to her, I will be erased. And if I'm going to be erased, I would rather get it over with now. You can't devise another way to pay me, because I can't spend credits if I'm dead."

Batacharia considered, frowning, while the others waited. "We will talk to your wife," she said.

*

During the next few days, Spalding seemed to go out of his way to help Paul spy for the police. Over dinner the first night, he stretched out his arms and said, "My house, your house. Pick a room—it's your own private office. I understand about the wife. I know how it is to get the boot, though I did finally litigate myself back into this place. Just relax and don't fall in love with Granny—she's a real heartbreaker."

Spalding had learned about the affair—from Jenny, he claimed—and he encouraged them to spend time together, even to go off on private walks in the garden. Paul could not have asked for a better opportunity for interrogation.

The garden was hideous, all lichen- and algae-stained trees, a mustiness of figs, ginger, and loam, creepy tangles of lianas, brown and hairy as tarantula legs, and bugs. Bugs in the air. Bugs on the ground. Bugs that looked like stems or leaves until he just about touched them and caused them to move. But the trees gave an illusion of privacy, which allowed him to have very open conversations with Jenny. Spalding might have had sensors monitoring their speech, but Jenny seemed to suspect nothing.

She was an excellent information source. Walks in the garden were a common pastime of hers, so she knew everything about every plant and tree, when each had been planted, illumination needs, even the respective phylogenies. "Botany is one of my hobbies," she had told him. "I've had a lot of time for hobbies." She also knew a bit about what Spalding was doing in the basement, since a number of his experiments had ended up in the garden, though she never mentioned the estate's secret levels.

She would point them out during the strolls. Even during their first night together, lying in the hammock, she had told him about one, though he had been too preoccupied to care. Even in the dim light from the loggia, he could tell that the palm trees holding the hammock had bright red heads of silk, not leaves. "The Lorax—I love this place," she had said, watching the trees' silken hair list in the breeze. "It's my favorite part of the garden."

He asked what was so special about stunted palm trees, and she gave a response that hadn't made sense at the time.

"They aren't real," she said.

"Yeah?" He gave the trees a glance but was still mostly interested in the brass rings holding her outfit together. "They look real."

"They're from a simulation of an old industrial fairy tale, my favorite story as a child. That's why I love them so much. Spalding brought them to life for me."

He murmured something inarticulate into her ear, assuming that they were inanimate models, and said that Spalding had been nice to create them. Then he had looked again at the creature in his arms, the bare feet, long legs, arms holding him, her lovely hair falling onto his shoulder, and tried to decide if they should meet again—or many times—and how long he should let it continue, less concerned right then with botany than with anatomy.

The full story had to wait until after the meeting in Phoenix, when he took her back to the hammock for a rendezvous, late at night, and lay there holding her again, less susceptible to memories of his wife. He asked her to repeat what she had said about the trees. This time he listened and realized that the tree was not a model, as he had assumed, but a true species, the morphed genome of a palm tree. Apparently Spalding had been building a set of tools for mapping an online organism to a zygote. He had made fictional insects, fictional flowers, even a Cerberus, which had been chained to the garden's stone wall until some jungle fungus had claimed it. Jenny pointed out the rusting iron ring where the Cerberus had been chained. These genetic experiments, illegal outside an accredited laboratory, resembled those of primitive man, except that their only aim was to map arbitrarily whimsical fictions into organisms that could live in the material world.

He sneaked this information to Beijing in a single encrypted syllable of a routine vidmail message to Banks. The reply came coded in the shifting scintillations of light in Banks' blue eyes: "THE COMPUTER HAS

HEIGHTENED ITS SUSPICION OF SPALDING. WE NEED ACCESS TO THE LAB. JENNY IS NOT SPALDING'S GRANDMOTHER. THE REAL JENNIFER BAINES DIED IN 2607. A JENNIFER BAINES IS ON FILE AT THE BUREAU OF LIFE INSURANCE, BUT THE RECORDS ARE FORGED. WE CAN'T READ THE MOLECULAR STRUCTURE, BUT THE WOMAN YOU HAVE BEEN INVES-TIGATING IS PROBABLY A MORPHOLOGY OF STELLA."

When the shock of the news subsided, he smiled. How fitting it would be for Jenny to be a copy of Stella; that would mean he was concluding his life with the same act that had triggered his whole mistaken existence. His life-line now appeared more predetermined than he ever would have imagined, drawn in broad strokes by hands he could not see, whether by the hand of fate or the hand of his original, he did not know. All he could say for certain was that he seemed destined, like his original, to forsake Claire for another woman. And then, only later, to seek forgiveness.

So while he sat on the pink balustrade that evening, swatting mos-quitoes and looking for monkeys, he waited for remorse, the final upswing of the pattern he expected to live. He searched for it in the knowledge of Jenny's duplicity, recalling the simple lust of their first night together, the trap—it seemed—Spalding had laid—but no sadness came, only bewil-derment. Why, he kept asking, why was she—or Spalding, for that matter—playing with his life? Who were they and what were they doing?

He wanted to pull some answers out of Spalding. But when the scholar came to the loggia for his evening meal, prudence forced Paul to pursue polite conversation, since later that night he would be risking his life to remove one of the dataseals. Any clues he could gather would have to be oblique and accidental.

"Jenny is looking for you," said Spalding, taking his usual seat in a lawn chair.

"Where is she?"

"Downstairs. She wants to give you a present."

Spalding's matter-of-factness was admirable, but Paul thought he could detect a nervous hesitation in the way Spalding spread the cloth napkin in his lap. He decided to see how well the scholar could lie. "What kind of present?"

"I don't know. Something outlandish, I think. She sure has taken a liking to you."

Paul came down off the balustrade. "Sure this doesn't bother you—me and your grandmother?"

"Great-great-grandmother. Relax. Our professional relationship is a temporary accident. I'm just glad you and Jenny are having some fun."

"She must come here a lot. She knows everything about the garden."

"She loves nature. Every chance she gets, she comes down for a walk in the garden or a look at the countryside. Nothing like this forest existed when she was young."

"You're lucky. I barely speak to my great-great-grandparents."

"The garden would completely fall to pieces if she didn't take care of it. It's Toril's baby, which she left behind after the divorce."

"I was under the impression that you were the one who selected most of the plants."

"No, Toril did that. She did it all." The scholar paused in the middle of cutting his meat and stared into the lush garden. A moment passed.

"This big estate must get awful lonely when Jenny isn't here." When Grandma isn't here, thought Paul, to water the plants and get you off.

"I get by," said the scholar, going back to cutting.

Paul's best instinct as a detective told him to berate Spalding about Jenny. It was like he had her—and all the Stellas—dancing on the ends of strings. Did he *own* her? Why did she cooperate? It made no sense. Paul kept thinking about what his son had said about Stella being programmed. That was what it seemed like; she played whatever part Spalding gave her, including, for whatever reason, the part of his guest's lover.

Too much, he decided. No reason to push his luck. Beijing would unravel the mystery when he removed the dataseal. He excused himself and went to find Jenny.

She was in her chamber, watching an old holomovie.

"Spalding said you have a present for me," he said in greeting. He was still wondering how to separate himself from her this evening, so he could sneak downstairs.

"He told you? It was supposed to be a surprise." She looked away from the movie and it paused automatically.

"He didn't tell me what it was."

"Well, he has *some* manners, then. I want to take you to the *Pleasuredome*."

"Where?"

"I have a room reserved. It's online, so we can stay a couple of days and you can still go to work tomorrow."

"That would be great." He was caught off-guard by the proposal. "But I can't."

"Why not?"

Because tonight I have to break into the basement, he thought. "Because—" The *Pleasuredome* could be a trap, like Stella's death simulations. "Because I have too much to do. I want to go over some files before tomorrow's interviews. I'm sorry. Maybe we can go later in the week. Do we need a reservation?"

As much as Paul distrusted Jenny, he remained somewhat sensitive to her feelings. She had suddenly slumped over the edge of the bed, inexplicably crestfallen. She said, "I thought you would be happy. It's the best simulation on the Net."

"I've never heard of it."

"It's on the A&M network."

Paul shrugged.

"You would love it. It's got little two-hour mysteries starting every hour."

"I'm not in the mood to play detective." He sat down on the bed. "Look, Jenny, I would love to go online with you sometime, but it will have to be a vacation, a trip far away from the World Police, and it will have to wait until this case is solved. The world is in great peril." He watched her eyes for involuntary dilation. He saw none.

"Just one night. Can't you forget that impossible investigation for a few hours?"

"The investigation is picking up. I think we're getting close to our criminal." Again, no reaction.

He put his arm around her and she followed his lead, laying her head on his shoulder. She was always quick to accommodate herself to whatever mood he was in. "There's something else," she said. "I have another surprise."

"Two surprises in one day. I'm a lucky man."

Jenny lowered her voice to a whisper. "I didn't want to tell you here."

"Why not?"

"Spalding. He would be upset."

"About what?"

She lifted her head off his shoulder. "Hey, I have an idea." Her face had brightened. "Why don't we go online for just a few hours. You can spare forty-five minutes. We need to talk about something."

She was not going to give up. Spalding must have changed her orders that afternoon. "Not today. Tomorrow."

"I have to talk to you today."

"Maybe I'll come down later. I have to get to work."

"We have to talk online."

He bent close so she could speak into his ear. "Can you whisper?"

There was a long pause, then she whispered, "If you stay offline, your ex-wife will have you erased. I don't want you to die."

Jenny was beginning to show her true colors. She was beginning to poke and prod like Stella. "What does that have to do with the *Pleasure-dome*?"

"I have a friend there. She can help you cross over."

"Over? Where?"

"To where you can't be traced, where you can live on stolen time. A lot of people do it. I know you're a policeman and would probably think it's wrong, but you can't just let yourself be killed."

"That's right: I'm a cop. You shouldn't be telling me this."

"I wake up every morning thinking, 'Today's the day: they're going to call him back to Phoenix and—poof!—you'll be gone.'" As he looked into her expressive brown eyes it was strange but he believed in the emotion behind what she was saying; a visceral fear seemed to grip every muscle in her body and to show itself through the skin of her face and arms. "We can't go on like this, Paul, living one ecstatic, final night together, night after night. I don't want to be your last fling. I want to be with you, for as long as we're happy together."

"Me too. But—steal computer time? I could never do that. Please don't mention it again. Yes, I'm a cop. I would have to turn you over to the police."

"Oh, wake up, Paul. What good's the law if it says you've got to die? You've let them make you into a datafile, something to be instantiated or deleted at their command. Stand up for your *life*, Paul."

"I have no life. My data should never have been copied." He believed what he said, but of course he wanted to live—and she could get him online. He had nothing to lose, actually, and for a moment he was tempted—a disposition Spalding, not knowing what Paul had seen from the garden a few nights before or even what exactly Beijing suspected, was probably counting on. But he could not go through with it. The investigation had reached a potentially terminal stage, and he was the crucial link.

Jenny put a hand on his knee. "Of course you have a life. Even a simulated moth has a life, a life worth keeping."

"I want to keep my life the way it is. We can go tomorrow."

Jenny was not going to take no for an answer. Falling back on her last means of persuasion, she began caressing his thigh, very expertly. He felt like he was being examined by the feelers of an insect. There was something disturbingly precise about her movements, as though Spalding had trained her to be like the women in porn simulations, constantly aware of posture, of vocalizations of pleasure, of whether her hair was obscuring her face. He was sure training like that had taken place, but there must have been more to it. He paid careful attention to what she was doing this time, letting her take off his shirt and kiss him a little. When he examined her eyes, trying to guess what was behind them, he thought he saw something sad, a muted pain trying to express itself, something hard to discern behind the strange light coming from the frozen holomovie. Spalding and Stella both had said something about the ideoplasm someday extending into the human brain. He wanted to ask Jenny if Spalding had done something to her, but he had to keep his cover.

When she reached under her short black dress and pulled down her panties, however, he could not fight back the revulsion. He was sure Spalding had done something to her, something to make her less than human. "I—I can't," he said abruptly, standing. "Not right now."

"What's wrong?"

He grabbed his shirt and pushed one arm into it. "I just remembered something. Banks needs a report I was working on."

"Can't it wait a few minutes?"

"I wish it could." He shoved his other arm into the shirt and pulled it over his shoulders. "I'll make it up to you tomorrow."

"I don't get it. Did I do something wrong?"

"No, no. Just relax. It's this damn investigation. I can't think about anything else."

She stood up. "I'm not going to let you go." She hooked an arm around his neck, locked it into a vice grip, and yanked him off his feet and onto the bed.

"Whoa! Hey!"

She clamped him to her body with her arms and legs, giggling loudly and—he thought—a touch frenetically. As he tried to pull away, she tightened the vice-like grip of her legs. Since she had left her underwear on the floor, he could feel her pubic hair against his hip, through his slacks. "Kiss me. C'mon, Paul. Don't you want to?"

"No!" he cried. "Let me go!"

Somehow the top of her dress had come unbuttoned. She was trying to wriggle free of the loose material. "Oh, Paul . . ."

He pinned her arms to her sides with his forearms and crawled his way into a sitting position. When he looked up a man had appeared in the dark doorway. He was holding what looked like a gun. "Spalding?" said Jenny. Out of breath, she rolled her fingertips back and forth over her exposed nipples, a sad look in her eyes.

"I've come for Paul," said the scholar, moving into the light where Paul could see him. "We've been watching from downstairs. His behavior is very odd, not at all what we were expecting."

Chapter 18

reporter: At the risk of undermining the scholarly intent of this press conference, I was wondering, Miss Mold, if you had any words to say to your public regarding you and your eminent ex-husband's separation and what effect it might have had on your—or his—recent work. I would not ask, except for the obvious curiosity regarding Dr. Morris's recent and controversial excoriation of the modern family.

Toril Mold: You have taken more than a risk, Mr. Jones. You have fairly successfully plunged this conference into the muck of tabloid news. But you are justified, and in fact I have a word or two to say. Frankly, Spalding Morris fashioning himself—all of a sudden—as a critic of domesticity strikes me as a gross perversion of nature. As I recall, the older our daughter became, the further he withdrew, gradually, into his study, cooking up his little academic notions of apocalypse. If he knows anything about families, it comes from books, not from his life. One does not have to look too deeply into his diatribe to see excuses— excuses for everything he did wrong while we were married. He's sore. Like a child, he's gone pouting to his room, where he's been dreaming up little fantasy stories—in his case, stillborn monsters of philosophy and cultural theory—and he really believes these little abominations are going to open their eyes, stretch their limbs, and populate our minds. He thinks they're going to remake our world in his image. He's somewhat of a megalomaniac, actually, who has lost the faculty of critical thought, who believes he can steer history with the power of his keen mind, who—I'm very sure of this conclusion—has long passed his prime as a philosopher of culture. You would do well to ignore his current efforts. Pardon me. I've said too much. My feelings for Dr. Morris, it seems, remain somewhat charged.

— press conference, March, 2908.

"You can't get away with this."

"Detective, you're amusing, always delivering the expected line at the expected time. You don't even know what it is I'm trying to get away with."

Paul was climbing down the ladder into the basement, unsure what was going to happen next. Spalding, above, had a dart gun directed at the top of his head. Paul said, "It doesn't matter what you do with me. Beijing will still arrest you. You can't win."

He reached the bottom of the ladder and immediately felt the cold muzzle of a gun press into the center of his back. "I always win." The voice sounded exactly like Spalding's. Paul did not have to turn around to know that this second man was an illegal copy.

The two copies of Spalding led him to a large chamber that looked like the control room of a spaceship. The walls were metal and fluted, the doors were automatic sliding panels, and around the chamber's perimeter technician's keyboards littered an array of bubble-shaped work modules. A giant panel filling most of the far wall looked like the front of an industrial-sized demiurge. Here and there other copies of Spalding sat on rolling chairs in the modules, half-concealed by holographic clouds of charts, tables, graphs, and—primarily—networks of what looked like neurons.

"Welcome to the intellectual center of Earth," said the first Spalding, the one who had taken Paul from Jenny's room.

"Welcome to the future," said the second Spalding.

The two Spaldings marched him to the industrial-sized demiurge, where they asked him to turn around and keep his back to the wall. "This won't take long," said the first Spalding.

"It's already too late," said Paul. "We know about your lab. You led us right to it."

"We know," said the first Spalding. "The computer would have selected us as a suspect eventually, so we decided to have our first brush with the authorities on our own terms. It's been a big advantage having an agent in Beijing."

"Getting rid of me will only delay the inevitable. You're already the prime suspect."

The second Spalding grinned smugly. "Inevitable. . . . We're the world's experts on inevitability."

"And we aren't getting rid of you." The first Spalding turned to a third Spalding, who was working at a nearby module. "Ready yet?"

"I'll let you know."

Paul was certain now that it was patterns of neurons flashing around the third Spalding. "What are you doing?"

"Reprogramming your mind," said the second Spalding.

The first Spalding gave the second a sharp look. "We're *overlaying* his mind," he corrected.

"We *program* the ultracortex. That's what I meant."

"The ultracortex is an interface."

"It becomes part of the mind. By programming the ultracortex we program the mind."

The first Spalding asked Paul to please excuse his colleague. "He's been heading the Ultracortex Group for fifty years. He's sort of lost track of the big picture."

"You can make me forget everything I know, and they will still come after you." Paul looked around the room, trying to imagine how this whole experience could be deleted, as if it were a scene in a holomovie.

The first Spalding spoke to the second. "See, you've already confused him." He said to Paul, "You won't forget anything, nor will you remember anything that didn't happen. Memories are almost impossible to add or delete. To be part of your brain they have to be meditated upon, compared, related—and that requires changes all across the mind, connections, impressions, changes that continue to occur for the lifetime of a memory. That's why we decided a hundred years ago to build a control system in cortex neurons, which interfaces with an already living mind."

"It's a pity," said the other Spalding, "because what we're really after is consciousness, which lies below the ultracortex."

The Spaldings seemed more interested in talking to each other than in guarding their prisoner. Paul, watching their dart guns waver, began to wonder if he could grab one without getting himself shot.

"This ultracortex is just a hack, really," said the first Spalding, "a cheap vessel for a personality construct."

"A necessary advance, though."

"True," said the first Spalding, expansively. "An important first step."

"You have to walk before you can run."

Paul was just about to leap when the second Spalding redirected his attention—and the gun. "So you'll still be conscious, sort of. Only you won't have any volition. They say it's like a meld-movie."

"It's quite maddening. If we could squelch your thoughts, we would, or if we could leave them intact, we would, but we have to settle for the middle ground. Fragments of awareness constantly being blasted away."

"Show him," said the second Spalding.

"He'll see in just a minute."

"Make Toril do her act. Toril?" The second Spalding scanned the room. He spotted Jenny, who was standing against the far wall, having followed them, passively, like a servant waiting to be given something to do. "Oh, there you are. Do your puppy act."

Paul felt no surprise when she obeyed, dropping down on all fours. He saw her clearly now, watching her caper around and make small barks. She was a computer program.

The Spaldings thoroughly enjoyed the performance. Several of them left their workstations to catch a glimpse of this poor morphed copy of their ex-wife. "It's time to go pee-pee," said one Spalding with a nasty grin. "Go pee-pee, Toril."

Jenny lifted up her leg, without regard for the minidress or her panties, and began urinating. Soon Paul could see urine running down the side of her leg, onto the floor. The Spaldings were smiling to themselves; one whistled at Jenny, and all of them eyed Paul expectantly, as though waiting for him to get the joke.

Meanwhile, a very human sadness came into Jenny's eyes, as though the ultracortex had for an instant relinquished control of her expression. She let the urine run down her leg, like an obscene ornamental fountain, the remains of whomever she might once have been pooling in her eyes, finding refuge there, mute, hurting, looking to Paul for mercy, or perhaps wishing mercy for him, knowing what he was about to become.

The second Spalding turned to the first. "We're frightening him. *You* get by, don't you?"

"Me? Well, yes, but all I have is a security cap. I don't have some foreign agent controlling my actions."

"A security cap?" Paul thought he had missed something.

"I'm the real Spalding," said the first Spalding. "The one with an official existence. Which means, ironically—" He gave his copy a wry smile—"that I'm the one who needs an overlain mind, in case I'm questioned."

"The overlay protects against lie detection," said the second Spalding.

"It will probably drive you crazy," said the other. "Every copy of Toril we uncap comes out a screaming banshee."

"We make her do things she doesn't like, however."

"Nothing terrible. Nothing she didn't ask for."

"It's not surprising she loses her mind."

In an incredulous tone, the real Spalding replied, "There's nothing wrong with the lives we give her. She gets to be romanced by fine gentlemen like our detective here." He gave Paul a sly glance. "That's not so bad, certainly not bad enough to turn her into that rabid monkey we've got downstairs."

"The interface still has a few bugs," said the second Spalding, shrugging his shoulders apologetically. "We think it damages certain brain centers."

"Changes them, to be sure." The real Spalding addressed Paul. "But you'll be fine—or act fine, at least—as long as no one removes the ultra-cortex."

Paul was trying to make a guess about their operation. There were probably hundreds or thousands of Spaldings, online and working in scan-time, doing research, working toward some psychotic vision—but was it the vision of social collapse Spalding had described on *Forgotten Planet: Spring*, or was it something more mundane, a vendetta against Toril? "Why are you telling me this?"

"Just making conversation," said the first Spalding. "It won't make a difference. You can't reveal anything once we implant the overlay."

"And in a day or two you'll be dead, anyway."

Schematics flashed off the Spaldings' round glasses as they looked at each other, at Paul, back at each other. They were completely deranged. "You know that Beijing is going to erase me. Why not just kill me now?"

"Not *you*," said the first Spalding, "all Paul Cramers. You're going to murder your original."

"And then you're going to kill yourself. It's a beautiful way to go, don't you think? You probably would have come up with it yourself, if you had our connections at the Bureau of Life Insurance."

"You see," said the real Spalding, anticipating Paul's question, "we're having all of your backup copies deleted. When you kill your original, he's gone, and the same will go for you."

"Isn't it just like a fable? The divided man, his inner emotional split dramatized with his own body, the pieces of his psyche fighting each other as beings, ending in self-destruction. You'll make headlines. You'll go down in history. Time will strip away everything about you except the final moment; you'll be like a god, a dim, collective memory of this century's bewilderment and desperation."

Paul was too stunned to speak. Death had been a reality for days, but what Spalding was describing was different; he meant the *end* of Paul Cramer, the termination of the timeline. What would happen to his family? Again, Paul eyed the scholars' weapons, waiting for a chance to escape. Toril still crouched on all fours in her urine, motionless as a stone.

"We aren't afraid of anything—least of all you or your ability as a detective. We could care less how many Paul Cramers are on our trail. We just think your death could be an interesting communication event. It would affect billions. We can't bring *everyone* online, not yet, but we can flash them a message. You can show them what they most need to know: death exists."

"And, more importantly, you'll be a dead hero, even more compelling in death than in life. Children will be watching holovision, holding their Paul Cramer action figures, seeing the two dead Paul Cramer bodies, and they will remember that moment for the rest of their lives."

Paul could not believe his ears. "You think you can pick heroes and gods for everybody else? That's a pretty classic symptom—isn't it? You sound like a psychotic demiurge personality that's totally off the scale."

"Your son, too," said the first Spalding dryly. "No one will care that he dies, but he suspects something. He's actually a greater threat to us than you are."

"Clay? You can't make me—"

"We're ready."

The neurons had disappeared from the third Spalding's workstation. "Any time," added the third Spalding.

"Beijing knows I'm down here. They're scanning us right now."

"Of course," said the second Spalding. "They'll be mounting a rescue mission this very moment, afraid I'm destroying evidence. When they question you, you'll tell them you saw multiple copies of myself, but the only one they will recover will be Number One." He gestured to the real Spalding with the muzzle of the dart gun.

"They'll find copy-making software, some genetic experiments, and evidence that I was using online copies of myself to accelerate research on my latest book, *Vortices in the Noösphere*, but nothing else."

"You won't reveal any other information."

Paul said, "The computer won't believe you bought all this equipment to research a book."

"It'll never suspect that we've developed neural engineering, which is the only secret we have."

"We don't care what they do to Number One," said the second Spalding. "Or even what they do to other copies they may find here and there. We're no longer an individual. We don't think as an individual, we don't act as an individual, and we can't be stopped the way you would stop an individual. We're a civilization, and even if you uncover a piece of our operation there will always—*always*—be some spore you've overlooked, and all it takes is one spore, one Spalding Morris, and the whole civilization can be rebuilt. We've used dozens of methods to hide our data, many of which exist only in our heads." He tapped his temple. "As long as our brains remain beyond your reach, so will we."

"You're just another scan-criminal," said Paul. "A little better prepared than most but no harder to delete."

"We're no kind of criminal you've ever encountered," said the second Spalding. "We've been online for a century, thousands of earth's most talented minds, all on scan-time, all thinking many times faster than offline researchers, pushing centuries ahead. We're from the next age."

"The Information Age," said Number One.

"You're still criminals."

"We only appear to be criminals," said Number One, "because we're from the future."

"We're freed slaves."

"We're a kind of person—or system of persons—the present age could never understand."

Epileptic smiles had crept onto the scholars' faces and died there; Paul wondered if the smiles were shaped by ultracortex software, or whether there was something imperfect or distasteful about the pleasure the Spaldings took from the thought of the Spalding Morris Society. "You aren't gods," said Paul. "And you aren't making a new age. All you're making is illegal copies, illegal science, and illegal simulations."

"We're changing more than you can imagine."

"Your son, for instance." Number One aimed his chin at Paul's forehead, looking down his nose—a scholar's habit of using his jaw to break the ice of his listeners' minds. "If you weren't about to kill him, he would never be the same person he otherwise was conditioned to become. He'd believe different things, he'd do different things. His field of possibilities would have been irreversibly widened."

"We would have changed his life. And his life would have affected others," said the second Spalding. "His online experiences would have rippled out, like shockwaves."

"We just need a few million like him, energetic and intelligent, to deliver the first blow of the chisel. Then cracks will form."

"You can't brainwash people into bringing about a future they don't want," said Paul. "That's what separates human beings from personality constructs: people have a sense of identity, and a willpower. Even Clay, as young as he is, has enough strength to resist whatever changes you think you can wreak upon him."

Chin now stowed away, Number One leaned in, his gaze the new source of malice. "Your son has about as much willpower as a wind-up toy. A week ago he was wound up on cheap violence, cheap sex, and pitiful little crumbs of pop culture. Now he's been wound by a different hand, the hand of history and self-knowledge. He's strong, and he's growing stronger, but not because of any special *self* inside of him; he's strong only because of the inputs he's received. His mind was a murky stew of unstructured flavors until we got it. We're providing a recipe. The same goes for the original copy of yourself."

Paul said, "Clay got sick of Stella and her simulations; don't be surprised if he breaks off in a completely different direction. He might even become your worst enemy."

"That's what I love about the human mind," said the second Spalding. "It has a boundless imagination."

"You're right in a sense, Paul. We can't predict the future, in any truly deterministic sense, but that's what makes everything so exciting. The historical rupture is going to be larger and more finely structured than anything we could engineer. It's like we're planting seeds of entirely new organisms."

"The last thing we want is to program the revolution," agreed the second copy. "It would be easy enough to install an ultracortex in everyone, but who wants to live in a world of personality constructs? It would be a fake future. We want people to embrace the future, because it's what they've been groping toward—life beyond immortality—and we want them to live in it, as real human beings."

"As impossible as it is for you to conceive, we're committing all these crimes for people like you, who can't understand the underlying cause of their discontent."

"What about writing self-help software?" said Paul. "Pretty good money, if you've got something to say."

"We want the world itself to be self-help software, so attuned and responsive to human needs that even simple-minded people like you and Claire will stumble their way to happiness. We want everyone to live online, where they can have all the children they want, where they can live in different periods of history, where they can endure hardships, struggle together—live dramatically, the way human beings used to live."

"What about love? People like Claire and me—we've done all right. We've stuck with each other—one way or another—and we haven't needed anything external, certainly not computer entertainment. We fell in love. We're still in love."

"Modern contracts and affection aren't love. The possibility of love won't even exist until we—"

"Remake the age."

"Change life. By altering just a few parameters."

Both Spaldings were so carried away with explaining their evil plans that the guns were now either pointing at the floor or, while the gun's owner was talking, lazily bobbing to the beat of a sentence. "The best we can do is put a hint of love in those like your original. We didn't need specific knowledge of Paul Cramer to help him. We put him in a world with adjusted parameters, and he responded. That's why he's the one restoring order, while you shear away out of the family structure with no inkling why."

"It's because I hate feeling trapped." Paul made a wild leap at the two Spaldings, snatching and lifting both weapons as he ran past. One gun came free, but somehow the other slipped away, and before he knew it he had been shot in the leg. A numbness in his knee caused him to stumble, and within seconds he was all rubber and being dragged by the feet back toward the huge demiurge.

He had to gasp out his words through rawhide lips. "It won't . . . work. They'll know . . . that it's not me. Someone . . . someone will know . . ."

"This isn't going to mess up the procedure, is it?" asked Number One.

The Spalding in the work module responded. "No, the machine's all ready. Throw him in."

Paul could hear the huge panel rolling open.

"We've learned a lot from our mistakes. You'll find that our software will give you an analytical awareness of your emotions. Your thoughts will have more structure, and you'll comprehend your family in the correct terms."

"If we didn't have to put in the suicide script, you'd be a much improved version of yourself. You'll see. You'll be conscious the whole time."

Chapter 19

Here ["in the deep course of the wisdom which has gone beyond"], O Sariputra, form is emptiness, and the very emptiness is form; emptiness does not differ from form, form does not differ from emptiness; whatever is form, that is emptiness, whatever is emptiness, that is form. The same is true of feelings, perceptions, impulses, and consciousness.

— "The Heart Sutra," 350 A.D.

And when oneness is not thoroughly understood,
In two ways is loss sustained:
The denying of reality is the asserting of it,
And the asserting of emptiness is the denying of it.

— Seng-ts'an, "On Believing in Mind," A.D. 600.

Paul felt his body step into the living room. He was home. Somehow Spalding had slipped his data to the telepod in France, and—he could think. His body moved by remote control, but his mind—

Where is everyone?

The voice came from far outside his mind, loud as a god's, turning his limbs to steel. His body made a swift circle around the perimeter of the room, liquid smooth and so automatic that he felt as though he was not moving at all, that everything around him was being tilted and turned, rendered by a machine. Spalding was right, he thought. This is like a meld-movie. A hyperreal meld-movie, only this is my house, my real life, and there's Claire in the bedroom, talking on a comlink. It's all coming at me like computer animation. Is this really happening?

Don't kill her yet.

The external presence strengthened, achieving a kind of spatiality, an enclosing quality. It was probing his mind for something.

Claire seemed to sense the danger. She broke off in mid-sentence, eyeing Paul fearfully.

This isn't me, he wanted to say; it's—

A surge of messages from the ultracortex replaced what Paul was thinking with noise, violent and information-rich but meaningless to the conscious part of his brain. Presently, Paul found himself saying, "I'm on my way to Phoenix. Please, I'm not here to beat a dead horse. I just want to see Clay. Is he around?"

Claire dismissed whomever she was talking to, then she rose, free to show her anger. "Get the fuck out of here." She came right up to him, as though she were going to hit him, and pointed to the telepod. "Go."

Her eyes were black and danced like spearheads. Don't hate me, thought his addled, half-functioning brain. I just want—

"Let me see my son one last time," he felt his mouth say. "Don't tell me I'm not his father. Don't tell me I'm not the right copy, or that I should be erased. I'm Paul Cramer, and I want to talk to him."

For a moment Claire hesitated, as startled as he was by this sudden tone of voice, then a set expression came onto her face. She threw her hair behind her shoulders with a deliberate toss of the head. "Get out of here. I told Batacharia 'no.'" She stiff-armed him back into the living room. "Computer, notify the police that the copy is here."

"No. Computer, cancel that command."

The computer said, "The police have been notified."

Apparently the machine had been serviced since his last visit.

He had to think fast. The police would be arriving any second. "Tell me where he is. He must hear what I have to say. It—"

"You can talk to him over a comlink from your cell in Phoenix."

"The original, too. I have to make my peace with both of them."

The telepod began to hum. *The police!*

His body back-pedaled along the outer wall and drew out the goo gun. He crouched behind the couch.

"Paul—Christ, what're you doing?"

The telepod door slid open, and before Claire could even shout a warning, he had sunk a dozen goo pellets into a uniformed policeman, who began to howl and writhe and change into clay. The officer pitched forward onto the floor, breaking into several pieces.

All at once Paul became aware of Claire's hysterical screaming, the vibrations of another police officer being instantiated, and, from the corner

196

of his eye, the original and Clay appearing, outside the window, just emerging from a forest path.

"You're totally mad!" said Claire.

"I don't need you anymore." He squeezed the trigger of the goo gun, filling her gut and chest with pellets. Ash-gray clay replaced the flesh of her neck, swift as spreading dye.

Her screams, horrible and choked into silence by the clay neck, were just loud enough to bring Clay and the original running toward the rear staircase. *Perfect*, he thought. He waited for the telepod to open, gunned down the other police officer, a woman this time, then took up position in the doorway of what once was his bedroom.

Oh, Claire! he managed to think, the lull in the action having released the ultracortex's grip on his mind. It's not me. I didn't do it. I didn't . . .

"Claire! What's wrong?" The voice—that of the original—was coming from outside. The veranda's wooden stairs resounded with footsteps.

Wait until both are inside.

Paul's dutiful body slipped deeper into the bedroom.

"Oh my god. . . ." The original fell silent.

Paul felt the ultracortex probe his mind. *He'll control his grief*, the answer came back. *He's already looking for me.*

Clay could be heard crossing the veranda. "What happened? Mom . . ."

"Get out of the house, Clay."

Go! Now!

Paul tried to catch them both with a swift spiraling motion of his arm, using the bedroom wall as cover, but the original had hidden. All he managed to hit were Clay's ankles.

The boy fell screaming to the floor.

"The telepod!" shouted the original from behind the couch. "Get to the telepod!"

Paul felt a smile form on his face. *He's behind the couch.* Into the living room he charged, wading through the body of his ex-wife. Claire's mud head squashed underfoot.

Claire!

The boy no longer appeared to be a threat. He was dragging his body across the carpet with his arms, a clay foot having broken off next to a leg of the coffee table. Paul went for the original.

This will be easy, he thought.

Before he could fire, a glass lamp, coming out of nowhere, struck the side of his head. He fell to the floor, stunned. When he regained his senses, the goo gun had slipped out of his hand. He got to his knees cautiously, just in time to see the original throw Clay's unconscious torso, which was missing a leg, into the telepod.

Almost in the same motion, the original snatched up a cut-glass vase and hurled it across the room. The vase shattered against the bench of the electric organ, inches from Paul's head. "Computer, instantiate a Mould Gun," said the original.

"No! Computer, stop." *Where's the gun?* He felt about for the gun, found it.

The panel of a demiurge slid open, to the far side of the telepod, while the telepod's panel slid shut. "Mould Gun complete," said the computer. "Storing Clay Cramer. Contacting Bureaus of Health and Life Insurance."

Where's the original?

Abrupt silence filled the house, like darkness. The original could have gone anywhere, the master bedroom, Clay's room, the side hallway to the dining room, even upstairs. One thing was certain: he would make a move for the gun; all Paul had to do was keep the demiurge in sight, wait until . . .

The ultracortex seemed to inhale information, like blood, making his vision dim and his head welter.

Hold on. There's another gun, the original's official firearm, which he keeps in the drawer of the night stand. He might go for that. In fact, he will; the one in the demiurge is a decoy.

The realization came just in time. A stun beam, buzzing the carpet where he had been lying, came close enough to tickle his heels as he slipped into the dining room.

A standoff developed, the original in the bedroom and Paul in the dining room. They had cornered each other. Neither could move without drawing the other's fire.

The original spoke first. "You maniac!" he shouted.

"I hate you! I hate you all!" To Paul's surprise, he had screamed these words, and . . . he had *felt* them; his emotions were being manipulated externally by the ultracortex. This is worse than a meld-movie, he thought. I don't have control. It's making me *live* this. . . .

All the jealousy, all the spite Claire's choosing the original had aroused in him, all the anger came seething together—*real* emotions, emotions he had felt, at different times, only not assembled quite in this way. He began hollering again, hysterically, and he believed every word that came out of his mouth: "You don't deserve her! You didn't come back for Claire; you came back because you were afraid you'd get caught."

"You can't kill me. I'll be reincarnated. All you can do is get yourself killed."

"Oh, you'll die. Your data—all of it, all backup copies—has been deleted."

There was a silence. "That's impossible."

"Believe it, Detective. The Bureau of Life Insurance can't do a thing to help. If I can't have her, neither can you."

The original said nothing.

"Talk to me, Detective," said Paul. "I don't want you slipping out a window." If he could keep the original talking, maybe he could catch him off-guard.

The reply was solemn, spoken softly. "This isn't about Claire. You just shot her, for chrissake. Why are you doing this?"

"I love Claire. It's you—it's you who—"

"Yeah? What do you measure that in? Kills? You don't even know what the word means."

"I love her." Paul said the words, but this time he did not feel the emotion. He was confused. The ultracortex had responded without drawing on his real brain.

There were footsteps outside, unnaturally soft on the wooden deck. Police, probably. Other officers—or perhaps copies of the same ones— would have been routed to the telepod of a neighbor's house. He should have anticipated them.

Only seconds remained before he would be surrounded. He had to act. "I love her!" he screamed, charging into the living room, firing into the bedroom. "I love her! I love her!" He howled the same words again and again, this time feeling emotion, not love, but an overwhelming paranoia, a sense that the entire world wanted, had always wanted, to kill him, and that he had to kill it first. He wanted to tear it all down, the walls, the ceiling, the men pointing guns at him. I want to try again, he thought briefly, before the stun blast, not knowing whether the thought was his own or generated from the outside. I want to start over. . . .

The world faded out, like the end of a game.

Chapter 20

Anchorwoman: Kay-Tell News reporter Rajeev Druma is in Beijing. Rajeev, how does the crisis look from where you're standing? (*Mr. Druma's image is overlain across a live back-drop of the many-domed government building, flags of the world waving.*)

Reporter: Frankly, Lucy, the questions continue to outnumber the answers. All we're hearing from law enforcement officials is that the situation is under control. They don't have much to say about the illegal copies, except that the copies are not armed and in no way pose a threat to the public.

Anchorwoman: Exactly how many copies are there? And how rapidly are they being produced?

Reporter: Not many. Thousands, perhaps tens of thousands, though the estimates we're receiving are probably on the low side. Everyone in government insists that replication is very slow. Apparently that is how they've kept the crime under wraps.

Anchorwoman: Any word yet on how long they have known, or on why they can't plug the hole?

Reporter: We're as lost in the fog as the rest of the world on that question, I'm afraid. Weeks very likely have passed, with no progress. No one knows why the leak can't be plugged. You can feel the panic in the air.

Anchorwoman: Thank you, Rajeev. We'll be checking in with Rajeev later, as the situation develops. Now we turn to Kay-Tell political analyst Newman Baldridge and his speculations on how an unsolved crime of this scope will affect President Smile's chance of re-election. . . .

— Kay-Tell News "Special Report," Feb. 1, 2997.

A mosaic of fear, relief, and horror came over Paul. He felt nauseated. Though Clay was okay, able to be reconstructed by the computer, and though Claire—thank God—still existed on the Life Insurance computers, he felt as though they remained in danger, like hunted animals, able to be reduced to bits of mud on the floor, to the messes he was watching get scraped up by the shovels of a police cleanup crew. It was horrifying. They had heaved Claire's new denim jumpsuit into the telepod like a sack of dung.

By the time Banks arrived he needed air. "Let's go outside," Paul said. "I want to talk."

"We don't have any idea how this could've happened. All the software . . ."

"Outside."

Paul slid open the glass door, stepped out onto the veranda, and went down the stairs, heading toward the sea. He felt better already. He kept moving, not wanting Banks to get an opportunity to speak.

When he had gone far enough, he swung around. "What do you see, Dave?" he hollered, gesturing to his house with a sweep of an arm. "What do you see?"

"The software . . ."

"What do you see?"

Banks blinked. "I don't understand."

Paul gestured again with an open palm.

"Your house?"

"My *home*. How many nodes must be sealed to secure someone's home?"

"Slow down. Just listen." Banks was breathing heavy and the veins stood out on his temples. His face was stark white in the midday sun. "Goddammit, I double-checked everything. Nothing could have gone wrong. The copy shouldn't have been able to come within a hundred miles of here."

"Claire told me a Beijing official was pressuring her to talk to the copy. She told her no. David, she said no. What the hell are the police doing?"

Banks looked away from the sun, down the deserted beach. "They made a deal with the copy. . . . They had no choice. But that's something else. The copy got past the dataseal on his own."

"I'm sick of the 'force playing games with my life."

"No one let him into your house. Christ, haven't you seen the news? The last thing anyone's thinking about is you and Claire. The curtain's come up on the investigation, Paul. The press is coming, and this time they aren't looking for heroes."

Paul looked past his friend at the small house. He had never noticed before how precarious it looked, balanced as it was atop a tangle of stilts. He felt capable of knocking it down with his fists—and part of him wanted to demolish the whole place and beam away, right now, as he had done before, beam away and start over, part of him, the old part, he supposed, not yet dead, despite a year online thinking and planning, not dead . . . Maybe he would never be able to kill it, no matter how hard he tried. "Aw, hell. I'd just gotten things back together. How could this happen?"

"Jesus, Paul, I wish I knew, but like I said, we don't know. You—the copy, I mean—doesn't know enough about computers to do what he did."

"He shouldn't even be alive."

A chilly salt breeze struck Banks in the face, making him wince. "We had no choice. He was the key to the case."

"There are a million other detectives in the world."

"He was the only one close enough to Spalding."

"Spalding?" Paul's tone was more bitter than surprised. He had hated being kept in the dark about the case. While the world fell to pieces, he was marooned here, on this beach, powerless to protect himself or anyone else. "The scholar?"

Banks nodded. "We thought he was our man."

"The Beijing official?"

"Though now we're not so sure. He's a strange bird all right; he collects old porn simulations, does screwed-up genetic experiments in his basement, and so on, but he doesn't seem to know about Stella. Everything checks out under X."

"What does . . . what does the copy think?"

"We could hardly get a word out of him. After the raid on Spalding's, he was pretty shaken up. All he would say was that the investigation was lost, or he would start crying and mumble things about the world being rigged and how he had no good moves—delirious nonsense. He demanded that we delete him immediately and put him out of his misery."

"Crying?"

"Yep. Like a baby."

Paul tried to imagine a copy of himself begging to be erased, a copy . . . driven to murder, suicide . . . How could it be? And how could Banks talk about it in such a casual, breezy tone of voice? "Why didn't you just kill him at the station?"

"We needed him for questioning."

Paul nodded in acceptance, though he would never forgive the department for its sloppiness. "I want to talk to him."

Banks shot him a quick look and quit fidgeting with his feet in the sand, reminding Paul that the department no longer considered him a detective, at least not regarding this case. "He's being interrogated right now."

"I want to see him before he's erased."

"Paul, I know from your perspective this investigation must seem somewhat mismanaged, and I know you want answers, but you have to understand. This is a very delicate time. Most of us want you back, but not now. Let us clean up this mess so that you can forget it and get back to a normal life."

"I have a right to question the copy. I want to know . . . Why the hell did all this happen? The department can let me do that, can't they? Pay a visit, like a relative or something?"

"I don't know. . . ."

"Run it by Sorenson. You were the ones who brought the copy into the world. You afraid of messes? What do you expect the press to make of all of this?" Paul waved in the direction of the house. "I can throw the doors wide open, David. I can throw them wide open."

"We—Yes, we—" Banks faced Paul, squinting in the bright light. "I'm sorry. I'll see what I can do."

*

Paul had the computer turn away every comlink request from a news organization, but the story got out anyway. Public opinion started to influence the investigation. Since most people wanted to hear what former world hero Paul Cramer had to say to himself, the interrogation request was granted. Everything would be recorded in 3D. Anything they said that didn't compromise the investigation would be made public, in time. The media was like a great beast of the ocean that needed constant feeding so that it would not come on land looking for prey.

A guard unlocked the door to the interrogation chamber, and Paul went inside. There he was: the famous Paul Cramer, seated in the small steel seat reserved for prisoners being questioned, visibly ashamed, dejected, still sallow and enfeebled from the blast of the stun gun. "I want to die," he said, not looking up.

"You'll get your chance." The department had been kind enough—or prudent enough—to leave this business to the Cramers; they were alone. "I will be happy to delete you myself, when the time comes. Right now, however, I have some questions."

The copy started to cry, holding his face, which seemed to want to break into a dozen pieces, each feeling a separate pain; he crossed his arms over his eyes and laid his head on the steel table. "Not again. . . . I can't go over it again!"

"Your own son . . . You tried to kill Clay. He was almost eaten up by goo pellets from *your gun*—a purely incidental matter for you, apparently, even though your son was screaming and parts of his body falling off! But what gets me is—how could you plan it out the way you did—cracking the dataseal, getting our Life Insurance archives deleted—plan it out, in such a rational, deliberate fashion, like a political assassination. Maybe you would fly into a rage, lose control . . . but murder? Throw your life away to get me and Clay. Why?" The copy refused to look up from where his face was buried between his arms, so Paul lifted the man's head by a fistful of hair. "Have you completely lost your mind?"

Eyes red, cheeks slack and wet with tears, his whole head puffy and deformed as though severed and mounted on a stake, the copy sobbed, "I didn't plan. The code was just sitting there, in a Canadian datavault. It worked. . . . I never really thought it would, but it did." Another fit of crying came over the copy.

This man is a total wreck, thought Paul. *Me*. I got this way. One of those people that kills his whole family then shoots himself in the head (only to get reinstantiated and thrown in jail). . . . How?

Paul threw the copy, by the hair, upright in the little chair.

The copy sobbed louder, his head lolling. "Just kill me," he said. "I want to die."

Paul eyed the hologram of vital signs and said, "I don't believe you. Your story checks out. The computer believes you, but I think you're holding out. If I hadn't seen it with my own eyes, I would have said you couldn't go through with something like that. What's the motive?"

"I don't have to tell *you*."

"You want this to be over, just make me understand what happened."

"You know *exactly* what happened. If it was you they brought back and you had this life you're supposed to fix but—oh, no, you can't touch it. Just do your job and step back into the telepod, please. Pretend it's a dream. You aren't really alive. . . ."

The copy kept going, yammering to himself in a half-dozen different voices. This was a breakdown in every sense of the word—the oldest sense, dating back to the industrial age. He remembered a debriefing about "breakdowns" he got from Stella after going through the Bedlam simulation. "We're all more or less machines," she had told him. "Once, we were like appliances. We went through our whole lives rusting, creaking at the joints, breaking down. Now we're just characters, constantly being rewritten and improved. It's hard to see, today, while the technology is so crude, but in the future everything we are, mind, body, soul—all of it will be rewritten all the time, by others as well as ourselves. We will live many lives, perhaps without even knowing it." The copy, it seemed to Paul, had malfunctioned, or had been rewired, damaged somehow, by all the stress and confusion of the illegal instantiation. He was no longer himself.

"Enough, enough already," said Paul.

Something flashed across the copy's face, anger maybe, or fear, but as quick as it had come it was gone. "You're the one that left," said the copy. He puckered his lips as though the words tasted foul.

"You're that same person, remember—the person I was. The old, heartless me."

"We both tried to delete the family—the Cramer family, and we tried to delete ourselves. The only difference is how we went about it. We both deserve to die." The copy slouched in the small metal chair and spoke very slowly, eyes fixed on Paul, completely calmed down. "We had a family because it's expected. Because it's a privilege. Now we're all sick of each other. We're bored and we're sick. It would be a service to the world if we—and everyone else made from the same mold—simply disappeared for good."

"Well, we weren't just going through the motions, in the beginning at least. We wanted a family. You have to admit that much."

"But now we hate just being alive. We should be killed. I'd do it myself, if I had another chance."

Paul stood up. He paced back-and-forth in front of the small, square table, every few steps examining the passive expression that had come over the copy. Finally, he stopped and leaned on the back of the chair with both hands. "Imagine Clay is here right now. I give you a goo gun. Do you shoot him?"

"I shoot you both."

"And you have no problem with the way we would die—watching your very own son screaming and burning and melting before your eyes?"

"My family is already dead to me."

Paul stared at the copy. He would have been shocked, had he not begun to understand what was going on. He smiled, enjoying the discomfort this seemed to cause the prisoner. "You can lie under X, you can lie to the whole world, but you can't lie to yourself."

"What?"

He grinned and pushed the chair under the table. "I have no more questions." He called the guards and had them take charge of the prisoner, once again feeling like the detective the world believed him to be.

*

Paul went to his old office, brought up some comlinks, and started giving orders. He had no official position with the police, but the Phoenix staff seemed grateful for the direction. He did not know how long his former superiors would tolerate the intervention—or if they would ever reconsider his suspension and the charges against him—but he finally had a hunch about the Stella mystery. All he could do was hope that the people in Beijing, hurt by the recent press attention, were not entirely immune to feelings of gratitude.

With these thoughts in mind, he told the lab people to run a comparison of the copy's data and his own.

"Yes, sir," said a perky young woman. She was probably a new hire, some kid hoping to be granted a child, in a hurry to live her life as soon as possible. "May I ask, sir, exactly what we're looking for?"

"Cells," said Paul. "You're looking for extra cells, or carbon data-crystals, particularly around the copy's brain."

"What should we do with them, if we find them?"

"Remove all discrepancies, then reinstantiate the copy and see if he lives."

The woman looked worried. "I'll have to get approval. . . ."

"Do what you have to, just get back to me within the hour."

"Okay, " said the woman, hesitating. "Yes, sir." She nodded and broke the connection.

Banks came in just as Paul was asking the computer to locate Batacharia in Beijing. "Sorenson is tuned into your office," he said. "He—and the rest of us—want to know what the hell you're doing."

"Just a hunch." Paul gazed at the far wall, though he had no way of knowing from what location Sorenson's eyes would be viewing the holodisplay. "I think I can get a confession out of Spalding. Give me two hours."

"What's your hunch?" said Banks. "The copy gave you the same line he gave us."

"Something my son suggested. I'll know when the lab results come back. In the meantime, I need to talk with Spalding. Can you help me get approval from Beijing?"

Banks lacked the proper authority, so Paul waited for someone monitoring the conversation to respond. Soon enough Sorenson was requesting a comlink.

"What's all this about a brain-scan?" he said in greeting.

"Not sure myself, but we'll know soon enough."

"You'll have to come up with more than that for Beijing. You shouldn't even be in the building."

"Let me interrogate Spalding. You guys wanted to bring back Paul Cramer—now's your chance."

A muscle near Sorensen's eyebrow was twitching uncontrollably, maybe a muscle that had been overly strained during weeks of meetings with worried officials. He appeared not to have the strength either to lift his eyebrows in surprise or lower them in disapproval. "Fine. I'll get approval. You'll have twenty minutes with the prisoner."

*

Hours passed before Paul got to meet the scholar. The red tape of getting clearance from the Beijing facility was straightforward, but he complicated everything by first insisting that a second copy of Spalding be instantiated and kept in a separate cell, just in case, and then that hyperwave jamming devices be installed outside both Spaldings' cells, as an additional precaution. No one in Beijing took him seriously until the results came back from the lab, after which they were very courteous and cooperative.

The staff in Phoenix was not celebrating, however. Against the satisfaction of learning how the criminals had beaten X was the discovery itself: a human brain had been altered, organically, to run the equivalent of a software program. In the latter part of the century, thanks to a long crime wave, police and citizens alike had grown accustomed to the fact that pieces of software could be corrupted or disabled, especially on the Net— but not the data of human bodies. Those files had always been safe.

The technician who gave Paul the news was speechless. She said only, "We found it, Detective," then she stepped aside so Paul could see the altered brain, which over the comlink was visible on holodisplays all around the technicians, caged in a sinister-looking structure of foreign neurons highlighted in red. A dozen faces around the laboratory waited for some kind of direction. "We have a new type of virus going around," he said simply, "a virus of the mind."

And Spalding, like all truly inspired criminals, had led them right to it, probably because he was proud of his handiwork. Paul couldn't wait to thank him. He went straight to the interrogation chamber.

The first thing he said to Spalding, turning the small metal chair sideways to have a place to put his foot as he asked questions, was meant more for himself—and, ultimately the media—than for the scholar, because the entity that would be answering the questions would be similar to what had controlled his copy's mind: "I've enjoyed the little odyssey you sent me on. It was somewhat lengthy for my taste, somewhat disruptive to my personal life, but educational; I certainly learned some things I won't forget."

The scholar did not comprehend. "Are you . . . are you the Paul Cramer I know, or are you the other one?"

"Oh, I'm sorry. We haven't met." Paul extended a hand. "I'm Paul Cramer, the original."

Spalding smiled faintly, still wondering, probably, what this was all about. "Glad to make your acquaintance. I—" He brightened. "I enjoyed the company of your copy immensely. He was a clever fellow."

Paul leaned forward onto his raised knee. "I don't think you'll like me nearly as much. Which is ironic, considering that if I'm different in any way it's probably due to the lesson plan you gave Stella."

"Actually, I'm sorry. I'm afraid I don't follow. What do I have to do with Stella?"

The holographic meters remained steady. "I have so many questions. I don't know where to begin. How'd you get the idea of using simulations from early history as therapy? That was inspired."

"I'm afraid I don't know what you're talking about."

"And the episodes from the animal kingdom. I guess that was to teach about bodies, physical interfaces with the world . . . Where were you going with that? I never found out, you see, because I never completed the sequence. I had to leave before I came to the ultimate lesson, which I understand to be—correct me if I'm wrong—that the body and mind should be configurable, temporary, or that they've always been configurable, on an evolutionary scale, but that they will soon be so within individual lifetimes, as evolution accelerates."

"I wish I could help, but . . ."

"You can help. Yes, your eyes give you away. You want more than anything to discuss your theories, but something is preventing you. An inhibition. Well, that's why I'm here, to help remove that inhibition, so that you can discuss your ideas once again. Because what kind of intellectual are you if you can't discuss ideas?"

The scholar was silent, the two parts of his brain wrestling, probably, with what to do.

Paul continued, "My theory is that you want to bring about the evolution of higher beings, on the Net, forms of consciousness more complex and powerful than a human mind. But we can discuss all of that later.

First, I want to tell you how the investigation has gone, so that you'll understand your present situation."

"I've already accepted my punishment, Mr. Cramer. I was wrong to do that work in my basement. I'm not a god, or a biochemist. I should have stuck to my books."

"Forget the biochemistry. For all I care, you could replace the whole Brazilian rain forest with Lorax trees and candy canes. But I don't think that was your plan."

"A forest of Lorax . . . You have quite an imagination. Actually, the thought had crossed my mind. My tinkering was always more for the sake of visual art than technical understanding. I wanted to be a painter, like one of the surrealists, from back when our perception of reality was just becoming fluid. I wanted to be the first painter of—sorry, a phrase from a recent paper—'the fluid real world,' the world that is coming."

"We're getting closer. You're opening up. Good. Let's talk about painting, then. I'm a fan of your work, though I don't know what exactly it all means. One painting in particular has been bothering me. I just can't put my finger on what it's meant to tell us. Maybe you could shed some light by way of an explanation." Paul told the computer to bring up the hologram of the copy's brain, where the virus was a lurid red spider.

A change came over the scholar's features. He suddenly appeared at ease, relieved. "So that's the ace up your sleeve, Detective? I wish you wouldn't play so many verbal games. How can we have a conversation if one of us speaks only in riddles?"

"Tell me what the painting means."

The scholar smiled. He seemed to be sizing up his adversary, then he said, "What's a painting without people?"

"This is a software construct with a body—it's a puppet, not a person."

"In time my talents would have improved. You're judging the work of an amateur."

"You aren't an amateur, Dr. Morris. You're not even an artist. An artist creates. You only pervert what already exists, take living, feeling minds and make them into gadgets."

The scholar shook his head in rueful disdain. "I'm afraid the fine arts is not your field. You've mistaken the paintbrush for the painting. Stella—or your copy, whose tragic failure, from what I've seen on holovision, has probably led you to your present state of awareness—is only a tool. The real painting is your mind. Like you said, if you're different from your copy, it's because of Stella. I'd even say that if you've made up with your wife, it's because of Stella. I saved you, Detective, just like I'm going to save everybody from the dissolution and ennui of the 'second childhood.'" The scholar chortled, very pleased.

The more Spalding opened up, the more he sounded like Stella. Paul recalled Stella naked in the moonlight of a world he had made, physically lovely but there only to parrot the same line of propaganda: "You are growing wise in ways you can only begin to understand. You take into your heart what other ages have felt and learned, what other species have always known, and it helps you understand yourself, your time, and the times to come." Very likely, the same computational entity controlled both of their minds. Paul wondered whether there existed a copy of Spalding somewhere in the world that was *not* under this kind of control, or whether even the scholar himself was just a puppet for some larger computational system. "Us mortals, we'd rather think for ourselves," he said.

"You just lack insight. The world I see coming—which will arrive eventually, with or without my help—will produce the highest state of existence possible to any sentient being. We will all be gods, each with his own universe as a plaything. We will all live a thousand lives, or more, as many lives as the human soul was once thought to live. We will be immortal, but unlike in the present age, we won't be dying of boredom."

"There will never be enough computer time for us all to be gods. And even if there was, someone would have to be tending the machines, and what kind of god can be deleted, at the whim of some computer technician? That's what you mean, isn't it? A world online, each of us lost in some simulation?"

"If you want to put it crudely. I think online consciousness, minds free to create their own existence, will make our species both wise and happy."

"Looks like you have a thing or two to learn from your own simulations. Life is more than dreaming and creating. Life is wanting something and not always having it. Working toward a goal. There have to be limits, or you don't exist. The gods you imagine would not be alive, in any real sense; they would be elaborate, expensive computer programs, churning out fantasy worlds, like perpetually dreaming children. No one would care what they thought or what they did, because they would be made from . . . What? Adventure simulations, vacations, pornographic meld-movies . . . just common entertainment. We can already conjure up our every fantasy, and that's what makes us so bored."

"Some of the universes would include failure, hardship, even death. The balance of success and failure would be up to the individual creators."

Paul considered saying more, curious how else the scholar, with all his learning and accomplishment, would justify his childish scheme, but the thing sitting in the chair beside him was just a construct. There would be more time for philosophizing when the virus was removed from Spalding's head. "But that brings me to the point of this interview. You're not a god, Dr. Morris, no matter how much you want to be. You're a man, and you have limitations, just like all men. We know that your mind has been altered, so that you can resist Exegesis, and we know how to change it back. Soon you will be telling the whole story, and your little dream of floating up to Mt. Olympus will end, like all dreams do, eventually."

"I appreciate your cunning. You have quite a flair, in addition, for the high-handed theatrics of a world-class detective. However, do you really believe that after all my preparations I would fail to have yet another line of defense?" The scholar reached the fingers of one hand into his mouth, as though he were pulling a tooth. "I'm going to be a lot harder to stop than you imagine."

Just then Spalding ceased talking and screamed. His gray tongue bulged between his teeth like a piece of metal. As Paul had suspected, the scholar had developed a goo capsule that would slip past the prison scanners. His lips and jaw were already dead-gray. In addition, given the man's connections within the police organization, the device was probably trying to talk to several computers, at the Bureau of Life Insurance and elsewhere, asking them to delete all extant copies of his data—and failing to be heard, thanks to the jamming device Paul had had installed. "We are aware of your next line of defense," said Paul. "That's why we have a second copy of Spalding Morris downstairs, in a cell much like your own, and a copy of your data on offline nanocrystal memory."

With satisfaction, Paul watched an expression of surprise freeze on the scholar's face, gray and changeless, like a black-and-white hologram. "Now, Mr. Morris, you are quite a work of art."

Chapter 21

Once again, the gratitude of the world shines its light on an individual, someone we remember well. We are safe tonight, thanks to him. Our children are safe. Our Network is safe. We will sleep well, our walls strong, our doors, once again, locked, our faith in the World Police restored. The noises we heard this morning, the footsteps in the dark, the prying open of windows—windows that open into the sanctuaries of all of our homes—these sounds were real. Someone was outside, trying to get in. But he is there no more. There is silence. His scheming has been stopped by one of us, who was up listening in the night, a guardian, an officer of the World Police, watching over all our homes, faithfully and effectively. We thank you and all your fellow officers, Mr. Cramer. You hold our world in your hands, our fragile world; you hold it firmly, and you have our trust.
— President Henry Smile, "Special Address," Feb. 12, 2997.

Overnight, the Beijing officials began to address Paul as "Detective Cramer." In official press releases, they glibly used the word "hero" and glossed over the whole two-month ordeal as though Paul had been hard at work the whole time, waiting for the case to break. Paul gladly played along. He felt like himself again. Secret online labs were found, staffed entirely by Spaldings, copies of Spalding began to be erased by the thousands, and he started to hear talk about another Eye Award.

He entered Batacharia's office a celebrity, which gave him a measure of power. It was with only mild alarm that he listened to her explain, very reasonably, the government's desire to reset his timeline. "We can't hide anything from the media anymore. With the case solved, the records will be made public, as a matter of law, and the whole story will become known. You have some experience with the process. As after the Walls case, you, primarily, will have to stand up to the cameras. You will represent all of us, the whole Bureau of Law Enforcement."

"I know what to expect."

"I don't want you to take this the wrong way, Paul. We trust you. We also owe you more than we can repay in words or awards. Many of us, in fact, owe our jobs to you, perhaps all the way up the ladder to President Smile. You helped stabilize not just the Net but the current administration. The media know this; they expect us to show gratitude, and we will. However, if you seem to embrace your life, the way you've lived it, you'll play into the hands of certain people in the media. Already a Kay-Tell reporter has been comlinking around the Bureau, interviewing for a piece entitled—intelligence forwarded a draft to me—'Ambivalent Hero: Cramer Bungles to Success, Saves World.'"

"Interesting angle."

"Next he wants to interview *you*. Certain people would like nothing better than to prove that our success was an accident—and that our most visible detective is insincere or 'ambivalent.'"

"I would be happy to set the record straight."

"The point is: no one is happy with the way the government handled the crisis. They're looking for villains as well as heroes. In your life, they could find anything—anything at all. They could make you into whoever they want."

"I can represent myself to the media."

"They have the defection, scan-crimes, your copy, then they have your personal life, which unfortunately is tangled up with the investigation at every turn: your affair with Stella, your marriage, the copy's affair, the behavior of your son . . . A soap opera. You'll never hear the end of it."

"I have answers. It's a question of acknowledging my mistakes."

"They're going to pick you apart, Paul. The reformists see a chance to prove that even the best of us are skeptical, that faith in the system is breaking down. You do see the need for damage control? Given your prominence in the media, even your slightest doubts could take on political dimension."

"Like I said, I made mistakes. But mistakes are how people learn. You don't learn to walk without banging your head a few times. And sometimes you don't get the right answer until you've followed a few false leads."

"Nice thought, but direct questions require direct answers. They will want some sort of gesture, a full renunciation of everything you did during December and January—a gesture, not just a statement."

"I came back. I restored my marriage, I helped the police . . ."

"The only gesture we believe to be strong enough is the resetting of your timeline. You must abandon the two months you spent away from the police and your family, make it clear to the world that you regret every minute, that it was an aberration, a malignant growth on your timeline that needs to be removed. Naturally, such a gesture will greatly commute your sentence. If you capitulate today, in fact, I can guarantee that your sentence will be eliminated. The last thing we want is live holovision coverage of you beaming into prison."

"I have a better idea. Let's tell the world that Paul Cramer was lost for a time, like many people, but that he found his way back home. Let's tell them that I've come back to the world more sure of myself and the Smile Crime Initiative than ever before."

"They would ask about . . . your time online. Details would come out, a slip of the tongue, who knows . . . things you don't necessarily believe, but things which could compromise the public's impression of you and the World Police. We think it's better to replace you with the earlier Paul Cramer, the one the public remembers."

"I'm confident I can communicate where I stand." Paul kept his eyes steady and voice as even as possible, trying not to betray any anxiety. She was right: the media would make a circus out of the case, but they would make it into a circus regardless of whether or not he stuck around to be the dancing clown. He did not mind being a clown. He wanted to live. For the first time in years he wanted to live.

"We don't think you can pull it off."

"There's only one way to kill a news story. I'll tell the truth. They'll get a thrill out of it for a while, but then they'll gradually get the picture. I'm still the same old Paul Cramer."

"Your visibility is higher than that. As long as you're willing to talk, someone will be taking notes."

"I'm not going to lay down my life for a few PR points for Henry Smile."

"Your son, too. We think it would be best if both of you returned to a more stable family situation, before any trouble started. That way, the journalists won't have anything but their own interpretations to go on."

"The last thing my family was back in December was stable. We were falling apart—that's obvious, isn't it? If anything, our earlier selves—if they don't give the world an encore performance of exactly what you want them to hide—will provide far more articulate statements of—what was it?—'skepticism?'—far more articulate statements of that and restlessness, disillusionment—name it. Clay and I are both much more reliable now. How can I prove it?"

Batacharia was beginning to retreat. She waited, a set expression on her face, guessing correctly that he was building toward something.

"I love my family," he said. "It's taken me a year scan-time, but finally I want to be exactly who I am. I don't want to go through that process again—or, worse, to never go through it, to just continue living in a stupor, like the copy, and I don't want Claire and Clay to be stuck with some depressed, run-down version of myself. This is my family you're talking about; you can't mix-and-match us. We're people. We're a family because of relationships we've built up over time. You can't assemble a family by cut-and-paste. You don't have that power."

"I'll give you one thing over the copy: you have conviction, at least. You're right that we can't make you reset your family. All we can do is make it attractive. I still believe it's the safest solution."

Painfully, Paul and Batacharia worked out a resolution, without convincing each other of anything. Paul would face his crimes—and the media. The World Police would support him, as they had to, and his sentence would be mild. It was in everyone's interest to blame his actions on Stella and her programmers, the real criminals, and to agree that the time he had spent with her had been essential to unraveling the case.

He beamed back to Phoenix, anxious to share his excitement over the day's events with David Banks, who had worked so long on the case. When he entered his friend's office, however, no sign of triumph or even happiness met his eye. All the rock-climbing posters had been torn down, as had the portrait of Commissioner Fairbanks, Banks' 29th century law enforcement hero. The holograms of his family, the big marble nameplate his daughter had made for him in school, the holomovie paperweights and other holiday junk given by relatives and friends over the years—all of it was gone, stuffed into the office demiurge, most likely, beamed home.

Even the drawers of the desk were pulled open and being emptied. "What's going on?" asked Paul.

Banks looked like he'd been caught in an illegal act. He froze, hands full of hardcopy magazines, halfway to the demiurge. "Word is that you cracked the case wide open. Congratulations."

"It's all over," said Paul proudly. "Beijing has enough to take apart the scholar's whole organization."

"That's wonderful." Banks proceeded, glumly, to the open panel of the demiurge, into which he threw the assorted magazines. He returned to the desk.

Odd behavior, thought Paul, for someone who had just heard that the Net's worst security leak in twenty years had been plugged. "Are you going to tell me what you're doing? Have you been fired?"

Paul waited in the doorway for a response, patiently.

Banks sighed, looking sad and worn out. He collapsed into the chair behind the desk, as though he could no longer bear to support his own weight. "I don't know where to go. That house has been my home for twenty-five years. I love Alaska. I don't want to live anywhere else."

"What happened?"

Banks eyed Paul quizzically, then his expression changed. "That's right. You don't know about Amy and me. It was the copy I told."

By now Paul knew what his friend meant. He listened without believing as Banks explained the plans for a divorce, the departure of his daughter for a boarding school in the Netherlands, the plans to sell the house—and he kept asking himself, When did all this happen? Banks—simple, changeless Banks—and Amy splitting up? I wasn't gone that long.

He told Banks what he was thinking, as though it would do any good, but his friend just shrugged away the concern. "We've been heading this way since Heather was born. Amy's become so remote and serious lately, wanting to go back to law school, open up a firm and all. I think it's a good idea, of course, but I guess I just don't share the excitement. And who knows what she really thinks of me." He leaned forward and pulled out one of the desk drawers. "She went off with a law professor from England, some guy she met in an ancient Greece simulation."

"David . . . I'm so sorry. It's not your fault. You shouldn't blame yourself."

"Yes I should. It was all me. I'm a self-made man. I stuck with this job so I could have a family and all, and never really gave a damn about being a detective, you know? Amy knew that. I'm really not much of anyone, so why should she stay with me, in particular, over anyone else?"

"You've been a solid part of this office for—what, now? Twenty years?"

"I'm good at keeping up appearances. Maybe I should become a politician."

"What are you going to do?"

Considering, Banks gathered another armload of material and started toward the demiurge. "I'm beaming into the new Titan simulation," he said, shoving the stuff into the compartment. "I'm going to climb the volcanoes. Methane ice is supposed to be the ultimate challenge. It's hard like rock but brittle." He told the computer to beam his possessions away. "I want to be alone. In the mountains." He kept staring at the demiurge, after the panel had slid back open, though nothing was inside.

Paul was caught short of something to say. It was unsettling, seeing his friend this way, so suddenly cast out of the life he had known. What *could* he say? The man seemed so spent, done being Detective David Banks, at least. The familiar product of a sick world, he thought. I was just like you, he thought, a few months ago. It hits us, all of a sudden, and it's always the same. Who we are just slips away.

As wrong as it sounded, Paul found himself wishing that Banks could just change into something—a bird, a spider, a moth, anything—the way Paul himself had been changed, by Stella, after leaving Claire. Just fly away into another way of living, for a while, a way of experiencing that could teach him to feel again. Living online was no substitute for a real life, but wasn't it okay—now and then—to escape? Paul had enough doubts not to say anything. Spalding's crimes, especially the tampering with people's minds, made the whole last year—all his time with Stella— seem deviously sinister. She had been a slave. Everything she had said had been scripted, all her phony affection and insight. When she spoke in his mind, he saw only the mad, grinning face of Spalding. And he did not know what pieces of her world—*their* world, he guessed, a world he had enthusiastically helped to build—should be kept, and which should be thrown away.

Nor did he know what to say to his friend.

Banks headed back to the desk for yet another load.

"Meet me at the *Hot Pants* after work?" asked Paul.

His friend looked startled, as though he had forgotten Paul was there. "Sure. Yes, I'd like to."

Paul excused himself. Maybe he could think of how to console his friend in the meantime.

*

He had one more stop. The copy. At last, deletion was inevitable— thank god—only hours away. He wanted to close his eyes and forget the copy had ever been made. Still, he thought the man deserved a visit. Would he remember what he had done? If so, he would be in a bad state, hours from death and prohibited from contacting his wife and son—even to apologize.

The distraught, almost deranged appearance of the copy bore out Paul's worst expectations. He was doubled over on the edge of the small cell's single bed as though he had a horrible stomach ache. He looked like a rag doll, made of cloth and stuffing, the life wrung right out of him. He reminded Paul—who during the past year had spent more time in the Age of Machinery, it seemed, than in the present—of an automaton from an amusement park of a primitive age, from a time when humans had little technology but still felt the urge to simulate. It was like the show was over now, and the power had been switched off. "Are you all right?" asked Paul.

The copy looked up, eyes hard with pain. Dimly, he seemed to recognize who had come to see him. "I have a headache," he said.

Paul entered, sitting down on a stool attached to the floor near a small desk. The face of his double was all cracked around the lips and eyes. A mask coming loose, he thought, breaking to reveal . . . what? The two of them sat this way for some time, in silence, contemplating each other. This is the future, thought Paul. The future of crime. As a people, we will invade each other's minds, wreck them, warp them. We will all end up like this: confused, rewritten remains of ourselves. All the world will be a simulation, each of us trying to be the only author.

He shuddered at the thought.

"Thank god everyone lived," said the copy at last, his reedy voice failing. "I wish Clay could forget everything, have his timeline reset or something. He must be overwhelmed."

"I haven't had time to reinstantiate him."

Morose, the copy said, "How could I . . . I wanted to kill him. That thing in my mind, it took everything bad I've ever felt about Clay and made me feel it all at once. I hated him. I would have strangled him."

Paul said nothing.

"It's like I've always wanted to murder him—and Clair—in some secret corner of my mind. I just needed a push in the right direction."

"You didn't want to kill anybody. That's absurd."

"I don't know. I don't know anymore."

The copy seemed so aware and contrite that Paul was inclined to believe his claim that the foreign neurons had given him a small "push" and nothing more. Who could say what it took to make a small frustration blow up in your face? In Tokyo, a little fooling around with Stella had sent him away from his job and family and turned him into quite a scoundrel, actually, in about eighteen hours. The truth was that he still did not trust himself; he was always changing, wanting one thing today and another tomorrow. If he had been denied Claire and his son, like the copy, perhaps he, too, would have had thoughts of murder, or suicide, and perhaps the effort to animate these thoughts into actions would have been small, as the copy claimed it had been. "The virus takes complete control," he said anyway. "You were a robot, like Stella, programmed. No one blames you."

Paul must have said something particularly terrible, because the copy immediately fell into anguished, almost frantic lamentation. "Toril! My god, you've got to save Toril! He's torturing her, that sadistic, twisted freak; you've got to get her away from him."

"Who's Toril?"

The copy explained about the scholar's wife, the divorce, and the years of psychosis that had followed. "He's out of his mind. He doesn't want a revolution; he just wants to make his ex-wife do what he says, endlessly, make her feel herself obey him, helpless."

"Take it easy. We're doing everything we can." Paul summarized what was happening in Beijing.

"He makes her crawl around for him, like a dog. He thinks it's funny."

"We will be able to find all of the copies, and we will delete them."

"Think what all the copies of Stella must be feeling right now, secretly, doing what they were programmed to do. That's what excites him, the broken vestige of his wife, everywhere, being punished. I can't believe we took so long to save her." The copy looked angry now, his face swollen with impotent hatred. "I wasn't even trying. It was all right under my nose, the whole time, but all I cared about was my little life. I was waiting for Stella, like everyone else, even if I didn't realize it, waiting to be lifted up into a simulation."

"You did what you could."

The copy was wringing his hands. His fingers looked red and sore.

"If you hadn't been investigating the scholar, failed, and been reprogrammed, we might never have guessed what he was up to. You were the key."

The copy smiled at this. "Are they going to have to make two action figures now, one to investigate the other?"

"This was a strange case," agreed Paul, surprised how distant he felt from the copy, how little the irony touched him. "Paul Cramer solved it; he had to split in two, but he solved it."

The copy nodded weakly. "Tough way to solve a case."

Paul didn't expect the copy to share his enthusiasm, under the circumstances. "You know that—this afternoon—they're going to delete you, right?"

The copy was staring at the floor, lost in thought, his face blank and bewildered; the brain damage was all too visible.

"Are you okay with that?"

After a long silence, the copy replied, his voice low and solemn, "I can't go on, not after what happened."

"Not the most glamorous way to die, I guess."

The copy ignored the question. "Are you and Claire all right?"

Paul tried to read the copy's hard, pained stare, waiting for the outburst that seemed right beneath the skin but which refused to come. "I think so."

"You and Clay?"

"We have an understanding, I believe."

The copy continue to stare at Paul, grave, like a patriot weighing his life against a sworn duty. "I'm fine then," he concluded. "I'm ready to die."

*

And so, without ceremony, Paul left. He would let the prison staff take care of the rest. Meanwhile, he had drinks with Banks, biding his time before the execution. He wanted the copy to be gone before he reassembled his family.

He told himself he should feel remorse or at least pity for the copy, but all he felt was relief. Thank god it wasn't me, he thought. A blink of the eye and I could have been the one locked up, my head filled with a hundred years of someone else's memories, someone else's loves. In fact, tomorrow I could step into a telepod and the same thing could happen; a second copy might be created, and I might be that copy. My life would be over, like that, and I wouldn't have done a thing.

Terrible thought.

He wanted to share it with Banks, but his friend was drunk and stunned by grief, muttering, falling into deep melancholic silences. Paul had little to say to his friend beyond general encouragement. The man would come through it, he guessed, on his own. In the end, he would have to. Hopefully the cliffs of methane ice (a little danger, perhaps a tumble or two, a simulated free-fall death) would clean away some of the sickness in his heart.

That left no one to listen to his comparatively minor worries about rebuilding his family. He certainly was not going to bother Clay or Claire with it. They would have their own problems, dealing with the vertiginous first days after a reinstantiation. They would need him to be stable, and so he would be.

Chapter 22

gritty male voice: [Double Trouble *theme music, gunshots*]
Cramer is back! [*shot of Cramer shooting gun*] Only this time he's
BAD. [*pan to other Cramer, running, dodging goo pellets*] He's an
evil mutant copy, Boss Crime's toughest gangster. One Cramer wants
to solve crimes [*shot of good Cramer, gleam in eye*], one wants to
break the law [*shot of bad Cramer, grimacing*]. Never before has so
much evil, so much peril, so much terror, awaited Detective Cramer.
He's the world's only hope, but is he smart enough, fast enough, and
tough enough to take on a copy of himself? Log in and see.
female voice: *Double Trouble*. On Funtime Online.

— ad for cartoon, Apr. 11, 2997.

From what Claire knew about dolls, the doll set was a cheap product.
Hastily designed. The Pauls were too stiff and plastic, like the cheaper
dolls she had been given as a child: savage expressions frozen on their
faces, as though the Pauls were perpetually shooting the goo guns molded
into their right hands. You could tell them to walk, fight, and hide, and that
was just about it. Clay was the same model, a generic "action figure,"
except shorter, without a gun, and covered in some weird nanite material,
which upon command morphed into hair, or back to skin and clothes. But
the Claire doll was the worst: a face either sweet and dreamy-eyed, like a
tranquilized princess, or contorted with dying. The doll had little capacity
for action. Like Claire herself in the news, it just stood around, smiling
sweetly, until it got shot.

She asked Paul for his opinion when he got home from work.

"I don't want to know," he said at once, turning away from the dolls and
the model of their house, which were sitting on the coffee table.

"Mr. Bowling wants you to approve—"

"He has my approval. He's the toy man. I trust him."

She followed him into the bedroom, where he began to change into swim trunks. "The dolls are pretty poor. I think you should take a look. All the Paul Cramer doll does is shoot and die."

"Mr. Bowling is the expert."

"I liked the old one better."

"The old one didn't even walk."

"It was more flexible. A kid could make it do things."

"All right." He struggled out of his slacks. "I'll take a look. But I have to get the net set up. Katherine wanted to play volleyball, remember?"

She had forgotten. They were having a barbecue. "Do I have to play?"

"You're the strong half of my team."

When he had changed, Paul came into the living room to look at the dolls. "I would rather forget about all of this, if you want to know the truth."

"Me too, but just take a peek at the expression on your face." She handed him a Paul Cramer doll. "The other one is identical. You can't tell the good one from the bad one. Is that how you want kids to think of you?"

Paul cast his eyes over the figure, then set it back down. "I'm one badass detective. Don't mess with Paul Cramer."

"I'm serious."

"To be honest, I don't care if kids think I'm a swamp monster. I'm just a figment of their imaginations, anyway. If Funtime can make us a quick buck from what people want to believe, great. We should be thankful."

"It's so banal . . . all the dolls . . ."

Claire felt a gentle, reassuring touch on her shoulder. "For twenty years I've lived in a world full of dolls supposed to be me, and the best thing, I've discovered, is just to ignore them." With that, Paul went outside to set up the volleyball net, leaving Claire alone with her thoughts.

She was the one with no memory of what had happened, yet she was the one who could not get the murder out of her mind. She had seen the forensic photos of her gooed body, with the other Paul's footprint where her head belonged, but it all seemed like a news story. She wanted to believe what everyone told her, that she had been killed, drawn into a world crisis, made famous, but her mind would not go along. She now knew how Paul had felt all these years. None of it had happened to *her*. She was someone else, taking her cues from other people, pretending, as though she had stepped into a prepared role. The demented dolls just made everything worse, more unreal.

Clay and Katherine arrived, both morphed as apes.

"Beautiful April day," she said in greeting. "Your father's outside putting up the net."

"Great." Clay approached the coffee table. "Are these the dolls?"

Claire nodded. "Mr. Bowling wants our opinions tomorrow."

Clay picked up himself. The doll was in "hair" state.

Feeling the doll with her fingers, Katherine said, "You're pretty skinny and mean-looking for a teddy bear."

"It's an action figure," Clay replied.

"You would be better as a teddy bear."

"I don't like what they've done," said Claire. "They make us look like a cop show."

"What does it do?" Katherine, having taken the doll from Clay, put it onto the dollhouse's veranda. "Does it talk?"

"None of the dolls say a word." Claire eyed the angry circle of dolls. "Mr. Bowling says that action dolls sell better if you leave the dialogue to the children's imaginations."

"They look fine to me," said Clay, without interest. He touched Katherine's hand, communicating a desire to go outside.

"They do have *some* sound effects, though," added Claire. "The Clay and Paul dolls grunt when they die. I scream hysterically."

The children exchanged glances, probably unsure what to make of this last bit of information. She was making everybody uncomfortable. What was the matter? The Claire doll had put her in a terrible mood. She was relieved when the children excused themselves and went outside.

I should be glad like the others, she reflected. If these dolls are half as popular as the old Paul Cramer dolls, we'll all be making good money for years. Clay will be able to afford a house, and I . . .

She scanned the dollhouse through the open back wall, seeing everything, all the rooms and furniture just as they were in the real house, the cherrywood bedroom set, the stately gray leather of the living room couch and love seats, the self-cleaning white carpet, the imposing length of the dining room table . . . She straightened the building to get a more direct look. The house had always seemed, in a sense, to belong to Paul, since he made the payments out of the doll royalties. That's where it had begun: the Walls case and the Walls-case residuals, movie rights, toy royalties; etc. Paul had seemed to recede, perhaps for other reasons, but recede, behind his money and all it was buying, while she had taken over raising their son. Their life had been split down the middle. With the development of the Claire Cramer action figure, however, she was gaining a certain financial existence. From now on they would *both* maintain the little coastal villa. She smiled. Perhaps Paul, too, would take on new responsibilities, spend more time at home. The quarantine had been good for him and Clay. They were closer now. They had been forced to spend time together, to figure out what sort of people they had become. All in all, the three of them had wound up for the best, she supposed. She could not complain. But still . . .

No. Paul was right. She would ignore the dolls. And the other popularizations of their lives, already in the works. And she would try to forget what had happened, the copy, the murder and everything, the month when Paul and Clay were away at prison, the stiff, holovised, creepily cheerful dinner in Beijing with the Smiles, forget and go on, as though the gap in her timeline had never happened, go on, while the royalties came in, quietly, and made her life a little easier.

"Hide, Claire," she told the Claire doll, which was standing on the toy veranda, a sunny expression on its face. It screamed and ran into the toy house.

Claire went outside, into the real sun, to play volleyball.

About the Author

As a child Sheldon J. Pacotti wanted to be an inventor. In his own laboratory at the age of seven he devised many inventions, including "soap water," aged spider juice, and other smelly corrosive fluids. Learning in college that real scientists study only one small area of knowledge, he turned to science fiction, literature, and programming—haphazard and therefore excellent preparation for a career in video games.

The highlight of his gaming career is *Deus Ex*, which won a Quantum Leap award from Gamasutra for being the video game that has "advanced game storytelling in the largest way." Despite writing for games and literary magazines, Sheldon carries on a stormy affair with computer software, creating odd experiments like a language for generating stories and a "dynamic voxel" video game entitled *Cell: emergence*. His other books include the novel γ and the short story collection *Experiments in Belief*.

www.ingramcontent.com/pod-product-compliance
Lightning Source LLC
Chambersburg PA
CBHW031219260626
47169CB00007B/2109